A FALSE DAWN

A FALSE DAWN

TOM LOWE

MINOTAUR BOOKS NEW YORK

This is a work of fiction. All of the characters, organizations, and events portrayed in this novel are either products of the author's imagination or are used fictitiously.

A THOMAS DUNNE BOOK

FOR MINOTAUR BOOKS.

An imprint of St. Martin's Publishing Group.

www.thomasdunnebooks.com

www.minotaurbooks.com

Library of Congress Cataloging-in-Publication Data

Lowe, Tom.
    A false dawn / by Tom Lowe.—1st ed.
       p.   cm.
    "A Thomas Dunne book"—T.p. verso.
    ISBN-13: 978-0-312-37917-9
    ISBN-10: 0-312-37917-X
    1. Human trafficking—Fiction. 2. Florida—Fiction. I. Title.
PS3562.O88423F35   2009
813'.54—dc22

                               2008036292

First Edition: April 2009

10 9 8 7 6 5 4 3 2 1

For Keri

ACKNOWLEDGMENTS

The publication of a book is a collective effort coming from a lot of people. I want to thank them all for their help in bringing my first novel to you, the reader. I will forever be grateful to Ruth Cavin at St. Martin's Press. Ruth has edited more books than she probably cares to remember, but she approached mine with a fresh passion that I wish I could bottle and savor during rainy days. Her keen eye for story and dialog is remarkable and inspiring. I am indebted to her and Tom Dunne for believing in the story and for giving the novel, and me, a home. Some of the other talented people at St. Martin's include Toni Plummer, an extraordinary and tireless associate editor, who always has time for the arcane questions I ask. The words in this novel were made better by the sharp talents of copy editor India Cooper. Art director David Rotstein did his magic and created a cover that captures the dark recesses of the story. My production editor, the wizard behind the curtain, is Bob Berkel. If you heard about this book before now, it was probably due to the attentive publicity efforts of Anne Gardner. To the tenacious folks in the sales department and the booksellers, you're the front line. My deep appreciation and thanks to you all.

Before this novel ever reached St. Martin's Press, it passed through a lot of hands. You won't find their fingerprints on the pages, but you will find their influence on me. Karen Gormandy was more than influential, she was motivating and challenging. She was the first literary agent to read the manuscript, and her suggestions made it a richer story. She will always have my gratitude. A life change pulled Karen away from the literary business, but she left me in the hands of an outstanding agent, Phyllis Westberg. Phyllis is a pillar within the industry, and her renowned agency, Harold Ober Associates, is legendary. Her insight into writing continues to astound me. Rebecca Krause is part of the agency's flawless teamwork.

Before all these pros left their imprints on the book, there is one person who makes perhaps the biggest difference in my writing and in my life. She is my wife, Keri. Her editorial skills and sense of story structure are intuitive and insightful. She knows what works, and to my admiration, what doesn't. These talents are equal to her infinite patience. She gives me the space, time, and opportunity to create. Most important, she gives me her heart.

Finally, to you, the person holding this book right now. I want to thank you because you bring our group into a circle. A writer's job isn't done and the story isn't finished until it's read. It's completed when the book is shared through the imagination of the reader.

I'm glad you're along for the journey. Come a little closer to the campfire . . . the story is about to begin.

A FALSE DAWN

PROLOGUE

It was Hector Ortega's turn with the girls, and he was nervous. He backed the nine-passenger van up to a run-down mobile home, turned off the engine, and said, "Make it quick. Don't like doin' this shit on Passover."

Ortega watched as Silas Davis, a black man with the build of a linebacker, got out of a parked pickup truck and entered the trailer. Ortega punched the radio station selector buttons. The pulse of Jamaican reggae rocked the van.

He opened the glove compartment, took out a small plastic bag of cocaine, shook a loose line on the back of his hand, and inhaled through both of his bull-like nostrils. Ortega closed his eyes, feeling the drugs enter his system and mix with the music.

When he opened his eyes a shadow moved. Beneath a live oak. Somebody watching. A single streetlight illuminated half a dozen ramshackle trailers. Ortega felt his night vision enhanced by the cocaine in his system.

1

The shadow was a man. Standing. Staring.

Ortega reached for the pistol under his seat. He turned on the van's lights, flashing the high beams. A farm worker wobbled from under the tree, holding a low-hanging limb for support. Ortega could tell the man was drunk.

The man ambled to a utility pole supporting a streetlamp. He leaned his back against the pole for support, unzipped his pants, and urinated in the dirt and mud.

Ortega lit a cigarette, took a deep drag, and blew smoke out of his nostrils. He set the pistol on the seat beside him and opened a bag of Fritos. He shoved a dirty handful of corn chips into his small mouth.

The farm worker finished urinating. As he started to walk, he held one hand up to block the glare from the van's headlights. He fumbled with his zipper, tripped, and fell down in the mud-soaked puddle of urine.

"Stupid fuck," Ortega mumbled.

Silas Davis escorted five women toward the van. They were all young and very afraid. "Let's go, ladies," Davis said as he opened the side-panel doors. The first four women timidly did as ordered, each taking her seat in the dark interior.

Angela Ramirez stood next to the van; light from a nearby trailer fell across her face.

"Let's go," Davis ordered.

There was no fear in her eyes. She looked at him the way a warrior might stand up to her sworn enemy. Resolute and bold. "I did not come to this country to be a whore!"

Davis laughed. "Get your ass in the van. We ain't got all night." As he reached for her, a dog let out a wolflike howl. Davis turned his head in the direction of the howling.

Angela bolted into the night. She ran behind the van and headed toward the dark of the tomato fields.

"Bitch!" Davis said.

"Get her!" Ortega shouted. He turned around in his seat and held the pistol so the other women could see it. "Don't make me bury any of you in these fields."

Angela ran as fast as she could, losing a shoe in the soft dirt. Davis easily caught her, lifting the screaming woman up over his shoulder and carrying her back to the van as if he were holding a kicking child.

"Shut up, bitch!" he said through clenched teeth. He tossed her into the van and slammed the door.

Ortega pointed the pistol directly at Angela's face and said, "Who do you think you are, huh? It's payback time! Now don't fuck with me, understand?" He threw his cigarette out the window. "'Cause of you, I'm going to have to use the child locks."

Davis leaned in the open window of the front passenger side of the van. He used the back of his hand to wipe a stream of blood from his cheek. "Look at this! Crazy bitch opened my face with her fingernails. She claws like a wildcat."

"She'll learn," Ortega said as he slipped an unlit cigarette behind his right ear. "Silo, one of your boys pissed on himself. He's lying over there in the mud and shit. Must have drunk some bad wine."

"They got to feed the fever."

"I'd leave him there." Ortega laughed as he drove away.

Davis strolled over to the man, who was passed out in vomit and mud-soaked urine. He kicked him hard in the buttocks, lifting the man off the ground and rolling him onto his back. The man slowly opened his eyes, squinting in the glare from the streetlight. His eyes were red, heavily bloodshot with disease and alcohol, smoldering like two pieces of ashen charcoal that had caught a breeze for a fleeting second.

Davis leaned over him. "Wake up, motherfucker, I want your ass on the bus at five thirty in the mornin'."

The man tried to focus on Davis's face. He held a hand up for a second, like a baby trying to touch something above its crib. He coughed up bile and said in a raspy voice, "Why you kickin' me? Ain't right to kick a brother when he's down."

"Not your fuckin' brother."

The man rested his spinning head in the mud, the red slits staring up into the cloudless night sky. "You can't be doin' this to folks. I'm a man."

The sounds of throaty snarls and hisses from feral cats fighting each other came from the shadows. They fought under one of the trailers with the exposed lightbulb over the door. From inside the trailer came a woman's terrified scream.

Gnats and moths circled the lightbulb in a silent cloud.

AS THE VAN PULLED onto State Road 46, Hector Ortega glanced in the mirror to check his cargo. All the women looked as well as could be expected. He didn't see the calm in the eyes of Angela Ramirez.

And he didn't see a black car pull out from a side road and start to follow.

ONE

Max saw him first. Then I saw him out of the corner of my eye. A hundred yards downriver from my dock was a man chest-deep in the river. He held a long pole, prodding underwater as if searching for something. Maybe it was because I'd clocked too many years in law enforcement, but it looked like he was searching for a body. He was coming my way.

"Think a gator will get him before he can make it to the dock?" I said to Max as she cocked her head and trotted to the end of the dock. Max, my nine-pound dachshund, let out a slight whimper as she watched the man in the distance. He didn't look our way as he poked and prodded the riverbed.

I turned and got back to the work I was doing, searched through my open toolbox for four-inch nails and found a hunting knife under my hammer. I glanced back at the man. He was still a good ninety-five yards downriver. I saw him put something in the pouch he carried.

After sniper training, after my time in the first Gulf War, I still calibrated distance in trajectory—what I had to do to make sure a .50 caliber rifle bullet hit a target the size of a grapefruit a quarter mile away. I looked at the river's surface. There was no wind. The man walking in the river wore a wide-brim hat. From where I stood, I could aim with a scoped rifle, if I had one, for the middle of the hat, right above the brim. From this distance, the bullet would hit him dead center in the forehead.

I blinked hard. *Enough.* Not everybody is a hostile. Not everybody is homicidal or a homicide suspect. I swatted a deerfly and inhaled deeply. It was spring, and the river carried the smells of renewing life. Alligators building nests out of sand, sticks, and river mud. Spoonbills and herons feeding live fish to squalling young. Honeysuckles and wild roses blooming.

I removed the knife from the toolbox and laid it on the wooden bench. I looked over my shoulder at the man in the distance and began driving a nail into the wood as I replaced worn and broken planks on the long bench. The morning was already hot, near eighty, I guessed. I was shirtless, wearing jeans. Sweat rolled down my back as I hit the nails.

My uncle Bill, a World War II vet who never spoke of the war, only the demons he fought after it, used to say that anger drives the nails into your own coffin. He also said that every man has his breaking point. After a thirteen-year career as a homicide detective, I began to understand what Uncle Bill meant.

It's gut rot of the soul, and it was the most pervasive part of the job in fighting crime. In homicide, I didn't fight crime. The crime had happened before we arrived. I fought the motivation, the detached switch that allowed someone to derail another person's life. And it fought back. It had pierced the scab covering a dark ember in my marrow, and the buried ash smoldered beneath the surface of night sweats.

I pounded another nail so deep into the wood I couldn't see the head. After my wife, Sherri, died of ovarian cancer six months ago, I moved here to this remote spot on Florida's St. Johns River, with Max. Sherri had bought the miniature dachshund when I'd been away on a three-day stakeout. She named her Maxine and allowed her sleeping quarters at the foot of our bed on her own "doggie blanket." When I'd returned home, my wife said that Maxine was the only other warm body she'd let in our bed. I couldn't argue that, and so this little dog, with her soft brown eyes, permanent eyeliner, and the heart of a lion, became our companion.

Now it was just the two of us, and Max was sleeping under the blanket on her side of the bed. I'd sold everything with the house in Miami. My new home was an old Florida cracker house with a large tin roof, plenty of rambling rooms, a huge screened-in porch, and a generous view of the river. The house sat on one of the few high banks overlooking the river. Most of them were bluffs of ancient Indian shell mounds. The native people had lived off the river, eating fish, clams, and oysters. They piled the shells and bones into mounds up and down the river.

"Dog's gonna be a meal for a gator if it gets too close to the edge."

I whirled around and saw the man, now less than fifty feet from my dock. How had he walked that quickly? Had I been pounding the nails so hard I didn't hear Max bark? Did she bark? She stood there, little paws at the edge of the dock, tail wagging, looking at the man in the river.

He wore an Australian outback hat that looked as old as Ayers Rock. He walked along the river bottom, water up to his chest, the pole tapping the unseen. Max finally uttered a low growl. .

"It's okay, Max," I said. She looked back at me like she didn't believe me. I glanced at the knife on the bench and looked at the man.

He held his hat and slowly dropped down into the river, the dark water covering him. Within seconds, he was gone.

TWO

I knew he had not been pulled under by a gator. His descent was too slow. He wasn't attacked. I stepped over to the side of the dock next to Max as she continued to stare at the spot in the river where the man had disappeared.

"Maybe he slipped in a hole, Max." She whined, her whimper somewhere on the verge of a bark. Suddenly, the man rose out of the river's surface like the Greek god Poseidon clutching his scepter. He used one hand to secure the hat on his head, water pouring from the brim, and the other hand gripped the metal pole. Then he dropped something into the leather sack slung over one shoulder. He said, "Couldn't get it out with my toes, had to use my hand."

"What are you doing?"

He closed his eyes and listened as he poked the pole into the river mud. His face was coffee brown, maybe Native American. He had smooth skin for a man I guessed was in his midfifties. His hair was long, salt and pepper, pulled back into a ponytail. He had a hawk nose that looked like it had been broken and set more than once. He wore a tank top, and his biceps rolled with muscle as he worked the metal prod.

I heard the pole strike something. With his feet, he seemed to be feeling the river mud. He lifted one foot out of the water and held something between his toes. He reached down to take the object, turning it over in his hand, studying it a few seconds before dropping whatever it was into the sack.

Max wagged her tail and finally barked. The man looked up and spoke in a slow, deliberate tone. "Dog's gonna attract gators. Saw a big'en here a month ago."

I almost laughed at the irony. "You're standing in the middle of the river, up to your chest, and you're telling me that my dog might attract gators."

He stopped his tapping for a beat. "I'm not in the middle of the river. Gator is most dangerous at night. You live around 'em long enough and you learn their ways."

"I'm glad you're in harmony with nature."

"Dog and a gator won't ever mix. Gator will stalk him. One day your dog will be barkin' here on the side of the dock and the gator will jump outta the river and grab him."

"What are you doing?"

"Retrieving artifacts."

"You're hunting for arrowheads?"

"Salvaging the past."

"Why are you searching in the river?"

"Because this is where they are." He squinted in the sun. "Lot of the ground's been picked over. This river basin was the home to thousands of my people. There's plenty of arrow- and spearheads in this river mud." He walked up to the dock, took his sack off, and emptied it on the wooden planks.

Max wagged her tail and sniffed. "Okay, Max, let's look at the past. The future is a little obscure right now." The arrowheads were all near perfect. Some small. Some large. They seemed to have been chiseled from different colors of flint.

He held up the largest. "They'd use a few like this to kill a manatee or a gator."

The man set the pole on my dock and climbed out of the river, mud clinging to his feet. He washed his feet in the water before standing.

"Name's Joe Billie." He stretched his long arm and offered a handshake. I shook his wet hand. I could smell sweat and river mud. His grip was strong. A knife was strapped to his belt and thigh.

"I'm Sean O'Brien. Do you often hunt for arrow—artifacts in the river?"

"Whenever I can. I can tell if I'm hitting flint or something like a beer can."

He bent down and scratched Max behind her ears. "Hello, dog." Her tail wagged. "Y'all live here long?"

"A few months. I'm restoring the place."

Joe Billie rubbed Max's head for a moment. He glanced toward my house. "Y'all ever see or hear things you don't understand 'round here?"

"All my life. I was a cop."

"No, here on the mound . . . you ever *feel* anything?"

"What do you mean by feel?"

"This is a sacred place, a burial ground. Should be treated that way."

"How do you know it's a burial mound?"

"Some mounds were for food waste. Others, the ones built overlooking the river like this, were for the spirits of the dead."

"Okay."

He looked at me curiously. "Protect what's left of this sacred place and you'll be protected."

I tried not to laugh.

He stopped petting Max, looked up at me, and rummaged through his knapsack. He pulled out a dark arrowhead. "Found this one near your dock. Take it. It's yours."

"Thank you, but I wouldn't know what to do with it. You keep it."

"It's rare. This is a very special arrowhead. No black flint in these parts. Somebody from a tribe out of the area might have used this arrowhead to kill someone or something. Maybe he died right here in or near the river."

"Maybe so."

"You ever use a bow?"

"I've got an old Pearson. Haven't shot an arrow in years. Today's arrows are a little more refined."

"When a warrior spent time sharpening one of these, he wanted to make sure he got a good shot."

He carefully laid the black arrowhead in the knapsack with the others and then rubbed a calloused hand across Max's head.

"You live around here?" I asked.

"I live on the river near DeLand." He studied my dock for a long moment. "Noticed some of your pilings could use replacing. I've set plenty of docks."

"I'll remember that. Did you walk in the river from DeLand?"

Joe Billie removed his hat and used his thumb to wipe the sweat from his brow. "I tied my canoe about a half mile upriver."

"Can I give you a lift back to your canoe?"

"If I walk back, my clothes will dry." As he started to leave, he paused, scanned his eyes from my home to the river, and said, "Protect what's left of this place."

He retrieved his things and walked barefoot up the path that leads from my home to the dock. He turned left, going toward the largest part of the mound, stopped, and dropped to one knee. He touched the mound with the palms of both hands and slowly raised his face to the sky. After a few seconds he stood, ducked beneath some of the low-hanging limbs from the live oaks, and vanished.

I decided to follow him. I wanted to see if he arrived in a canoe or by car. Was he casing my home? Maybe the ex-cop in me was too guarded. Screw it. Something was coalescing in my gut, something about Joe Billie was making me suspicious.

I left Max in the kitchen, put a shirt on, slipped the Glock under my belt, locked the house, and started my Jeep.

THREE

As I rounded a bend in the road I knew I'd see him. I'd try to drive slow enough to see if he hauled the canoe in a pickup truck. Maybe see a license plate. He was nowhere to be seen. I remembered an oyster shell road that led from the county road down to the river. The jaunt to the river was less than a hundred yards. I pulled up next to the river and got out of my Jeep. No Joe Billie. No canoe. Nothing.

I looked closely at the spur road. Since last night's rain, there were no tracks, no impressions from a car or truck anywhere in the damp mud, shell, and gravel. How did a barefoot man beat me as he walked a half mile to his canoe?

I watched the river for a moment. An invisible curtain of wind came upriver, rippling the surface like someone playing piano keys across the water. A mob of gnats swarmed near the shore. The air was building in heat and humidity. I felt a drop of sweat roll down my spine. There was the hint of rain in the air.

As I started toward the Jeep, I heard a noise in the thick trees. A crashing sound of attacking wings and aggression. There was a shrill protest from a bird and then silence. A bright red feather floated to the ground. I looked up. A great horned owl, yellow eyes unblinking, stared down at me. The owl had captured and killed a cardinal. The body of the limp redbird lay still under the owl's talons. I knew these big birds occasionally hunted in the daylight, but I never expected to witness it.

I watched a smaller feather from the dead cardinal float on an air current toward the river. It was then that I saw the sliver of lemon yellow that looked strangely out of place. Maybe it was a piece of trash that had washed up in the current. But trash doesn't move by itself. As I approached the spot, the sliver of yellow became the blouse of a woman who was either dead or near death.

The woman had been severely beaten. Her left eye was swollen shut. I knelt down and reached for the hand that lay across her stomach. Her pulse was weak. She was young. Maybe eighteen. Lower lip split. A wound in her upper chest. Her breathing was labored, a slight gurgling sound coming at each inhalation. Dried blood at the corner of her mouth and nostrils. Her blue jeans were stained with blood.

"Can you hear me?" I asked.

She opened her eyes. There was no connection. She seemed to stare at a place somewhere above my head. She was distant and dying. I gently squeezed her hand and lifted a strand of hair from her face. She gasped and pulled away.

"I'm not going to hurt you."

She started to shake. She was going into shock. Her life was compressed into minutes. I held her hand. "There is a phone in my car. I'll call for help."

Her lips trembled, and she whispered something in a language I didn't recognize. "*Atlacatl imix cuanmiztli*" she said in a labored breath.

What did it mean? There was a slight reflex from her hand. A single tear escaped through swollen flesh and shattered blood vessels, past the slit of an eyelid, down her face, and vanished into mud and river sand. One of the bruises on her cheek resembled the letter U.

I ran to my Jeep and dialed 911. "Come on!" An answer on the third ring. I explained to the sheriff's dispatcher that an ambulance would be too slow. The victim needed to be airlifted by helicopter to the hospital now. I took a towel out of the backseat of the Jeep and ran back to the girl.

"You're going to be okay," I said in the most convincing voice I could. My heart raced. "Medical help is coming! Do you hear me?" There was only the sound of air escaping her chest. I applied pressure to her wound. She was slipping away.

Where the hell are they?

She looked at me for a long moment, the clear eye seeming to connect. It was now a pleading, frightened eye, an eye too wise for its host. From somewhere lost in history and heritage, she looked at me through the saddened eye of the elders. She wept silently. I never felt so helpless.

The wail of sirens sounded in the distance. I heard a helicopter far away. But the look in her eye was further away as it peered through time and space and found me.

I held her hand, my own eyes suddenly watering. "Stay with me! Okay? Stay with me! I'll find the person who did this to you."

FOUR

The feeling was almost surreal. For years I had investigated crime scenes. Now I was the one being questioned. The initial battery of Volusia County deputies had been efficient, articulate, and polite in asking most of the right questions. Had I known the victim? Did I see anyone? They scribbled notes, eyes panning my face while I explained what happened. I gave them permission to search my car as a team of forensics people started sifting through the surroundings.

Then the detectives arrived. A man and a woman got out of an unmarked Crown Vic. Another man, who was alone, parked behind them and stayed in his car with a cell phone welded to his ear. The detectives huddled with two officers for a few minutes, heads nodding and glancing toward me. Then they walked in my direction.

She was in her midthirties, an attractive brunette with an aggressive, no-nonsense walk. The man was a little younger. African American, light skin, square shoulders. They both carried notepads and small tape recorders.

She said, "Mr. O'Brien?"

"That would be me."

"I'm Detective Leslie Moore, and this is Detective Dan Grant, homicide." Detective Grant removed his sunglasses and nodded. The woman continued, "I understand you worked homicide for Miami PD?"

"Thirteen years."

Detective Grant said, "Well, you ought to be used to this. What'd you see?"

"You never get used to it." I told them the entire story. They didn't interrupt. I concluded by asking them a question. "Is she alive?"

"We don't know," Detective Moore said. "She's in surgery."

Detective Grant folded his notepad, looked out across the river. "You move up here from Miami, left a place where you investigated killings, and now you find one not far from your house. I guess you're pretty unlucky, huh?"

"Detective Moore just said the vic's in surgery. So, at this moment, it's not a murder. As far as I could tell, the young woman was raped, stabbed, and left for dead."

"How'd you know she was raped?" he asked.

"It was obvious."

Detective Moore interrupted. "Mr. O'Brien, when you spoke with this man"—she paused and looked at her notes—"this Joe Billie . . . with your background, did you sense anything suspicious about him?"

"I was intrigued that he'd been walking in the river. Not many people do that."

"What is your occupation now?"

"I don't have one."

"Does it get boring sitting home all day after a career with Miami PD?"

"I don't sit home all day. I'm remodeling the old place."

17

She smiled. "We appreciate your cooperation. I'd just like to know where we might be able to locate you if you're not home."

"You have my cell."

"Sometimes people forget their cell phones."

"I spend time working on an old sport fishing boat I have at Ponce Marina."

"You in the charter fishing business?" Detective Grant asked.

"Thinking about it."

The detective who had been sitting in the car approached. His shaved head glistened in the sun. He stepped in front of the other two detectives and came a little too close to my personal space. I could smell his aftershave and perspiration soaking into his starched collar. A blood vessel moved beneath the skin near his left forehead and pulsated like a worm crawling under his scalp.

"I'm Detective Slater. We appreciate your cooperation here, Mr. O'Brien. In your excitement, and it happens to lots of folks who stumble upon a crime scene, you didn't compromise anything, right? You know, pick up any possible evidence."

I looked at my reflection in his sunglasses and saw myself grin as if I was just asked how long I'd been potty trained. "I tried to save a young woman's life."

He glanced down at my hands. "How'd you get those cuts?"

"I'm restoring an old house. Replacing wood. House looks better than me."

"I guess the scratch on your chin came from the dock."

"That's right."

"You never saw the victim before today?"

"That's correct."

"You saw nobody around? Just happened to walk up on a dying woman?"

"While you were on your cell phone, I explained to these detectives why I was here. Prior to that, I gave a full report to the officers."

"You told the deputies that a man approached your dock." He paused for effect. "Let me get this story straight . . . you said he walked out of the river?"

"He seemed as serious as the guys with the metal detectors, but he was looking for arrowheads. Had a sack full of them."

"How'd he get in the river?" Slater asked.

"I suppose he walked."

"According to your statement, the man docked his canoe a half mile from your home and walked into the river hunting arrowheads."

"That's what he told me."

"Kinda risky. Gators are mating and building nests. They get very territorial."

"The man's probably native Seminole. They've dodged gators for centuries."

"Why were you looking for him?"

"He'd offered to help me repair my dock, but I didn't get his number before he left. The man wasn't acting like someone who'd raped and beaten a woman."

"How'd you know she was raped?"

"It was evident—blood, a lot of it."

Detective Slater took out a handkerchief and wiped his bald head. He carefully folded the handkerchief and tucked it into his pocket. "Mr. O'Brien, you're using a lot of supposition. We assume the victim was raped, but we haven't received a report from the hospital. And you say this Joe Billie, a man who walks on water, didn't 'act like' someone who'd just committed a heinous crime."

"I worked homicide for thirteen years. Miami."

Slater slowly removed his sunglasses. He seemed to be seeing me for the first time. "You look a little young to retire."

I said nothing.

"Did the victim say anything to you? Anything at all?"

There was something different about the way he asked the question. His eyes too eager to get an answer. The body language edgy. I thought about mentioning what I heard the girl say, but I didn't. "She was going into shock when I found her."

"Too bad. Just a short description of the perp would help."

I turned to leave.

Slater said, "We found a gun under the seat in your Jeep."

"I have a permit to carry it."

"No doubt."

He handed his business card to me. "If you remember any other details, here's my number. It's an interesting coincidence, Mr. O'Brien. You worked homicide in Miami, you move out here, and you walk into a crime scene that might become a murder."

I DROVE SLOWLY EAST on State Road 44 as I tried to put the pieces of the morning together. I needed to sort out the smallest details of what I'd just experienced. I decided to drive to Ponce Inlet, buy a new bilge pump, breathe some salt air, and install the pump on *Jupiter*. I'd try to forget the look in the girl's eye.

There was one problem: I couldn't forget.

FIVE

It was late in the afternoon when I finally arrived at the Ponce Marina. Finding and buying the right bilge pump took longer than I expected. Now it was less than two hours before sunset, and the posts on the marina docks cast long shadows toward the east.

Five months ago, at a DEA auction, I'd bought a thirty-eight-foot Bayliner for ten cents on the dollar. The boat was nine years old. It had an ample cockpit for fishing, a dive platform, two cabins, a salon, and a fly bridge. I'd picked it up not long after selling *Eternity*. Sailing was a love, but sailing without the woman I loved was no longer fun.

My new-old boat was called *Jupiter*. I had it overhauled and painted and the zincs replaced before I piloted it up the Intracoastal to Ponce Marina in Ponce Inlet.

Today I wanted to work with my hands—to center my thoughts on something other than the girl I'd found. I twisted bolts and did some minor rewiring on board *Jupiter* as I tried to will the bilge pump into place. Every time I refocused on the job at hand, my thoughts would shift to the girl. Was she going to be all right physically? Maybe. In the heart, never. Who was she? How'd she get to the river?

I reconnected the wires, got out from the depths of the bilge, and switched on the power. The pump hummed, and a steady pulse of water splashed into the marina bay. Within a few minutes the bilge was dry.

A slight breeze moved across the mangroves on the western side of the bay, and I could smell the saltwater rising in the tidal flats. The tide was creeping up on the oyster beds, spider-legged mangrove roots, and sandbars.

I went below, shucked off my T-shirt and faded swimsuit, and was soon soaping up in the shower next to the master cabin. The warm water beat against the back of my neck. It's easy to remove the dirt, but how do you wash away a mood?

With my eyes closed, I could see her face. Her unharmed eye looking at me. Looking into me. I let the water run over my head and closed my eyes for a full minute. Something in my mind popped to a pixilated image, a subliminal portrait of another victim now blurred by time and fatigue. I tried to frame it before the image faded like fireworks in the night sky. Gone. There was something about this girl that I'd seen somewhere else. What was it? Where? I tried to concentrate on each detail I saw at the crime scene.

I could still feel her weak pulse on the tips of my fingers. Under the drone of the shower, I heard her labored breathing. The frantic weight of her struggle dropped around me like soot.

I visualized her beaten body. Face. Swollen jaw. The bruise in the shape of a U. The nose. The lips. What was it? What had I seen somewhere else? I pressed my forearms against the shower walls, steadying myself and keeping the walls from closing in around me. The shower now sounded like a roaring waterfall.

I dried off, put on fresh shorts and a clean T-shirt, and pulled a Corona from the farthest and coldest ranks of the bottles in the fridge. I found an aspirin bottle, shook out two of the little white gods, and tossed them down with a swig of beer.

I punched in a stored connection on my cell phone. My former Miami PD homicide partner, Ron Hamilton, picked up the phone with his customary greeting.

"How the hell are you, Sean?"

"What did you ever do before caller ID?"

"It's got its pluses and minuses. Tips are way down. Nobody wants to get involved. Nobody wants to leave a trail. But the nuts still call. They don't give a shit." He paused for a moment. "Why haven't I heard from you in, what . . . four months?"

"No real reasons, you know, still trying to put the pieces back together again. I'm hoping I'll figure it out before I'm broke." I paced *Jupiter*'s salon.

Ron was one of the few friends I had left inside Miami PD. He and his wife, Alice, had been there through Sherri's illness, death, and funeral. They helped take care of arrangements. All I did was to honor Sherri's wishes and scatter her ashes at sea.

I told Ron about the girl's death, described her features and what she was wearing. I filled him in on what I knew of Joe Billie.

"Think Joe Billie is the perp?" he asked.

"Don't know. Guy's a little odd."

"So are you, Sean. For Christ's sake, you're supposed to be moving on with your life. Let the locals handle it. You made a promise to Sherri."

"And I made a promise to the girl I held today. I said I'd find who did it."

"Just walk away, Sean. Okay?"

"She almost died in my arms. She might be dead for all I know."

"The more you get involved, and I've seen it a dozen times, the more obsessed you get. I've heard you say that someone has to speak for the dead, the unsolved murders. The sheer volume is like being in a war, maybe like some of that shit you went through in Afghanistan."

I said nothing. I could hear him breathing hard into the phone.

Ron said, "I'm not a psychologist—"

"That's right. You're not."

"You were a damn great investigator. You take justice personally, but it doesn't work that way, bro. I saw how this tore you apart from people in your life. People who are or were alive. Sherri and—screw it! You are who you are. Sorry, Sean. Just let it be, old buddy."

I let Ron cool off for a long moment before I responded. "You ever hold a dying girl in your arms?"

"No." His voice was flat.

"I do get obsessive when I see a human being victimized that way, and I feel the investigation is a lot weaker than the perp who did it. You know it's the first forty-eight hours that shape it. I don't think the lead detective up here has a sense of urgency. But I *held* her, for God's sake. Did everything I could to keep her alive. Her life and, if she died, her death do take on a personal priority."

Ron's voice was softer. "In homicide, we aren't called to the scene before they die. Must be fucking awful to stumble on one alive . . . barely."

"There was something about this girl . . . something I've seen before."

"What's that?"

"Don't know. I can't place it because, like you said, I was trying so hard to save her life that the usual details I always scrutinized became a film shot at high speed through adrenaline, and I can't seem to play it back in slow motion. Maybe it was something she said. The way she looked. Exotic and fragile. She said something in a language I didn't recognize. She said, '*Atlacatl imix cuanmiztli.*'"

"Wonder what it means?"

"Not sure. She might be here illegally, smuggled. Maybe connected to the migrant camps, but I don't think the vic had spent an hour in the fields. No calluses on her hands. The way she was dressed. Maybe it was a lovers' quarrel that got way out of hand, or something with deeper repercussions."

"What do you mean?"

"Not sure yet."

"I'll check missing persons reports. Might want to touch base with the feds."

"And I might want to try bungee jumping."

"You remember Lauren Miles in the FBI's Miami office?" Ron asked.

"We've crossed territorial paths."

"That's her. Too bad, she's such a looker. Easier to dislike if she wasn't."

"What about her?"

"The *Herald* ran a story on one of her investigations a few months ago. She's investigating missing persons, mostly young women, or at least she was. Florida's kinda the epicenter for runaways and people that simply vanish."

"They vanish because their bodies are never found. Others are stolen, maybe sold in some human trafficking ring. They might as well be dead, too."

"Yeah," said Ron, "but unless they're somebody's neighbor, they become yesterday's news real fast."

"They're all somebody's daughter. I owe you one, Ron."

"You owe me nothing. You do owe Sherri, God rest her soul, a promise to do something else with your life. Sounds like you stepped in a big shit hole. Ask yourself if it's worth it. Remember the price you paid."

Ron was gone, but his words lingered in the salon like foul cigarette smoke.

SIX

I had to get some fresh air. I tossed my phone on the sofa in the salon, went out the sliding glass doors leading to the cockpit, and climbed the ladderlike steps to the fly bridge. This was the perch I liked most. I unzipped and folded up the isinglass, exposing all four quadrants of the fly bridge to the coastal breezes. I sat in the captain's chair, swiveled around, propped my feet up on the console, and sipped the beer. Another hour and the sun would be setting beyond the expanse of estuaries and flat, tidal marshes. A half dozen brown pelicans sailed effortlessly across the marina.

I held the cold bottle to the left side of my forehead. The alcohol and aspirin seemed to work in unison, the throb becoming less of a pain and more of a state of mind. As I looked across the marina toward the wide Intracoastal, I thought of the last time I sailed with Sherri. I closed my eyes and could hear her voice.

"Hey, Sean! Got a minute?" It was Dave Collins, standing on the bow of his boat, rinsing off the swim platform.

"Sure," I said.

Dave Collins wasn't one of the boomers who dreamed of sailing around the world. Before retirement, he was employed by American oil companies. He'd worked in countries like Saudi Arabia, Sudan, and Israel. He had been in "human resources," a recruiter, so he said. Dave had two daughters and one grandson living in Michigan. His boat, *Gibraltar*, a forty-two-foot trawler, was a few slips away from *Jupiter*.

Dave shut off the water and put away the hose. In his early sixties, he was silver-haired and broad-shouldered. No beer belly in spite of his love of dark beers. Like me, he'd lost his wife, but his loss was because of divorce.

As Dave stepped onto *Jupiter*'s cockpit, I said, "Get a beer and come on up."

He whistled as he rummaged down in the galley and then climbed the bridge ladder, beer in hand, with the agility of someone half his age. "You had a visitor."

"Who?"

"A detective. Said his name was Slater."

"What else did he say?"

Dave sipped his beer. "Are you in some kind of trouble?"

"By default." I told him about finding the girl.

Dave set the beer in the cup holder. "I saw a little piece on the news. They didn't have much. Said an unidentified woman was found beaten and stabbed near the St. Johns River. The reporter said police are questioning a 'person of interest.' By the detective's line of questioning, I bet you're that 'person of interest.' You think this Joe Billie did it?"

"I wish I knew."

Dave made a slight grunt and sipped his beer. "Tell me again what the victim said, the words she uttered to you?"

"*Atlacatl imix cuanmiztli.*"

Dave wrote it down on the back of a napkin. "Wonder what it means?" He folded the napkin and placed it in the pocket of his Hawaiian-print shirt. "If English isn't her first language, what is? Where's home?"

"She looked exotic, sort of like the people I've seen in areas of Central America. I'd held her hand waiting for paramedics. There were no calluses. Nails were painted, lipstick smeared. She wore tight jeans and a blouse."

"What are you thinking?"

"I'm wondering if she made it. Who's her family? Where's she from?"

"Sean, this detective is curious about you."

"What else did he say?"

"Didn't seem like your typical sleuth."

"How?"

"Poor listener. Knew answers to questions before he finished asking them."

"What sort of questions?"

"The usual. How much time did you spend on the boat? Did you ever bring women here? Any rough stuff or noises? He was trying to see if you fit a profile."

"What'd you tell him?"

"I told him you were a loner and came to the boat only on the night of a full moon and on a high tide." Dave chuckled and swallowed the last ounce of his beer. "I didn't tell him a damn thing, really. Nothing to tell. You're one of the good guys, Sean. A burnout, but one of the good guys. Seen my share of the bad ones."

"Bet you have."

"Let me know if there's anything I can do."

"Thanks, Dave."

"Maybe I can catch you for eggs and issues in the morning."

Dave never referred to the morning meal as "breakfast." It was always called "eggs and issues" because it was when he liked discussing the morning newspaper.

"Tiki bar at eight for breakfast," I said.

THE ROAR OF A DOZEN Harleys arriving carried across the marina. The bikers seemed to parade through the marina's gravel parking lot, disembarking in front of the Bayside Bar and Grille. Black leather and jeans stepping from the shiny chrome, like cowboys tying up horses in front of a saloon at sundown on a Saturday night.

I could smell the smoke from blackened Florida redfish coming from the Bayside, which was an outdoor tiki bar with a roof of dried palm fronds. The hangout catered to tourists, boaters, bikers, and a few vagabonds that fell between the cracks and landed on bar stools. The tiki bar sat on stilts over the water.

Maybe I'd stay on *Jupiter* for the night, make sure the bilge was performing well. As I debated whether to make the drive home, I thought about Max and her tiny bladder.

So it would be an evening with a wiener dog. I'd call Dave and cancel breakfast.

I CROSSED THE DUNLAWTON BRIDGE just as the sun was painting the Halifax River in shades of flattened copper and deep merlot reds that simmered across the water like a river of blood. The day's events seemed a lifetime ago. Was the girl okay? No, she wasn't okay. Never would be. Was she alive?

Then I turned my Jeep around and drove fast toward Halifax Hospital.

SEVEN

Death has an odor unlike any other. The smell is often the first thing that greets you at a murder crime scene. In Miami, the heat and humidity would accelerate the decay process. Some cops seemed to get used to it. I never did. It was resurrected the moment I walked into the hospital emergency room.

The intensive care unit of Halifax Hospital is a sanitized place where the whiff of death isn't permitted. There was the smell of misery, though. I could detect it between the layers of disinfectant. It was the scrubbed hint of diarrhea, bleach, vomit, adhesive bandages, medicines, and human stress.

Nine adults and three children sat in the ER waiting room. I looked at each face, trying to determine a connection between the victim I'd found and anyone in the waiting room. Three of the grown-ups were black; the half dozen others were white.

A nurse seated behind the desk ignored me as she keyed information into a computer. "Excuse me," I said. I waited for her to pause and look up. "A young woman was airlifted in here this morning. Can you tell me how she's doing?" I noticed that a doctor stopped writing for a moment and looked over at me.

"What's the patient's name?" the nurse asked.

"I don't know. She was young. Face injuries. Probably a rape victim."

"I need a name."

"Look, this woman was severely beaten. Is she going to be okay?"

"Are you a family member?"

"No."

"I can't release that information unless you're a member of the family or a police officer. Sorry." She dropped her eyes from me and began typing on her keyboard.

I almost instinctively reached for a badge that I hadn't carried in a year. "My name is Sean O'Brien. I found the victim. I was a homicide detective with the Miami PD. Here's my driver's license. All I'm asking you is to let me know her condition."

"That information is private. Hospital rules."

I started to tell her that I couldn't care less about hospital rules when the doctor nearby stopped writing and approached me. He motioned for me to follow him from the reception desk into an alcove. He studied me a second or two through dark eyes that looked tired yet compassionate.

"I'm Dr. Saunders. Did I hear you say that you found the girl brought in by air ambulance today?"

"Yes. How is she?"

"No one has been here except the police. We don't even have an ID for the deceased—"

"Deceased?"

"We did everything we could to save her. She was brutalized."

I said nothing. Acid burned in my stomach.

"She'd lost a lot of blood. We had to remove her womb to try to save her."

"What?"

"She'd been so abused there was no option. It's tragic. I hope her killer is found." He paused and started to leave, then hesitated. "I heard you say you were a homicide detective. Are you going to search for whoever did this to that poor girl?"

As I started to answer, his name was paged.

Dr. Saunders swiped an ID card through a slot, and a set of double doors opened to a labyrinth of treatment rooms. I stood there a moment and watched him walk down a long corridor of hope and despair.

The sounds of my surroundings seemed more acute. The pulse of digital monitors connected to misfiring hearts. Soft sobs came from behind a curtain. A baby cried.

Outside, I inhaled the night air, filling my lungs to capacity. I wanted to purge the medicinal smells of human pain from the back of my throat. There was the scent of blooming roses, fresh-cut grass, and pine. Lightning illuminated clouds over the ocean.

Exhaustion was sinking into my chest and the back of my neck. I looked forward to seeing Max. She was such a damn good listener. Never talked back, always seemed to care about what I was saying. I hoped she could hold her little bladder a while longer. Half an hour and I'd be home to let her out, feed her, fix myself some leftover chili, and end the evening on the porch with Max on my lap and a scotch in my hand.

I was almost to my Jeep when two people stepped from a row of cars.

"That's far enough, O'Brien," one of them said. "Put your hands where we can see them."

EIGHT

Detectives Slater and Moore cautiously approached me the way officers do when they think a gun is present or an arrest is imminent. Detective Moore carried something in one hand. She looked nervous, her lips tight, eyes wide, ready for confrontation.

Under the parking lot streetlights, I could see a pulse beat in one side of her neck. She said nothing, allowing Slater to throw out the first pitch.

"Mr. O'Brien, we meet again. How's the vic?"

"She's dead, but you knew that."

He was silent, searching my face for a beat. "Where have you been since I last saw you, if you don't mind me asking?"

"I do mind. I'm not a convicted felon. You're not a parole officer. So why don't you two tell me what you want and we can enjoy the rest of the night in separate places."

"I'll tell you what we want. We want your DNA. Detective Moore is prepared to take it. Don't suppose you're wearing your gun."

"Not tonight. I usually do wear a gun in a hospital to see how fast security can respond. Part of my consultant business."

Detective Moore almost smiled. She said, "We appreciate your cooperation."

Slater said, "Then you don't mind turning around and placing your hands on top of the hood. Spread your legs."

"Glad to oblige, Detective." I placed my hands on top of someone's BMW and spread my feet apart. I could hear the sirens of an approaching ambulance a few blocks away racing toward the hospital. Slater frisked me.

"All right," he said with a sound of satisfaction. "Turn around. Why were you at the hospital?"

"If there isn't a new law against hospital visitations, I'm leaving."

"Not yet," he said, holding his palm out like a crossing guard. "We'll take that DNA sample. Leslie, why don't you go on and secure a sample from Mr. O'Brien."

"Why don't you ask my permission before you start reaching in my mouth?"

Slater's eyebrows rose as if an animator had drawn them high on his forehead. "We can do this at the sheriff's office or we can do it here, Mr. O'Brien."

"I don't have a problem with a DNA sample. I do have a problem with your method of getting one."

"If you don't like police protocol, take it up with the sheriff." His jaws hardened.

"This'll be fast," said Detective Moore, as she took a swab from a plastic kit that she held. "Please, open your mouth."

"Do I say ahhhhh?" I asked, opening my mouth, allowing her to take the saliva sample, which she did.

"Thank you." This time she did smile.

Slater rocked on the balls of his feet. "When we did the search at the crime scene, we found blood in the back of your Jeep. We tested it. Came from the victim."

"As I told you, I tried to stop the bleeding from her chest. I ran back to my Jeep to call for help and to get a towel. I must have touched something."

"What did you think when you heard she'd died?"

"What did I *think*? I was saddened. She was someone's daughter."

"No one's claimed the daughter—the body. Don't have an ID. Makes it hard to alert next of kin. Right now she's a Jane Doe, unless you know her name."

I said nothing.

"I'm looking forward to the results from the DNA," he said. "Why'd you really leave Miami PD in the prime of your career? I checked on you. Seems you took a medical leave after you shot and killed an innocent man at a crime scene. Was the line gettin' a little blurry for you, O'Brien?"

"Why would I assault this girl and stay at the crime scene?"

He grinned. "We're eliminating suspects. You haven't been eliminated."

"I'm not your perp, pal. He's out there, and chances are he'll do it again if he hasn't already. Now either arrest me or get the hell out of my way."

"I'd watch that temper if I were you, O'Brien. Leads to stress."

I walked between Slater and Moore. I hoped Slater would reach his sweaty hand out to try to stop me. He didn't.

I DROVE WEST on Highway 44 toward DeLand and the St. Johns River. I watched a quarter moon play hide-and-seek with me through the trees near the road. I hadn't been home in almost fourteen hours, and I felt bad for little Max. I made a silent promise that I wouldn't even raise my voice to her if she'd peed on the floor.

The day's events played back in my mind. What had the girl whispered to me? *Was* the bruise on her cheek the letter U or something else? I knew that somewhere there *was* someone who loved her and *was* never going to see her again.

I flipped on the Jeep's high beams as I came around the last curve in my drive. The headlights panned across the house. I looked for a moving shadow or anything that appeared out of place. A fat raccoon scurried across the oyster shell drive. After I shut off the ignition, I sat and listened. There was the ticking sound of the motor cooling, the crescendo of frogs, and the whine of mosquitoes. I moved the dome light button to a manual off position, reached under the seat for my pistol, and slowly opened the door.

Stepping from the Jeep, I heard the deep-throated grunt of a bull alligator across the river. Under the moon, the live oaks were solid, shadowy giants with dark beards of Spanish moss that hung straight down. There was no breeze, and the night was warm and humid. I could smell smoke from a campfire in the national forest. A cloud drifted across the moon, drawing a curtain of black. Mosquitoes orbited my face in a halo of whines that screamed in my ear for blood.

I silently walked up the three steps leading to the screen door on the porch. I could feel that it was slightly ajar. Had I left it that way? I backed down the three steps and walked around the outside of my house.

I unlocked the front door and heard the pulsating beep of the twenty-second delay on the alarm. Max barked and scampered down the hall to greet me. "Hello, lady!" I said. Her tail was a blur. "Come on, Max, let's see if you can make it outside."

I opened the door, and Max bolted between my legs in a mad dash for some earth. I flipped on the floodlights and would have laughed if I hadn't felt so bad for leaving her home alone for hours. She squatted and peed for a full minute, looking up at me through eyes that seemed to ask, "Where the hell have you been?"

"Chow time, Max." That's all it took to see her charge across the threshold and beat a path to the kitchen. I poured a cup of her favorite dog food into her bowl. For me, it was leftover chili. I pulled a cold Corona out of the refrigerator, managed to fit the bottle in my back pocket, and picked up my chili bowl and Max's bowl, and together we headed out to the back porch to dine.

As Max ate, I took a long swallow from the beer, set the food on the table beside my chair, and looked at the moon's reflection across the river. I reached for the bowl of chili and noticed something on the far end of the table.

I recognized it. The black flint arrowhead I saw Joe Billie pull out of the river. It was lying on the table like a black diamond. The arrowhead was fitted into a long wooden shaft, trimmed with eagle feathers and notched at the end.

NINE

The next morning, the St. Johns was a late sleeper. No visible current moving. No ripple across the surface. The humidity was already building, and it was a little before 8:00 A.M. The beards of Spanish moss hanging from my live oaks seemed to sweat as the rising sun evaporated the heavy dew.

A shaft of sunlight crept around a tree and broke through the screen, directly hitting the black arrowhead on the table. In the light, I could see that the arrowhead still retained its edge. I glanced down at Max, and she looked up at me.

"So where do you think that arrowhead came from, Max, at least originally? We saw Billie pull it out of the river, but how did it get there?" Max wagged her tail and half barked and half whined, a signal she uses to encourage me to let her outside for her morning ritual. "Just a minute, I have an idea before we heed nature's call."

I got a plastic trash bag from the kitchen and a pair of barbecue tongs and carefully lifted the arrow into the bag. I sealed it. "Max, we'll have the lab see if Billie left any prints on it. What lab?" I wanted to call Ron back, to send the arrow to him for processing, but at that moment I didn't feel like a lecture.

Something moved down by the river. Through my kitchen window, I could see a small boat chugging in the river. It belched smoke from the engine like puffs of blue fog.

I poured a cup of coffee and escorted Max down the steps and into the yard. We headed toward the dock. I'd seen the man, usually very early in the morning. I figured he was a commercial fisherman. I waved, which caught his attention, and signaled him to come to my dock. He made a half circle in the center of the river and steered the boat toward Max and me.

"Good morning," I said.

"Mornin'," he said, killing the small motor.

He was in his midsixties. His face and hands were dark, basted by sun, work, and water. The left side of his pewter beard was streaked a dark eggplant color. He leaned over and spat tobacco juice.

"Toss me a line. Want some coffee?" I asked.

He tossed the line. "No thanks. Got me a thermos in the boat."

"I'm Sean O'Brien. I moved here a few months ago. Thought I'd introduce myself. I've seen you on the river. Usually at the crack of dawn."

"Name's Floyd Powell. I was lookin' at stringin' a trotline from near here to the opposite side. But the river's too deep. Catch nothin' but cats and rays."

"You a commercial fisherman?"

"Yep." Another spit. "Cute dog. Keep him away from the river's edge. Dog's even too close at the end of the dock. He's a little bit, but he's big-time gator bait." Floyd used a paddle to lift the top off a cooler in the center of the boat. Dozens of large catfish and one bass thrashed in the sunlight. "That's what I done so far this mornin'." He placed some Red Man in his cheek and listened, his eyes constantly looking back toward the river, scanning. Watchful.

I remembered seeing a photograph on a fish camp wall of a man twenty years younger than the man in front of me. In the photo he was barefoot and shirtless, standing in front of a shack with a girl about age five or six standing on his shoulders. His arms were outstretched to help her balance. They stood next to a monstrous alligator that was tied by the neck with chains and suspended high in the air from the blade of a front-end loader.

"Are you the same Floyd Powell in the picture on the wall at Raven Moon Fish Camp, the one with the huge gator?"

He cocked a gray eyebrow and spat tobacco juice. "You recognized me in that old picture? Damn, that's impressive. You a cop?"

"Not anymore."

"My daughter was five in that picture. She's twenty now. This river's got some bigger gators than that. Right here in this bend, I seen one that'd go ever bit of fifteen feet. I hunt gators in season, and I'm licensed by the state to hunt nuisance gators. Had a little processing house about ten miles downriver where the power lines cross north of Hontoon Bridge. I'd butcher the gators, sell the hides, meat, whatnot. Some fellers bought the place recently. Said they was part of a fishin' club. They didn't look like people who fish. I used to guide. You can usually tell." He glanced at Max. "How'd you make the connection between me and the old picture?"

"Didn't at first, but your name was written below the photo with the length and weight of the alligator. I've had some practice remembering names and faces on photos."

"Bet you have."

I broached the next question so I could get a good look at his eyes. "Let me ask you something." He glanced up from his boat. "Did you hear about the murder yesterday on the river?" His eyes were as dark as the water. No looking away. There was a slight nod of the head. "It happened about a half mile south of here. A young woman was found. She'd been beaten and stabbed."

He chewed the tobacco thoughtfully, quiet for a long moment. The catfish beat at the side of the container. A hawk cried out. "Not much in the paper. No picture. Law ain't arrested nobody yet."

"I wonder if you or anyone may have seen something."

"Such as?"

"Anything out of the ordinary."

"What'd you drivin' at?"

"Do you know Joe Billie?"

"Know of him. Can't say I really *know* him."

"Where's he live?"

"You do sound like a cop. I've had 'nough experience in that area. Used to do a little poaching." He stuffed some tobacco leaves between his gum and cheek. "You might find Billie at Hangin' Moss Fish Camp."

"Thanks. That's not too far from here."

He looked at me like I had said I was going to swim across the river in the dead of night. "You gonna question Billie about the killin'?"

"Why?"

"It's not 'cause you said you ain't a cop no more."

"Then what is it?"

"They say Billie's a descendant of Osceola. It was Osceola who gave the guv'ment hell during the Seminole Wars. Never beat him. Few years ago, a bone hunter was caught diggin' up one of the Seminoles' sacred burial sites. This Indiana Jones fancied himself to be an anthropologist, but I heard he was sellin' skulls to some devil-worshippin' cult. The fella had been warned by Game and Fish to stay the hell outta the wildlife refuge and the protected mounds. A state biologist I know said he'd heard this idiot went and dug up a medicine man's head. You just don't do that to the Seminole people. They didn't get the name 'unconquered' for nothin'. Rumor has it that Joe Billie tracked the guy, caught him doin' a dig, hog-tied the ol' boy, carried him down to the glades. The bone hunter ain't been seen since."

"You recall his name?"

"Best I recollect, feller's name was Clayton Suskind."

"How long ago did this happen?"

"Less than a year."

"Did Suskind live in Volusia County?"

Floyd smiled, his teeth the color of baked beans. "If you hadn't told me you was once the law, I coulda figured it out by now. Why you so interested in Joe Billie?"

"He was here the day the girl was found. Walked out of the river."

"I've seen him collectin' stuff outta the river."

"Hanging Moss Fish Camp, right?"

"Best be careful if you start jerkin' Billie's chain. He might hang you by your scrotum if you fuck with him. And you're a big feller." He smiled, spat over the side of the boat. "Got to get these cats to the fish house. Runnin' low on ice."

I saw a small spiral notebook in his shirt pocket behind the to-bacco pouch. "If I can have a piece of paper out of your notebook there, I can write down my cell number."

"Sure." He pulled the pad out of his pocket.

"If you come in contact with anyone who might have seen or heard something in the area where the girl was killed, please call me."

He yanked the motor cord. The old Evinrude started on one pull, smoke encircling the small boat. Before he put the motor in gear, he looked at Max and then at me. "Y'all are new to the river and all. Best be careful, know what I mean?"

I watched the silent river flow around the elbow, the crooked bend across from my dock, and I remembered holding the girl's trembling hand. I felt there was something very evil around the corner. It was quiet as the current in front of me and darker than the water. I felt its presence just beyond the corners of my blind spots. It preyed on the helpless, the fragile—those broken in mind, spirit, and body.

I looked at Max. "There have been warnings, Max. What are we to do?"

She barked and trotted to the end of the dock, then glanced back at me. I followed her and we looked down and saw our reflections off the black water.

I wondered if there was anything just below the surface watching us.

I PACKAGED THE ARROW for overnight delivery to Ron Hamilton at Miami PD. I marked the box: CONFIDENTIAL. I sat down and fired off an e-mail to him:

> Package will arrive in a.m. Please rush the workup the best you can. See what you have on a missing person, Clayton Suskind, d.o.b unknown, last domicile, Volusia County. Check bodies recovered from Everglades in the last two years.

TEN

The morning sun was topping the tree line down by the river when I started for the door. Max followed me through the house, where she sat down on her rear end and watched me lock the door. She cocked her head. I almost expected her to open her mouth and speak.

"Stay here, Max, I'll be back in a few hours." She looked up at me with disbelieving brown eyes. Yesterday I told Max the same thing and almost caused her to develop a kidney infection. "All right, you can come along. Let's go ask Mr. Billie a few questions. You're the only backup I have."

THE WHITE LETTERS on the cypress plank sign leading into Hanging Moss Fish Camp were faded, but I could still make out the words. It read BAIT, BEER, BOATS. Under a dozen live oaks and cabbage palms were single-wide trailers, rustic cabins, and a vintage silver

Airstream trailer closer to the river. I parked the Jeep in front of the bait shop.

A gunshot popped.

Max barked.

"Hush, Max!" I half-zipped the isinglass windows on the Jeep just high enough to keep Max from jumping out. I shoved the pistol under my belt in the small of my back. I could see no one. I eased out of the Jeep. "Stay, Max! Keep your head down!"

A second shot fired. It came from the direction of the river. I darted to a fifty-five-gallon trash barrel next to an embankment that gave me a vantage point to look down at the river forty feet below me. I followed a worn flight of wooden stairs to a boat dock.

A shirtless man, bare feet grungy, blurred tattoos on both forearms, stood holding a 12-gauge shotgun. Two boys in their early teens watched something in the weeds. One boy said, "I'll get it with a paddle, Daddy." He took a paddle from one of the johnboats and reached into the weeds, lifting out a large water moccasin. Half the snake's head was blown away.

"He's still alive!" the younger boy yelled.

"No it ain't," the man said. "That's just dying nerves twitchin' the tail. Set him down, boy. Coon'll come along tonight and eat it."

The man spotted me and said, "I was cleanin' some fish over there, turned around, and that damn snake had a whole crappie in his mouth. Like to eat it right off my stringer. That'll teach the sons-a-bitch."

"Don't think it'll be back for seconds," I said.

He set the shotgun down, shook a cigarette loose from a Camel pack, lit it with a Zippo in his pocket and inhaled a long draw. He looked out toward the water as he exhaled. "River's full of them. Moccasins are mean motherfuckin' snakes."

I looked at his catch. "How's fishing?"

"Pretty good," he said after exhaling smoke. "I bring 'em boys up here every year. We usually do good, exceptin' three years ago when the river was so high."

"Do you know Joe Billie? He lives here at the camp."

"Don't know nobody. You can check with Doris in the store."

"Thanks."

He nodded and flipped his cigarette toward the dead snake.

Max poked her head out one of the airholes I'd left for her. She watched me silently as I opened the bait shop's screen door. The image that hit me was of an old Florida bait shop with a faded postmark and no return address. Hanging behind the counter was a six-foot rattlesnake skin, filleted open, shellacked, and tacked to a cypress board. Pickled eggs and hoop cheese were sold next to alligator-claw backscratchers.

No one was in the small store, but the images of ghosts were tacked to one wall. A father stood next to his daughter and helped the girl hold a stringer of catfish. A barefooted man in bib overalls held up a bass the size of a roasted turkey.

"Help you?" He stood at the threshold of a side door and wiped his hands on a towel. Friendly face, ruddy, perspiring skin.

"Is Doris here?" I asked.

"She's off. I'm Carl. I was skimming shiners out of the tank. Didn't hear you."

"Do you know Joe Billie?"

"Doesn't ring a bell. He rent here?"

"That's what I hear."

"He a friend of yours?"

"He's a handyman. I have some work I need done."

"I haven't met anybody named Joe Billie. You could ask the witch in the blue and white trailer about two hundred yards on the left."

"Witch?"

"I wouldn't go there unless you really need to find this guy."

"Why?"

"If you stop there, you'll find out."

ELEVEN

As I drove slowly through the fish camp, I tried to match any one of the trailers or cabins with Billie. They all looked pretty much the same. A 1950s feel. Sagging trailers with aged aluminum the tint of potato peels. The wooden cabins were painted in varied shades of army green. Most had screen doors. All had tin roofs.

A middle-aged woman stood next to a vintage trailer and watered flowers that looked plastic. A sign in her patch of green yard read PSYCHIC READINGS BY REV. JANE.

I stopped and stepped out of the Jeep. Her head didn't turn, but I could tell she was watching me. Her hair was swept back, covered by a strawberry-colored scarf. She wore a smocklike dress, dark blue with the images of yellow owls on it. I stepped closer. Her skin was alabaster white with tiny blue spider veins just below the surface on her forehead. Wide emerald green eyes masked detachment.

A breeze picked up across the river, and wind chimes began tinkling.

The chimes hung like holiday ornaments from the lower branches of an oak.

She waited for me to speak. "Do you live here?"

"Two years now. Moved up from a spiritualists' camp in Cassadaga."

Her voice was beyond flat. It was more distant than the moon.

"Saw your sign. Thought you might have some information. I need—"

She held up one hand. "I know why you're here. You want something."

"Good guess. Let me guess, you're Reverend Jane, right?" She nodded and watered a sunflower the size of a pie plate.

"It wasn't a guess. You want something. Everybody who comes here does."

"And what do you want, Reverend Jane?" She ignored me, turning to water her flowers. "Sure, I'd like some information."

Her colorless lips pursed for a brief moment. "Come inside."

I looked toward Max, who watched without a bark. Not a good sign for Max.

"Maybe I can just ask you a couple of questions here in the yard."

She turned off the water and dropped the hose. "I don't do readings outside."

"Not looking for a reading."

"I know what you're looking for."

"Everybody is searching for something."

"Not everybody is hunting for who you want."

"Who's that?"

"The Indian. I don't work for free." She turned to go inside. I followed her through a curtain of beads into a dark room illuminated by three burning candles. The scent of candles was layered with the odor of cigarette smoke, cat urine, and incense. We sat at a round wooden table. Tarot cards on its surface. Cup of black liquid to one side.

She looked up at me through eyes now the color of a fresh-cut lime. "Your dog's okay where she is. Nobody's gonna mess with her." She sipped from the black drink. "Would you like tea?"

"No thanks."

"He's not here."

"Who's not here?"

"Joe Billie. Isn't that who you want?"

"I suppose you know the answer to that. Did Carl in the bait shop tip you off?"

"Questions like that don't bother me. Not anymore."

"You know who I'm looking for. Where can I find him?"

"He'll find you. That's if he wants to. He's mostly Seminole. Which means he's mostly found if he wants to be."

"Does he live at this fish camp?"

"He's here sometimes. Visits the reservation, too. Where he really lives, even I can't see that."

"Where does he stay?"

Her eyes dropped back to mine. "The silver trailer next to the river."

"Thank you." I stood to leave.

"That's twenty dollars."

As I reached in my back pocket for my wallet, she stared above my head, her eyes narrowing, mouth opening like a baby bird.

"She fears for you," said the woman, her voice now with a hint of compassion.

"What are you saying? My wife? Sherri?"

"Angela is her name."

"Ask her who killed her!"

Catlike, the lime green in the woman's eyes changed shades, darkening some. Her skin twitched once below her right eye. She was silent.

"What's her last name? What's Angela's last name?"

"I see nothing else." She closed her eyes for a few seconds. "I'm tired."

I dropped a twenty-dollar bill down to the table. It landed directly on one of the tarot cards, covering it. She opened her eyes and looked at the money for a long moment, picking it up and slowly turning over the single card. A red patch appeared on her neck. She continued staring at the card. "Be warned of the three men. He'll send them first. If you survive, then he will come."

"Who?"

"You'll know."

"Know what?"

"He wears the mark of the serpents. If you see the mark . . . it will be too late."

"Stop the riddles and cut to the chase."

"This is not a riddle. It's a prophecy." She seemed to breathe for the first time since she sat down. The dark green eyes were now tired eyes.

"Who and what are you talking about? Is it related to the murder of the girl?"

"I don't know. I can't see anything now. Whatever I said, it's up to you to decide if you want to believe it. I need to rest." She looked away, folded the money, stood up as if her body hurt, and slipped through another set of beads.

Angela. Was that the girl's name? Had she appeared to the woman? All of my training and experience in investigations told me it was phony. Smoke, mirrors, and bullshit. Even in the stale, recycled air, my neck felt hot. The room seemed oppressive and dark as a dungeon. I looked down at the table before leaving. The single card that the woman had turned over depicted an armored skeleton riding a white horse.

At the bottom of the card was one word: DEATH.

TWELVE

I closed Reverend Jane's front door and wondered if Max could sniff the darkness on my clothes that probably clung to me like a curse. I could smell rain in the wind coming across the marshes. Two purple martin gourds hung from a pole, clanking into each other in the stiff breeze. The wind chimes were sounding like angry bell ringers.

Max was unusually silent as I approached the car. Maybe a spell had been cast on her or me. "If I stink like a dungeon, Max, I'll put the windows down to get some air in here and blow the ghosts out." Her tail resumed its normal blur. Spell busted.

There was no car in front of the silver Airstream. I drove by the trailer and parked about one hundred feet away under the boughs of a live oak.

"Max, I'll be right back. Anybody fly by on a broomstick—bite 'em." I pulled out my shirttail, hiding the pistol that was wedged under my belt.

The Airstream looked like an advertisement in a page from an old *Saturday Evening Post*. There was no mailbox. No address.

I strolled around the parameter like a lost fisherman circling the small backyard, which was fifty feet from the river. A canoe was turned upside down, supported above the ground by two sawhorses.

The trailer had no rear door. Approaching the front door, I wasn't sure whether to knock or kick through it. The only backup I had was a nine-pound dachshund. I knocked hard. I couldn't hear anyone moving inside. As I turned the handle, the door opened with a squeak. I pulled out my pistol and entered.

The smell of burned wood, dried grasses, and rich humus came from the shadows of the interior. The tiny living room had a worn rust-colored couch, an unfinished wooden rocker, and a bookcase. On the shelves were a dozen small canning jars, each sealed. Most were about filled with tree bark, roots, leaves, soil, and dried berries.

I searched the premises, not sure of what I was looking for or what I might find. Was he a sex offender? A murderer? Was he simply cut from a different branch?

The kitchen was smaller than most bathrooms. No sign of eaten food. No empty cans in the trash. The bar-sized refrigerator had no food in it.

There was a closed door leading to what I assumed was the only bedroom. My grip tightened around the Glock as I slowly turned the doorknob with my left hand. How many times in Miami had I felt the same thing? Entering a rat hole where a killer, high on drugs and adrenaline, was coiled like a snake. Would Billie be on the other side of the door with a bow pulled back, the tip of an ancient arrow ready to impale me to the wall? I raised the pistol and shoved the door open.

Dust danced in the streaming light coming from a single window. There was a cot next to one wall. A multicolored Seminole blanket lay folded neatly at the head of the cot. On the blanket was an eagle feather. I knelt down and looked carefully at the feather. I spotted a long gray hair on the blanket.

The room grew darker as storm clouds blocked the sun. There was a clap of thunder, and rain began to beat the aluminum trailer like a thousand drumsticks. I sat on the cot, laid my gun down, and picked up the eagle feather. Holding it, my hand trembled. I could see dried blood at the base of the quill.

LATER THAT NIGHT the rain tapered to a gentle drizzle. After I fed Max, I poured two ounces of Irish whiskey and took down a photograph of my wife from the old river rock mantel. I walked to the porch and sat. A whippoorwill sounded across the river. A sonata of frogs filled the rainy night air. Under a cone of light spilling from the kitchen onto the porch, I looked at Sherri's face. I touched the image, my fingers moving across cold glass. I longed for her warmth, her smile, her laugh. God, how I missed her.

WE WERE ON a much delayed vacation. Sailing from Miami to Key Largo. It was late in the afternoon, and the sky was splashed in purples and gold. The sails stretched in a southeast wind. *Eternity* made a *whoosh . . . whoosh . . . whoosh* sound cutting through water, the setting sun reflecting the blush of a twilight sky. Sherri held the ropes near the bowsprit, her hair dancing in the wind. Suddenly, one on each side of the boat, two porpoises began leaping out of the water in unison.

Sherri laughed. "Look, Sean! Not only do they have a smile on their faces, it's in their eyes. What a fabulous way they see the world around them."

Six months later, she was in a hospital bed. Through her fight with ovarian cancer, the chemo treatments, an arsenal of pills, the constant blood work, her eyes never lost their light. The last week before Sherri's death, she asked me to take her home. She wanted to be in our bedroom, surrounded by her books, little Max curled up next to her.

The night Sherri died, I held her hand and wiped the perspiration from her face. She said, "Remember the dolphins, Sean?"

"I remember," I said, trying to be strong when my insides were tearing apart.

"Remember their smiles . . . let it remind you how to smile. Somewhere . . . you've lost that . . . I miss it in you . . . Promise me two things, Sean. Promise me you'll move away from the dark side— the side you enter to try and make a difference. You need to reclaim yourself. That's where you will make the difference in the lives of others. And promise me you'll watch over Max. She loves you almost as much as I do." Her hand trembled as she stroked Max, who had snuggled next to her.

I leaned over and softly kissed Sherri's lips. They were cool. She smiled one last time as I looked into her eyes and saw the light fade.

I PLACED HER PICTURE on the porch table, sipped the whiskey, and felt it burn in my empty stomach. I called Max over to my chair and lifted her up. She licked my chin and lay down in my lap. I scratched her behind the ears and stared into my dead wife's face.

I finished the drink and realized the rain had stopped. A slice of moon perched far beyond the live oaks. I sat there in the dark until after midnight watching fireflies play hide-and-seek along the banks of the river, their tiny lights reflecting in the dark current like meteor showers in the night sky.

THIRTEEN

The next morning I drove with Max to near the spot I had parked when I found the girl. Was her name Angela like the Reverend Jane said? She was now a body under a sheet in the coroner's cold storage filing cabinet, tucked away like another crime statistic.

Max followed me to the spot where I'd found her. I knelt down and began to search the area. Max sniffed blades of grass. She seemed to sense that something was wrong here. Deer tracks, wide and deep. The deer had been running. Had the deer been frightened by the person who had killed the girl?

"Let's see where these came from, Max." She ran ahead, barking and wagging her tail. Max and I were now backtracking, following a trail in reverse, hoping it might lead to the start of how the girl got to the river.

We were within seventy-five feet of the road when Max stopped. This time the fur rose along her spine, a whine coming from her throat. She found a single shoe, a woman's shoe. It had a short heel and a closed toe. I took a pen from my shirt pocket and lifted the shoe from the ground. It was the shade of cherries. No brand name.

I held the shoe with a handkerchief and carefully poured some of the contents from the toe area into one of the Ziploc bags I'd brought. The soil trickled out of the shoe like coal dust. Holding it to my nose, I could detect the faint odor of phosphates, possibly man-made fertilizers.

I lowered the shoe back where Max had found it and looked around for a second shoe before calling Detective Slater on my cell. "I found what I think may have been one of the victim's shoes."

"Where? Under your car seat?" Slater asked.

"It's where you should have found it if you'd searched the crime scene the right way." I fired back, regretting my comment the instant I said it. "Look, Detective Slater, she wasn't wearing shoes when I found her. This shoe is another two hundred yards north of the river, near Highway 44. Maybe she lost it running from the perp. Maybe she'd been in his car. Or she could have been some poor kid in the wrong place at the wrong time hitching a ride. The shoe's here. I'm leaving it right where I found it."

I could almost hear his mind crunching through the phone. "I'll be there in an hour. Don't touch anything. And don't leave."

"I wouldn't think of it, Detective. Did you get an ID on the girl?"

"No, but we have the autopsy report."

"You took a DNA sample from me. I know there was no match. But I don't know exact cause of death or who she was. I was hoping you could tell me that."

"Stay put until I get there."

"I'll make this easy. I'll tie a white handkerchief on a tree limb next to Highway 44. You pull off the road and walk about seventy-five feet straight north from the tree and you'll find the shoe, but you won't find me. Do your own police work, Detective."

I hung up. Max had vanished. "Max!"

Silence.

There was the noise of something moving in the brush. "Max." Nothing. Then there was a sound you never forget—the sound of a rattlesnake.

"Max!"

I stepped around a large pine tree and stopped. The snake was as thick as my arm. Body coiled, ready to strike. The eyes were trained on Max like heat-seeking weapons. They were dark, polished stones. The snake's tongue tested the air in flickers of black.

"Max! Stop!" I blurted. She paid no attention to my command. Here was an animal she'd never seen, and it was shaking a new toy. Playtime with death.

The next few seconds switched to a film in macabre slow motion. Max's nostrils quivered. She froze, mesmerized by the unblinking dark pearls. The snake coiled tighter. Head poised to strike.

"Max, move!" My scream sounded distant. The strike was a blur.

The snake was dying before it could bury its fangs into Max's face. An arrow had gone right through the rattlesnake's head, impaling it in the ground. Its body wrapped around the shaft in a death grip, the rattle growing quiet, softly caressing the yellow quill feathers as constricting muscles and nerves died. The black pearls seemed to stare somewhere beyond Max.

I turned around as Joe Billie stepped from between two tall pine trees.

FOURTEEN

Where'd you come from?" I asked.

He looked at Max, who seemed as bewildered as I was, and said, "Ever think about getting a Lab? Don't think you'd see a Lab playing with a rattlesnake."

"What are you doing here?"

"Passing by. Thought you could use the help."

He held the long bow to his side. He had a hunting knife strapped to his belt. There were no other arrows. No quiver. "Where are the rest of your arrows?"

"Usually carry one. You aim better when there's no second chance."

I glanced at the dead snake. "Where'd you learn to shoot like that?"

"Had good teachers."

He approached the snake, placed a boot on its head, and slowly pulled out the shaft and arrowhead.

"Why'd you leave that arrow at my house?"

"You said you had a bow, thought you might appreciate it one day."

"I do appreciate your gift, but I was surprised to find it on my porch."

Billie said nothing.

"I'd hate to use something that ancient in my bow. Seems it ought to be in a glass case to protect it."

"It might protect *you* one day." He threaded the bowstring in the notch on the arrow shaft and pulled the string all the way back to his right cheek, arms knotting. He held the draw, rock solid, sighting a pine tree as a target. "You hold your breath. Draw back. Keep both eyes open. Block everything out but the spot. Then let go."

"A young woman died near here the same day I met you."

Joe Billie didn't flinch. No emotion. No visible changes in breathing. He slowly eased the bowstring back down, removing the arrow.

I said, "Seems to me like you'd have passed by her if you walked down the river."

"Where'd she die?"

"I'll show you." I scooped up Max with one arm and headed for the river with Joe Billie following me. I thought about what Floyd Powell had told me sitting in his boat at the end of my dock. *The bone hunter ain't been seen since.*

"Stop," he said abruptly.

If I turned around, would I be hit with an arrow through the heart? I slowly turned to face him. He was reaching toward a bush, examining something.

"You remember what the girl was wearing?"

"Yellow blouse, blue jeans."

He pointed to something caught on a palm frond. "It doesn't look like a thread from blue jeans, but it's blue," he said, reaching for the bright blue thread clinging to a barb on the frond.

"Don't touch it." I used my pen to carefully lift the thread off the thorn. I pulled a second Ziploc bag out of my shirt pocket, lowered the thread into the bag, and sealed it.

"You always carry those?"

"When I get into a murder investigation and I'm the one they're investigating."

"That why you're curious as to my whereabouts? You think I killed the girl."

"I didn't say that."

"Didn't have to."

"There's a lot more room to hide a body in the Everglades, don't you agree?"

He slowly turned his head toward me, his brown eyes searching my face for a long moment. "I didn't kill him."

"Clayton Suskind?"

"Someone digs up your grandfather, cuts his head off, sells it. How'd you feel?"

"Angry. But not enough to kill."

"I told you, I didn't kill him. It was the last moon after the Green Corn Dance. I took him in the rock chickee to sweat out his demons with the fire and smoke. I gave him the black drink of our ancestors to show him the wrong he did."

"And it poisoned him?"

"No, it guided him. He heard the spirits that night. When the sun broke, he said he was moving to Arizona. Said he was being called there to teach . . . university."

I said nothing, not sure what to say. Max barked at a lizard, and I said, "It does seem odd that you walk down the river and don't see the girl lying near the bank."

He pointed to the thread in the bag. "I saw that."

"It wasn't easy to spot."

"Things that aren't a natural part of the surroundings can stand out." His eyes moved slowly from the branches to the ground. "Things like this." He stepped over to a palmetto thicket, knelt down. "Don't think that little plastic bag of yours will hold this."

Max followed me, sniffing, growling, and uttering throaty barks. It was a domestic animal's reaction to the aberrant, to the incomprehensible—to evil.

"No, Max!" I shouted as she started to sniff a long stick covered by a dark stain. I looked closer and could see a single hair stuck in the bark and blood.

Billie sat on his haunches, pondering, as he looked at the stick. "Was she raped?"

"Yes."

"Looks like whoever did it wasn't satisfied with the sex part."

"For this guy, it wasn't about sex. It was about power and humiliation."

Billie stood and searched the area, stopping every few feet to turn a leaf or stick with the tip of his bow. "Here's something."

Almost hidden under the dried palm leaves was a piece of gray duct tape.

I stared at the tape and felt my chest tighten. My palms were moist. I touched it with the end of a pencil. I could see a dark hair stuck to one corner of the tape.

At the river's edge, I could smell the odor of dead fish and honeysuckles. A half-eaten catfish, probably ripped from a trotline by a gator, had washed ashore.

"Here." I pointed to the spot where I'd found her. "She was on her back here."

He looked over the premises, lifting a dead leaf or a broken twig, eyes moving like a bird of prey. "When I came upriver I was over on the far bank with my canoe. That's Dickensen Point. I crossed to this bank about another hundred yards down. Pulled the canoe on a sand-bar and walked in the shallows until I came to your dock."

Max looked toward the east and uttered a low growl.

Joe Billie smiled. "I'm startin' to gain more respect for that little dog."

"Why's that?"

"Because she knows somebody's coming."

FIFTEEN

Within three minutes, Detective Slater arrived with a posse. Two unmarked cars and two Volusia County sheriff's cruisers pulled up, lights flashing, dust trailing. Max barked as the detectives and deputies spilled out of their cars at once.

Detective Leslie Moore wore her hair pinned up. Her partner, Detective Dan Grant, followed her. Slater took his time, staying in his car, cell phone on his ear, eyes on me. He waited for the others to almost encircle us before he appeared.

"So, what do we have here?" Slater asked. "O'Brien and the crocodile hunter?"

Billie ignored the comment.

Slater continued, "We have a man with a bow and arrow and a hunting knife. What are you hunting?"

"Artifacts. Spear- and arrowheads," Billie said.

"You won't find arrowheads here unless the victim was stabbed with an arrow."

I said, "Detective, we've found a couple of things that may have slipped through your first investigation. Between here and the road, less than a quarter mile, you'll find a woman's shoe, a bloodied stick, and a piece of duct tape. The tape looks like it has a hair stuck to it. I'll show you where we found them." I wasn't going to tell Slater about the thread or the dirt I'd taken from the shoe.

Slater turned to Billie. "I'd like to take a look at that arrow." Billie handed him the arrow. Slater removed his sunglasses and studied it. "I see tiny pieces of something between the stone and wood. We'll run DNA on it."

"Unless you're storing rattlesnake DNA in your database you won't get a hit," I said. "He saved my dog's life when a rattlesnake was about to strike her."

"This man shot a rattlesnake with a bow and arrow, huh? Don't see that every day." He adjusted his sunglasses. "Arrow's going to the lab. That skinning knife, too."

Billie unbuckled his belt and handed Slater the knife.

"What's your name?" Slater asked.

"Joe Billie."

"Got an ID, Mr. Billie?"

"You mean driver's license?"

"That'd be a good start."

"No."

"It's against the law to drive without a license."

"Didn't drive here."

"Are you and Mr. O'Brien carpooling?"

Billie stared at Slater for a moment, then looked toward the river.

"You live around here, Mr. Billie?"

"Most of my life."

"Where?"

"Hanging Moss Fish Camp."

Slater glanced at my Jeep. "Hanging Moss is way upriver. How'd you get here?"

"Canoe."

"Where's your canoe?"

"Behind those trees." Billie motioned toward some willows near the riverbank.

Slater turned to a deputy. "Check it out." The deputy nodded and left.

"What were my DNA results?" I asked.

"Negative," said Detective Moore. Slater looked hard at her. She ignored him and said, "Where is this physical evidence you just mentioned?"

"About a ten-minute walk from here."

"Mitchell," she said to Slater, "want me to check it out?"

"Maybe you both should see this," I said before Slater could speak. "The more eyes, the less chance something might not be seen."

A muscle below Slater's left eye twitched. He started to say something but was interrupted by the deputy, who was returning.

"There's a canoe tied up down there."

A DEPUTY ROPED OFF a rough rectangle between the scrub brush and pine trees. Detective Grant took digital photographs of the evidence and the surroundings. They collected and bagged the shoe, duct tape, bloody stick, and leaves and dirt from the area.

I stood out of the way, holding Max and watching Detectives Slater, Moore, and Grant work. Moore and Grant were thorough, organized. Slater smoked three cigarettes and looked at his watch four times in fifteen minutes. They approached us.

Detective Moore removed her gloves and petted Max. "Cute dog."

"Thanks. Her name's Max."

Slater lit another cigarette and sucked a mouthful of smoke into his lungs. "Let's cut the chitchat and get to the point. Mr. O'Brien, you are a person of interest in this investigation. Now, so is Mr. Billie. We'll be taking Mr. Billie in for further questioning. Mr. O'Brien, we're not done quite yet."

I said, "You're eloquent. I called you, remember? Now you have some hard evidence in your bag. Let's see what you can do with it, Detective."

He turned to Billie. "If you have no history, you're a mystery. I solve mysteries."

Detective Moore said, "Mr. Billie, we'd appreciate it if you could come to the department to answer a few questions. If you don't have a car, we'll provide transportation back to your home or to your canoe."

Billie said nothing. He looked in the direction of the river. A red-tailed hawk alighted on the top of a pine tree. It seemed to watch as Billie was led away.

I stood there and saw the hawk fly to a cypress tree. Even with Max, I suddenly felt alone, out of sync with everything around me. The faraway sound of a train whistle beckoned down the St. Johns. It was a lonesome sound, a hymn carried by trestles crossing rivers of time to bridge the soul. In two weeks the girl would be a cold case. Forgotten. But I couldn't forget the promise I made to her and to my wife.

A gut feeling and a heartfelt promise often don't mix. No easier than good and evil can sleep together. My gut told me one thing while my heart spoke another. I hadn't asked to be tossed into this ring, but some choices are already made for you.

The girl I found had had no choice.

"Come on, Max. We're told her name was Angela. Let's see if we can name her killer."

SIXTEEN

It was Monday morning and I rose before dawn. As I sat on the outside steps to the screened porch and laced up my shoes, the sunrise broke, resembling a ship's light in a mist over the tree line along the river.

After a mile or so at a fast pace, I stopped to catch my breath. I stood there, sweating and watching the silent St. Johns for a minute. There was the scent of damp moss, orange blossoms, and honeysuckle.

My cell rang. Its chirp sounded like a bird that didn't belong in the forest.

"You sound out of breath," Ron Hamilton said.

"Trying to get back in shape. Running again."

"There's another killing. Similar MO. Female. Young. No ID. Raped and strangled. Could be the same perp."

"Where'd they find the body?"

"Brevard County. Not too far from you. Two teenagers on four-wheelers found the vic. Word I hear is the feds are making a half-ass effort to look into this one. Not much is done about it until it grabs the girl next door."

"What did you come up with on similar cases, missing or unsolved homicides?"

"Florida's got two things more than any other state. The coastline is the longest and so is the missing persons list. I tried to triangulate it into stats that would correlate with the ethnicity, age, and sex of your vic and the one found today. Went back five years. There are ninety-three reported missing. Nineteen known homicides. Out of that number, four people have been convicted. So that gives us fifteen where the perp or perps are still out there. In each case, the bodies were found in some remote spot."

"Was the cause of death the same?"

"Looks that way. Necks broken. Raped and sexually mutilated. But because he's not killing college coeds, like Danny Rolling or Ted Bundy, it becomes old news fast. Look how long the Green River Killer kept killing prostitutes. The people least likely to be reported missing."

"For every girl reported missing, I wonder what the ratio or percentage is of them found alive or dead? What's the death quotient?"

"There are girls missing that nobody files a report on because their families live in some other country. Human trafficking. Sex slaves. All here in the good ol' U.S. of A."

"You got it, partner."

Ron grunted. "Out of the fifteen we know about, one body was found the first year. The second year produced two. The third season, if you will, there were three killings, about one a quarter. Year number four produced four dead girls. And this last year there were five. These killings were scattered in counties from the northern part of Florida to the tip of the Everglades."

"If all the bodies were found, and it's the same perp, he's killing

more each year, getting bolder, or an urge can't be satisfied for as long. What'd you get on Joe Billie?"

"The print on the arrowhead could be from Billie. There's no record of his prints anywhere. No criminal record. Nothing in DMV. Seems he doesn't exist. The blood on the feather you sent matches the DNA of the hair follicle you found on the cot. Came from the same man, Billie, if that's his hair. No hit in CODIS. Why his blood is on the damn feather, I can't help you there, bro. I'll send the arrow back to you."

"Did you find anything on Clayton Suskind?"

"Ph.D. in anthropology from Florida State University. Suskind was arrested in 2008 for unauthorized digging of a national historic site, the protected Crystal River Mounds. This is probably the biggest Indian burial ground in the Southeast. He knows, or knew, where to dig. Collectors pay a lot for this stuff. The good professor is another missing person who has never been found."

"Check with colleges and universities in Arizona. See if he's on staff."

BACK AT MY HOUSE, I dialed the Volusia County Sheriff's Office. I asked to speak to Detective Slater. "There was a killing in Brevard County. Maybe the same MO."

"We're on it. You're not a cop anymore, O'Brien."

"Do you know where I can find Joe Billie?"

"Why?"

"He left something with me. I'd like to return it. Have you charged him?"

"Not yet. He's probably lying low on the Seminole reservation. Sovereignty and all that shit. We're watching him. Just like we're watching you."

"What's that supposed to mean?"

"You know what it means."

"Did you come up with an ID on the victim?"

"That's not your immediate concern."

"I haven't figured out your attitude yet, maybe it's a turf thing, Detective, but your incompetence made it my business. I assume you haven't got an ID. Maybe the killing in Brevard is related. It might be a way to help ID the girl I found."

"I don't need you to tell me how to do my job."

"I think you haven't come up with an ID yet or a real suspect."

"This isn't *CSI: Miami,* O'Brien. Push me, I push back. Promise you that."

"Here's a promise: If you don't find out who killed the girl, I will."

He slammed the phone down. I gripped the receiver hard, my knuckles like cotton.

I looked out at the stillness of the river and thought about my conversation with Ron. A second murder. Was it the same perp? *Atlacatl imix cuanmiztli.* I heard her garbled words through the whisper of air from her punctured lung.

The room suddenly seemed cold.

There was a noise near my driveway. I picked up my Glock, looked out the window, and saw a car parked under the live oaks at the far end of my drive. By the time I got to the front door, the car was gone.

SEVENTEEN

I skipped breakfast the next day, loaded a case of beer and Max into the Jeep and drove straight to Ponce Inlet Marina. I was looking forward to a quiet Tuesday, on *Jupiter*. I'd planned to install a GPS system on the boat.

As I walked by the tiki bar, on the way to my boat, Kim, the bartender, smiled one of her thousand-candlepower smiles and held up her hand for me to stop. She was in her early forties. Easy smile. Dark hair and brown eyes that had their own sense of humor.

"Looks like a party," she said, glancing at the beer and then at me.

"I always seem to get thirsty when I work on the boat all day."

"Hi, Max!" Kim bent down and picked Max up, kissing her head. "So you're the lucky girl who's first mate." Max's tail wagged nonstop.

"Sean, were you on *Jupiter* a couple of nights ago?"

"No, why?"

"I was closing and thought I saw a light on your boat. Like a flashlight."

"Sure it was *Jupiter*?"

"Not positive. But it looked like it was your boat."

"Did you see anyone leave?"

"No."

"Thanks, Kim."

She set Max on the ground to follow me. "No problem. That's what I'm here for, neighborhood watch."

The breeze across the Intracoastal delivered the scent of a receding tide, barnacles drying on pilings, exposed oyster bars, and mullet feeding across the mudflats.

The *St. Michaels* had returned. Nick's fishing boat, with its Old World look and feel, seemed to rest quietly in its slip. On the dock next to the boat, his calico cat sat on its haunches, chewing a severed fish head.

Jupiter sat waiting for me like an old friend. I stepped into the cockpit and began carefully examining everything I owned. Deck chairs, cooler, ropes, anything that might look out of place. I raised the hatch to the engine and began looking for any sign of intrusion or something that didn't belong in the bowels of *Jupiter*. Nothing.

I opened the salon door lock and stepped inside, Max following at my heels.

The first sign. Max darted around the salon sniffing every piece of furniture. The fur raised slightly on her back. "What do you smell, Max? Let's check below."

The second sign. Sherri's picture had been moved, slightly, but I could tell. A faint dust line on the shelf gave it away. If it were not for Kim tipping me off, and Max's antics, I might not have noticed that someone had been on *Jupiter*.

I examined the rest of the boat and could find nothing stolen. A few things seemed slightly out of place, but nothing gone. I would check topside in a moment. I didn't think I'd find anything taken from there. If robbery wasn't the motive, what was?

Through *Jupiter*'s portside window, I saw the feet with the flip-flops. A few seconds later, Nick Cronus bellowed, "Permission to come aboard." Nick eased down like a sloth from the dock into the cockpit. He had thick curly black hair, a mustache, smiling dark eyes, and skin stained the hue of creosote. A lifetime at sea, pulling nets and traps and battling storms, had given him a Herculean build tempered with the survival skills of an Argonaut. Nick was a blend of Zorba and Will Rogers. He had a string of ex-wives, children, girl-friends, and creditors in his circle of acquaintances. He had the heart of a St. Bernard, too, loyal and trusting where his friends were concerned. I was glad to be included as one of them.

By his slow movement, I could tell he was slightly hungover. I would wait a few minutes before asking him if he'd seen anyone around *Jupiter*.

Max ran out to greet him, her tail fanning. He leaned down and lifted her up using one hand like a giant with a toy. He held her over his head and said, "Hot dog, you come to sea with me! I feed you some octopus, give you a starfish for a chew bone, and let you bark at the porpoises. It'd be a good life, yeaaaah!"

He did a 360 spin, holding Max even higher in a Greek dance. It was more excitement than Max's bladder could hold. She let loose a trickle that ran down his arm. I yelled and Nick laughed. Max looked dizzy.

"Hot dog! What you do to me?" Nick set Max down as if she'd turned into a nine-pound glowing coal. She looked up at him through sad brown eyes. "Little one, don't be ashamed. It's often the effect I have on the woman."

"Let me get you a towel," I said.

"No, Maxine is trying to tell me something."

"What's that?"

"She hates me so much she pee on me, or she say, Nicky my buddy, you need a shower and I'll encourage you to take one." He looked at Max, peeled off his shirt, opened the door from the transom to the dive platform, kicked off his flip-flops, and dove into the water. He swam out about fifty feet and turned over to float on his back. He bellowed, "What a fine bathtub!" He swam like an Olympian competitor back to *Jupiter*.

I tossed him a towel. "You're lucky the tide's in. Otherwise a Max urine shower might be cleaner than the marina."

"I don't think about it, at least not long enough to stop me from having some fun." The gold cross hanging from a chain around his neck winked in the sun as he dried off.

"Nick, have you seen anybody on my boat, or around it?"

"Lemme think. I've just been back one day. Had a little too much ouzo last night and slept like a dead man." He closed his eyes for a moment as if steadying himself. "When I first brought my boat back to the marina, I was working against the tide. I remember two people I haven't seen on the docks walking away from your boat. Man was as bald as an onion. Couldn't see the woman's face, but she had a nice ass."

I told Nick about the murder, the investigation, Slater, and how I'd become involved. After I finished, he looked up at me through eyes so dark you couldn't see the pupils and said, "Wanna beer?"

"It's a little too early on my clock for a beer."

"Come fishing with me, storms and shit send your clock into a Twilight Time Zone, man." He shuffled into the galley with Max following him, tail wagging. I could hear him chatting with her like she was human. He returned with a Corona, popped the top, and took a long pull. "Sean, you got some dick with a hard-on for you. You find a woman 'bout dead, call for help, and he thinks you did it. What's his gig?"

"Don't know, but I do know someone broke into *Jupiter*."

"They steal from you?"

"Don't think so. Can't find anything taken, but things have been moved."

He leaned back into the sofa in the salon, held Max in his lap, and propped his flip-flop-clad feet up on a shellacked cypress table. He set his beer on the table and picked at a small scab on his dark forearm. "Think that cop was the one on your boat?"

"Maybe. Why not search my house? It's closer to the crime scene."

"He coulda been there. Maybe you just don't see it yet."

"Or there could be another reason he was on my boat."

Nick finished his beer. "What reason?"

"What if he wasn't hunting for something?"

"Huh?"

"What if he was leaving something?"

EIGHTEEN

The noise from the big diesels in the charter fleet sounded like a semi truck passing in front of *Jupiter*'s bow as the boats headed toward Ponce Inlet Pass.

"What you mean?" Nick asked.

"Stay right where you are, Nick. Don't move."

"I got nowhere to go." He shrugged.

"Hold Max."

I found one of my three marine flashlights. It had fresh batteries and was capable of shining a beam a mile across the water. I turned it on, stepped back up to the salon, and began slowly panning the light across the floor.

"What you looking for?" Nick asked.

"I looked for something taken. Now I'm searching for something left behind."

"Looks like you are hunting for a lost contact lens."

"Come down in the master and shine the light across the mattress while I squat down for a close view. Set Max in the cockpit."

He nodded, put a perplexed Max out the door, and followed me to the master. I handed Nick the flashlight. "Pan it slowly above the bed."

"What are you looking for?"

"Hold it right there."

"What you see?"

I stood and stepped into the galley for a moment, picking up a pair of tweezers and a Ziploc. I knelt down and inched closer to the pillow on the right side of the bed. "Hold steady, Nick." I reached for the hair follicle, picked it up with the tweezers, stood, and looked at it in the light. It was long and coal black. Roots intact.

Nick grinned. "You had some company. Good, man."

"I haven't had a woman on this boat, and when I bought *Jupiter*, she was cleaned. This is new. And I know where this hair came from. It's as dark as her eyes."

"What woman?"

"She's dead."

"How'd a dead woman's hair get in your bed?"

"Planted. Whoever planted it will return. With a search warrant."

I lowered the hair into the Ziploc and sealed it.

We both felt *Jupiter* move. Nick started to say something, but I silenced him by holding a finger to my lips. He nodded at the same time Max barked. I reached for my Glock on the nightstand and left the master cabin for the salon, pistol ready.

Dave Collins saw me the second I saw him. Instinctively, he held his hands up. "Sean, it's me!"

Nick followed me, and Max followed Dave from the cockpit to the salon.

"Why the gun?" Dave asked.

"Sean just lifted a girl's long black hair outta his bed," Nick said.

Dave smiled. "A brunette or a naturally blond woman?"

"It came from a dead woman," I snapped.

Dave said nothing, his expression one of disbelief.

Nick said, "I congratulated him till he told me somebody put the hair in his bed."

"Put it there?" Dave asked.

I pulled the folded Ziploc out of my shirt pocket. "Here it is, and I believe it came from the head of the victim I found."

"Why would someone place evidence in your bed?"

"Because someone wants me to take the fall for her murder. Might be the person who killed her, or might be someone covering up for the person who did it. If it's someone covering for the killer, then what's the reason?"

"Sounds confusing," Nick said. "I'm gettin' a beer. You want one, Dave?"

"No thanks."

As Nick made his way into the galley he said, "Sean, somebody wants you to get the death penalty. You got an Indian leaving an arrow at your house. This cop thinks you killed the girl. Man, I thought I got into a lotta shit."

Dave said, "I did some translating on what the victim said to you."

"What'd you find?"

"It's an obscure, almost dead language called Nahuatl. Originally spoken by the Aztecs. What she told you was *'Atlacatl imix cuanmiztli,'* and the translation is 'He has the eyes of the jaguar.'"

Nick whistled softly. "Who has eyes of the jaguar?"

"Do me a favor, Nick," I said. "Keep a lookout for anybody suspicious."

"To me, everybody's suspicious."

"If anyone comes too near *Jupiter*, or climbs on her, get their names and what they're doing. Then call me." I stood to leave.

"Where you heading?" Dave asked.

"Would you mind watching Max for a couple of hours?"

"The little lady is always welcome on *Gibraltar*."

"I'm going to buy a tiny camera. It'll be one that will be able to transmit, online, a live video feed to a laptop I'd like to place on *Gibraltar*, Dave."

"I get the picture," Dave said, grinning.

"What's that?" asked Nick.

"The picture will be of the guy who placed the hair on my bed. He'll come back to find it, and he may have a search warrant, but he won't suspect that the evidence will be gone. He won't know his every move will be recorded on a hard drive—and, gentlemen, that will be entertaining to a grand jury."

NINETEEN

I found exactly what I needed at a RadioShack less than twenty minutes from the marina. Within two hours, I had installed and tested the hidden camera I had placed between stacks of books in the master cabin, its fish-eye lens pointed at the bed. The trap was set.

After I finished, I called Dave over to show him my handiwork. "I'm setting the laptop up here on the table in the salon. I'll go back into the master cabin and walk around. You can watch it on the laptop. All wireless."

"Essentially like television," he said.

"Picture isn't ready for prime time, but it'll work for crime time." I stepped down into the master cabin and heard him applaud.

"Sean, I can see the entire cabin. You have a certain flair for the covert."

I came back up to the salon. "How'd you know about covert activities?"

Dave only smiled.

"We can stow that laptop on *Gibraltar*. Signal will go the distance."

Max did one of her half barks and half whines, which added up to a total command. "Max is ready for dinner. You hungry, Dave?" I was hoping to bounce some thoughts off Dave's brow.

"Let's eat," he said.

"I'll leave a note on Nick's boat. Maybe he'll be back in time to join us."

I turned the camera on, locked *Jupiter,* left a note on Nick's door, set the laptop on Dave's table, and walked with him toward the tiki hut, Max following us.

ALTHOUGH THE FISH WAS COOKED over hardwood to perfection, I had very little appetite. Max had a small hamburger patty served medium well. She ate from a paper plate on the wooden floor next to our table.

Kim brought us fresh Heinekens and said, "Max has better table manners than most of the people I serve." Max cocked her head and seemed to nod. Kim beamed. "Coffee?"

"Grey Goose over ice and a squeeze of lime, Kim," Dave added.

I said, "Coffee sounds good. It'll keep me awake for the drive home."

Kim almost frowned. "You have a perfectly good boat to sleep on. At least I imagine it's perfectly good for sleeping. Why the hurry?"

"I'm expecting visitors."

After she left, Dave said, "I think she likes you."

"Maybe. Maybe she's just a little lonely. We know for sure Kim likes Max. She gets the free meals." I sipped the Heineken. "Do you know much about human trafficking?"

"Big market overseas, especially in the sex trade. The women are stolen or duped into believing they are getting legitimate jobs in more prosperous countries. They incur false debt for transportation. They're forced to work it off, on their backs."

"It's happening right here in America."

"No doubt. You think this is somehow related to the girl you found?"

"I do."

"How?"

"I think she was connected to one of these migrant camps because some soil in her shoe smelled like chemicals—fertilizers—something with a high phosphate count. She wasn't used as a farm worker, though. Maybe she was forced into prostitution and ran."

Kim brought Dave his drink. He swirled the vodka and ice in his glass. "Modern-day slavery, forced prostitution, human trafficking—right here in the land of the free."

"I think this murder, and the one that came a few days later, are the work of the same killer that's cutting one out of the herd when he feels the urge."

"And victims are the least likely to be reported missing," Dave said.

"The victim I found, she was just a kid. I think she was in the area and running from someone, maybe bolted from the perp's car. She escaped and ran toward the river. He caught her. Probably thought he'd killed her on the banks of the river."

"You say she was barely alive when you found her. Maybe she played dead and he left. Or perhaps someone scared him off."

"I investigated some similar cases in Miami. The perp was called the Bagman because he asphyxiated his victims with a plastic bag during the rape. There was duct tape near the victim I found. This tells me it was planned. I never caught the Bagman. Now I know there have been at least fifteen sexual murders of Hispanic women in

Florida, rural areas, starting after the Miami murders dwindled down to nothing."

Dave stirred his ice. "The duct tape could be a similar MO, but maybe not."

"You translated the words the girl whispered to me. *He has the eyes of the jaguar.* The only victim to survive the Bagman said she could never forget his eyes. She said they were like the eyes of a wildcat."

TWENTY

I had awakened at dawn back at my river house. I let Max sleep in as I sipped a cup of coffee on the back porch and watched shadows fade away across the river. I slipped on my running shoes, went out the back door, and ran along the riverbank.

Later, when I climbed the steps to the back porch, Max was barking as she went toward the front door, stopping to see if I was coming as her backup.

"It's okay, Max. Could be someone asking for directions." As I said this, I picked up my Glock and wedged it into my shorts near my lower back.

The knock at the door was soft, almost apologetic. I opened the door, startling Detective Leslie Moore. "Mr. O'Brien," she said, embarrassed. "Good morning."

"Heard your fan belt the first time you drove by. Makes surveillance difficult."

"I wasn't on surveillance." She looked at my damp T-shirt and my shorts and running shoes. "Is this a bad time?"

"If you're here to arrest me, it's a bad time. Something else, not so bad, maybe."

She smiled. "No, I'm not here to arrest you. You'd be the first to know I wouldn't do that without backup. May I come in?"

"Door's open." As she stepped into the foyer, Max ran up, barking.

She knelt down and greeted Max. "Good morning! How are you?" She petted Max's head, instantly winning a friend. "She's so cute."

"Sometimes it's like having a kid. I have to find a babysitter when I'm gone."

"I wouldn't know. I don't have a dog or a baby."

"Max was my wife's baby. Now it's just Max and me. We're river rats."

"I know that your wife died. I'm sorry."

"I bet you know that. Good cops usually know the bios of suspects. So you're not afraid to be here alone with me?"

"As far as I'm concerned, you're not a suspect. Never really were."

I said nothing.

She hesitated a moment. "Is there a place where we can sit down?"

"Sure, follow me." I led her to my back porch.

"The view is beautiful," she said, standing next to the screen and looking at the river. "This must be paradise, living way out here. The river is gorgeous."

"Always something to fix. Paradise needs a lot of Band-Aids."

Detective Moore laughed. Her eyes danced as she watched a blue heron and a white egret take ballet steps in the water. "This is like a wildlife documentary. The birds seem oblivious to us."

"They can't see us. Factor in sunlight, trees, and porch screen. It's a window to nature. Would you like something? Coffee or water?"

"No thanks."

"You didn't drive here to look at wildlife. How can I help you, Detective?"

"This is my first murder case with Mitchell Slater." She paused and looked toward the river. "We don't have an ID on the vic yet because I'm not so sure we're working that hard to find one."

"Meaning?"

"We've run all the channels—DNA database, state and national, prints, photo sent to the FBI, and elsewhere. Nothing."

"Someone knows who she is."

"I wish they'd come forward. Of course, we'll store all the dental, anthropological, and DNA records, but the body will be interred tomorrow. Buried as a Jane Doe. A number on the marker. No name."

"Is there a connection to the Brevard homicide? MO? Anything physical?"

"We're working with Brevard, sharing information and resources. So far, nothing to correlate the two deaths except each victim was young, female, pretty, and Hispanic. I'm having a hard time following leads, not that I have a lot."

"What's the difficulty?"

"Slater."

"Not surprising."

"He doesn't go out of his way to follow up on anything. And what I bring to the table he dismisses like it was a bad idea. He is pursuing you, and to some extent Joe Billie, but there's nothing there. He knows it, but he's like a bulldog."

"What's his agenda?"

"I'm not sure. I've been watching him, and I think he knows it. I believe he's on the take from somebody—somebody with power and influence. He seems to be living way above his pay grade. Wears a

Rolex when he's off duty. Connected in the community and with the old Florida money."

"Any of this old Florida money coming from agricultural interests?" I asked.

"Probably. There are rumors he's about to run for sheriff. If he could pin the murder on you, and convince the DA he had a winnable case, he'd get the press and probably announce his intent to run."

"How do I know you aren't here to try to implicate me?"

"I hoped you'd trust me."

"Trust you? I don't even know you. You stick a cotton swab in my mouth, collect some hard evidence that I found, take a nonsuspect in for questioning, come to my house, pet my dog, and ask me to trust you. Why?"

"Because I don't have anyone else," she said, nostrils flaring.

I said nothing.

"I'm not sure who I can trust in the department. My partner, Dan Grant, is honest and dedicated, but he's only been a detective six months. I don't know who's in Slater's camp. Thought maybe you might help. If you weren't a former cop, I wouldn't be here. Maybe I'm wrong, but based on the way you acted at the crime scene, I believe there is something in you that seeks justice."

I was silent.

"Will you help?" she asked, her eyes searching.

"Detective Moore—"

"Please, it's Leslie."

"All right, Leslie. I'm Sean. Now that we've got the formalities out of the way and we're on a first-name basis, I'll help. But it's got to be a two-way street. You give me what you have and I'll see what I can do."

"Okay, what's first?"

"The physical evidence near the scene. What were the results?"

"The blood on the stick came from the victim. No match from the

DNA database with the hair on the duct tape, but we do know it didn't come from the vic. We found skin under her fingernail, but it didn't match DNA found in the hair from the tape."

"Meaning she was raped by two different men, or she was in a fight with someone before the last perp raped and killed her."

I retrieved the Ziploc bags. One contained the soil I'd collected from the girl's shoe. The other had the thread Joe Billie spotted on the thorn. I handed them to Leslie.

"What's this?"

"Run an analysis on this soil. See what's in it, where it might have come from."

"Is this why you mentioned agricultural interests?"

"Maybe. It could wind up being pay dirt. The thread was hanging on a palm thorn. I'm betting it came from the killer's clothes, probably a shirt. Find any commonality you can on the two victims. If we can find that, we're on the trail of this guy. I believe he'll keep killing until he's caught. Give me your cell number."

I reached in a drawer and found the sealed envelope with the single follicle of hair. I opened the envelope, took a pair of scissors off the table, cut the hair into two pieces, placed one in an envelope, and gave it to Leslie. She watched as I put the second half in a separate envelope and sealed it.

"What's that?"

"I was hoping you could tell me."

"Is that the vic's hair?"

"Your forensics ought to tell us. I found it on my boat. Someone planted it."

"Planted it? I hope you don't think I had anything to do with this."

"Somebody did."

"You still don't trust me, do you?"

"No, but I'm willing to take a risk."

"I'm taking a risk just coming here."

"Have you ever been on my boat?" I watched her eyes.

"What?"

"My boat at Ponce Inlet Marina. I noticed a few things out of place."

"I wouldn't board a boat without a warrant. I was there, though, with Slater."

"Did Slater board her?"

"No. We questioned a few people about your comings and goings. Everyone there, from the bartender to the dock master, seems to like and respect you."

"If you told them you were investigating a murder, there is now a marina full of people wondering if I might slit their throats in the dead of night."

She pushed a strand of hair behind her right ear and smiled awkwardly. "I'm sorry. Sometimes the innocent get bruised. I should go now."

I followed her to the door. She started to say something, hesitating for a moment. "Can I ask you why you quit as a homicide detective? According to the people I've talked to, you have some ability, maybe a rare gift, to really read suspects. To tell if someone is lying the first few seconds you talk with them."

"Sometimes I got lucky, that's all."

Leslie smiled. "I don't think luck has anything to do with it. It's the kind of thing the FBI teaches in its behavioral profile classes. Was it a skill you developed?"

I wanted to change the subject. "Don't let your research into my background skew your judgment. I made mistakes—so many I quit."

"You don't seem like a quitter. Maybe one day you'll tell me about it."

"Nothing to tell."

"Somehow I don't quite believe that." She smiled and opened the door. "I'll have the results of these samples in a day or two."

As I watched her get in the unmarked patrol car, I thought of an unmarked grave. It was then that I planned to attend a funeral.

TWENTY-ONE

The next morning I drove to the Volusia County Cemetery, a potter's field. I parked and stood under a lone water oak tree and waited for the crew to finish. A blackbird alighted on one of the limbs not far above my head. There were only two men, the backhoe operator and a man with a shovel. When the grave was deep enough, the men slid the wooden coffin out from a county truck.

They held opposite sides and carried it as if they were carrying a junk sofa to the curb for pickup. They lowered it by hand, then I heard one of them say, "Hold it! On three. One . . . two . . . three." The coffin dropped into the hole with two thuds, body against wood.

"Show some respect!" I yelled, stepping from the water oak. The man working the shovel stopped and stood erect. He was tall, well over six feet, Viking stock with dirty blond hair gelled in a flattop. He held the shovel with one hand, resting it against his wide shoulder. The other man, light-skinned black and overweight, shirttail hanging out, climbed on the backhoe and turned over the diesel, ignoring me.

I stepped to the open grave and looked at the pine box at the bottom of the hole.

"You don't have to drop the body. The casket could splinter."

"Don't matter," said the man with the shovel. "They's nobodies." He lit a cigarette. He inhaled the smoke, flipped an ash into the grave, and said, "Ashes to ashes."

"Her grave isn't an ashtray!"

"You related to her?"

"I didn't have a lot of time to get to know her."

"Fuckin' nut." He shoveled in dirt.

The man on the backhoe shrugged his shoulders and began scraping the dirt into the grave. The man with the shovel was angry, tossing in dirt like someone covering up a hole that hadn't produced buried treasure.

Within a few minutes they were done. Eighteen years of life covered in eighteen minutes of work. The man with the shovel tossed his cigarette into the grave and covered it up with dirt.

I grabbed the wooden end of the shovel with one hand, catching him off guard. "Dig out the cigarette!"

"Kiss my ass!" he shouted above the noise from the backhoe. He jerked the shovel out of my hand and swung the blade at my head. It missed my nose by inches, the grit and sand spraying my eyes, blinding me for a moment. He hit me with the wooden handle. The blow landed on my jaw. There was the instant taste of blood in my mouth.

The backhoe man turned off the diesel and shouted, "Bust his ass, Lonnie!"

The blackbird sounded right above me. I dove in the opposite direction of the man's shadow. Dropping, spinning, and tackling him to the ground. We rolled across the fresh grave, the taste of sand in my mouth now as well. He swung at my face. I smelled stale cigarette smoke, sweat, and beer through the man's pores. I closed one eye to focus. I hit him hard on the jaw. The sound was like Sheetrock smacked with a hammer. He flailed at my head, a gurgling sound coming from his throat. The man on the backhoe slid out of his seat. I picked up the shovel and held it like a baseball bat.

"Don't take another step!" I ordered.

The man lying across the grave tried to stand. He was dazed. His threats sounded synthesized, like a voice coming from an animated character. I heard, "Gonna bury you."

"Pack up your backhoe, get in your truck, and leave," I said. My head pounded.

The black man loaded the backhoe on a flatbed behind the pickup truck.

"Come on, Lonnie," he said. "Leave this crazy fucker in the graveyard." The man called Lonnie limped to the truck. He pulled himself into the cab and slammed the door. A half minute later they were gone.

I was alone in a field without flowers. Nothing but the sound of a blackbird in the lone water oak. What do you say at a funeral that no one attends? The hot sun licked the back of my neck.

I knelt in the dirt staring at a county-issued cross at the head of a fresh grave. I smoothed out the warm soil with my trembling hands and looked up at the water oak.

The blackbird was silent.

TWENTY-TWO

I wasn't sure how long the phone had been ringing when I finally rolled over and lifted it from the nightstand. I felt like I was awakening from surgery. My jaw felt swollen. I managed to utter a sound into the receiver that was similar to "hello."

"Sean? Is that you?" asked Detective Leslie Moore.

"Yeah."

"Are you still in bed?"

"Not now."

"It's almost noon."

"That means the drugs have worn off, and I don't have to feed Max breakfast. We can just dive into the midday snack." I sat on the edge of the bed.

"You sound different."

"I feel different."

"Did something happen?"

"I don't do funerals well." I stood and took the phone into the bathroom. I squinted into the mirror. My left jaw was slightly swollen. I could see a halo coming from the bathroom light.

"Are you okay, Sean?" Leslie's voice sounded alien and far away.

"Yeah, I'm all right." I headed toward the kitchen to fix an ice pack.

"I have some information back from the lab."

"Shoot."

"The soil didn't match any of the surrounding soil where the body was located or where the shoe was found." I steadied myself on the bathroom counter and listened. "The soil had traces of three commercial grade fertilizers and a fungicide."

"What else?" I asked, wishing I had taken more aspirin last night.

"The single cloth thread was silk. Probably came from an expensive shirt. Maybe Italian. If we could find it, we'd match it."

"And if we could find the bastard that left hair in the duct tape, we'd nail him, too. Trouble is, we have no one."

"We have more hard evidence than suspects," she said. "I'll get the DNA results on the long black hair, the one from your boat, in a day or two."

"What big agriculture interests are within a hundred miles of the crime scene?"

"What do you mean by big agriculture?"

"Those using migrant help."

"Oh, I see where you're going. Could explain why no one has reported the girl missing, the soil samples you asked for, and why no one claimed the body."

"The Brevard murder," I said, now starting to feel blood moving through my bruises. "Anyone identify the body?"

"Not yet. Autopsy indicates she was raped and her neck broken. Both vics could have been employed by any of the big farms. Most of those farms are owned by old money, old Florida families. Multinational companies own some of the others."

"Much trouble on these farms? Any reports of beatings? Human trafficking?"

She was silent for a few seconds. "Our files are full of missing person reports. Hispanics and lots of others tossed in the mix. And with all the lakes and swamps and hundreds of miles of coastline, it would be easy to dispose of bodies."

"I did some cross-checking with my old homicide partner, Ron Hamilton, at MPD," I told her. "In the last five years, there have been nineteen known homicides involving young Hispanic women. All were between the ages of seventeen and twenty-five. Out of that, four men were arrested and charged in four separate killings. Fifteen of the murders remain unsolved, now cold cases. The women died the same way. Rape, necks broken."

"If it's the same perp, how has he stayed under the radar so well?"

"Selective kills. Covers his tracks well, if it's the same perp, but he didn't finish what he began with the girl I found. I think something caused him to cut and run."

"No witnesses, of course, have come forth."

"Leslie, you'd mentioned that Slater has political ambitions, connected to old Florida money. How?"

"Lawyers, developers, and agriculture."

"Any specific farmers?"

"He's been seen at a few fund-raisers for Richard Brennen, the heir apparent to the family farming business, which is a very big business."

"Who's that?"

"He's running for a state senate seat. Brennen's family is SunState Farms. Been in the family for generations. They've got thousands of acres in three counties."

"Where's the headquarters?"

"Polk County."

"What else do you know about Brennen?"

"What I read in the papers. He's confident, charismatic, and rich."

"Run a check on him all the way back to first grade, if you can."

"Okay. What are you going to do?" Leslie's voice was softer.

"I'm going on a field trip."

"Without a badge, I don't know how far you can get with these people before they have you arrested, or worse. Be careful, Sean."

I chased two aspirins with orange juice two weeks beyond its expiration date. As I started for the shower, the phone rang. It was Nick. "You sound like I woke you," he said.

"Someone else beat you to it."

"What's wrong, man?"

"I hate funerals."

"Know what you mean. Hey, some people were hanging by your boat."

"Who? You talk with them?"

"Kim saw them."

"What'd she see?"

"They weren't messin' with your boat. They were asking questions about you."

"They? Who? What kind of questions?"

"Don't know. Kim told me to tell you if I saw you. Been tryin' to call you. Thought somebody killed you and tossed you in the river. Almost got on my bike and run out to your place, but I'd had too much Greek wine."

"How did Kim describe these people? Was one bald?"

"It was a he and a she. Two of 'em. From the FBI."

The throb above my left eye became more pronounced. I popped a beer, sipped it on one side of my mouth, and thought about taking another aspirin.

TWENTY-THREE

After resting my jaw for three days, I was becoming anxious to do what I knew in my gut I had to do. It was the feeling I got before combat during the first Gulf War. It was the mood that came over me when the hunt was closing in on a suspect in the streets or corporate offices of Miami.

I made arrangements for my neighbor to take care of Max while I was away. I didn't know if I'd be gone a few hours or a few days. I did know that the FBI was interested in me, but why? The stories were now being carried by the national wire services. There were rumblings of a serial killer loose in the Sunshine State, the land of Mickey Mouse and Shamu. The feds were being more reactive than proactive.

My immediate decision was whether to let them come find me, or go to them. I thought about it for less than a second before turning south on Highway 27. I wedged the Glock out of sight between my seat and the gearshift console.

I unzipped all of the windows on the Jeep and invited the wind along for the ride. The air was cool and mixed with smells of freshly plowed earth and orange blossoms. I drove through cattle country, sliced by drainage canals and dotted with orange and grapefruit trees. It was a cloudless morning, and the sky was so deep blue it was as if I were looking into a bottomless indigo bowl.

Glancing in the rearview mirror, I saw a car following about a quarter of a mile behind me. I accelerated from fifty to sixty-five. My cell rang. I didn't recognize the number. I did recognize the man's voice.

Floyd Powell, the commercial fisherman, said, "I run into my nephew this morning. We got to talkin' about that killin,' you know, the one with the girl. He told me he was frog giggin' near there that night. Had his light on the bank where the frogs is at and he says he seen what he thought was two people having sex higher up on the bluff. Says it wasn't but a few seconds later when he saw a car headin' down the dirt road toward State Road 44. Bobby said he thought it was odd 'cause the driver never turned on his lights until he was on blacktop."

"Can your nephew identify the guy?"

"Says he was too embarrassed to look good when he caught 'em in his light."

I thanked Floyd and hung up. Now I knew why the girl I'd found hadn't suffered a broken neck. The perp was frightened by the boat lights and fled the scene.

The approaching car in my rearview window caught my attention, but the driver kept his distance. Then I kicked the Jeep up to more than eighty miles an hour. It didn't take a full mile for me to be certain that I was being followed.

The driver was good, staying far enough behind to appear that he or she had lost me. I tapped my brakes, slowing back to about sixty.

The car drifted at a distance behind me. The car grew smaller in my rearview mirror. The driver suddenly whipped off the paved road, the car kicking up a long rooster tail of dust as it sped in another direction going down a dirt road.

I dialed Leslie Moore's number. "Leslie, you mentioned that the chemical found in the vic's shoe isn't used to grow citrus. What does it grow?"

"Primarily tomatoes, at least in the concentrations we found."

"What does SunState Farms grow?"

"They're one of the largest growers of tomatoes in Florida."

"Text the directions to SunState for me. I'm two miles north of Lake Wells."

"Okay. I got the DNA results back from the black hair you found in your boat."

I was silent.

"The hair came from the vic you found. Someone is trying hard to set you up."

"Wonder who that might be? Is Slater there?"

"I haven't seen him in a couple of hours. Why?"

"Nothing. Just wanted to see if the pit bull was out of his yard."

"Slater met with two agents from the FBI. They showed up yesterday right after I arrived for work. Asked to meet with Slater. They met behind closed doors for about a half hour. Slater didn't say anything to me about what went on."

"Maybe Slater called them."

"That's not his style either. If there is any truth to the rumors that he's considering a bid for sheriff, maybe he's using the FBI in some capacity to help with this case. I don't know. I think—" She abruptly stopped talking.

"Is someone there?" I asked.

"When will the car be ready? Good, please check the brakes, too." She hung up.

I drove silently for the next fifteen minutes. Then my phone beeped with a text message. I read the directions to SunState Farms. I also read her last line, which said, *Slater knows I rode out to your place. Be careful!*

TWENTY-FOUR

I was soon driving through the farm community of Lake Placid. The marquee on the Lake Placid Theater read RET RN OF THE JED

As I pumped gas at the Circle K, I watched a dozen or so farm workers in the parking lot. Jeans and T-shirts stained dark green from harvesting tomatoes and peppers. They sipped Mountain Dews and Dr Peppers and ate sausage biscuits and microwaved enchiladas while attempting to avoid my eyes.

At the register, a large black man was buying cases of cheap wine. MD 20/20 and Thunderbird, enough of the stuff to give a platoon a hangover for a month. He glanced across his shoulder at me, black irises floating in twin pools of yellowish white, spattered with tiny specks of bloodshot veins. There was a look of suspicion as he turned away from me to face the female clerk who had finished ringing up the wine.

A scratchy voice came through vocal cords worn thin from years of cigarette smoke and nicotine. She said, "Comes to a hundred twenty-nine dollars and two cents."

The man reached in his pants pockets and pulled out a thick wad of bills. He peeled off two one-hundred-dollar notes and handed them to the woman.

"Where's the dolly at?" he asked.

She snorted, clearing mucus deep in her throat. "Where it always is, in the corner, behind the mop, next to the ice machine."

She looked at me. "You payin' for gas?"

"Yes. The Jeep."

"Be anything else?"

"No thanks."

"Forty-nine fifty."

I waited for change, watching the black man load the cases of wine on the dolly. His biceps strained the T-shirt, which read O-ROCK 107—THE CHRISTIAN ALTERNATIVE.

The clerk handed me the change and reached for a smoldering cigarette.

"Can you tell me how far I am from SunState Farms?" I asked her. The black man stopped loading the last case of wine for a second as he listened.

The woman exhaled smoke through her leathery, pitted nostrils. "No more than nine or ten miles east on Highway 66." She looked at the black man. "Silas, why don't you have him follow you, if you're goin' to the farm?"

He leaned the dolly toward his gut and said, "I ain't goin' there."

"No problem," I said. "Wherever you're going, it looks like it'll be quite a party."

"Somethin' like that." His tone had a challenge. "Who you want at SunState?"

"Richard Brennen. I understand he's running for office."

"So I hear."

"You know where I can find him?"

"Depends. If you're sellin' stuff, he ain't the man to see. He got people for that."

"Maybe I want to make a campaign contribution."

He looked at me through eyes cold as black lava that had turned to stone a lifetime ago. His disdain soaked into my skin like a coffee spill inching through a paper towel. I noticed a two-inch scratch on his left cheek. He gripped the dolly with two hands and backed out the door.

I wanted to give him time to load the wine and beer. I bought bottled water and then walked to my Jeep as he finished stowing his cargo in a decade-old Ford van. I watched the van head east on Highway 66. I let him get a good distance down the road before pulling out to follow.

The first SunState Farms sign appeared sooner than I anticipated. The sign was not large, but its message was:

SUNSTATE FARMS

VISITORS REPORT TO OFFICE

TRESPASSERS WILL BE PROSECUTED

I drove another half mile and saw a second SunState Farms sign. I was beginning to appreciate the size of the operation when I drove nearly a mile farther before coming to the entrance. A truck, loaded with tomatoes, came out of the gate.

I thought the man driving the van would pull into the main entrance to SunState. He passed the gate and picked up a little speed. Another mile and the van turned off the road. I slowed just enough to see that the van had stopped about a hundred feet down the dirt road. The man the clerk had called Silas was urinating in the bushes.

I kept driving. I'd let a few miles pass before turning around and going back to the dirt road.

As I made a U-turn, my cell rang. It was Nick. "Sean, the cops are here."

"What?"

"The onion-head dude. He's got two real cops with him. They're walking to your boat."

TWENTY-FIVE

I knew they'd come with a search warrant, and I knew Slater wanted to find me on *Jupiter* to make it work. "Nick," I said, "casually walk down the dock toward *Jupiter*. Chances are they won't break into the boat. They may ask you if you know where I am. Tell them I'm due back Sunday for a morning fishing trip."

"No problem. Where're you?"

"If you don't know, you can't say."

"Man, you don't have to worry about me. I don't say nothin'."

"I'll call you later." I ended the connection and pulled back onto Highway 66 heading west. Soon I was turning down the dirt road where the black man had urinated.

A quarter mile down the sandy road, I entered a third world country on a few acres in Florida. Dozens of trailers, many dilapidated and supported by cinder blocks and rusted jacks, lined both sides of the road. An old school bus, tires flat, wheels rusted, sat near a trailer.

A brown-skinned little girl, no more than two, belly swollen, wearing a diaper sagging from urine and feces, stood in the open door of the bus.

A barefoot woman, late twenties, sat on a metal folding chair under an Australian pine and breast-fed a baby. She watched me without reaction and then lifted a hand up to chase flies away from the baby's face.

An open ditch flowed with liquid that resembled molasses. The bloated body of a black cat was lying on its back in the water. A turkey vulture paid no attention to my Jeep passing as it tore into the dead cat's belly. The air carried the caustic scent of human waste, farm chemicals, green tomatoes, and burning trash.

An underfed dog, part black Lab and part unknown, barked and tried to chase my Jeep. It stopped short, the dog's right hind leg stiff with atrophy and disease. Chickens scattered as I drove slowly through the community.

The place was about the size of a football field. Everything was bordered by rows of tomato plants as far as the eye could see. The double-wide and single-wide trailers were mixed with a few tar-paper shacks and a graveyard of old pickup trucks, cars, vans, tractors, a backhoe, and other farm equipment.

One trailer, a single-wide, fairly new and well maintained, seemed to serve as some kind of store. A dark-skinned man came out of the door with a loaf of white bread and a six-pack of Diet Pepsi in his hands. Another farm worker walked up the three steps leading to the open door and went inside.

I drove on slowly but couldn't find any sign of the van I'd followed or its driver. As I came to the end of the row, I noticed a lone trailer isolated from the rest of the camp. All the blinds were down, and the trailer looked unoccupied. As I turned and started to drive in the direction I'd come, I looked in my rearview mirror and saw a black man stepping out of the trailer. I stopped. As he came closer, I recognized the T-shirt. I turned off the motor and waited for him.

"Don't like peoples following me," he said, standing by my door.

"Didn't see any No Trespassing signs. I was trying to find Sun-State Farms. I guess I made a wrong turn."

"Guess you did. SunState is on down the road. Only a blind man would miss 'em." He braced his big hands on both sides of my door and leaned closer to me. A worn toothpick was in the left side of his mouth. His breath smelled of last night's beer, onions, and decaying beef jerky. "What are you doin' here?"

"I told you, I'm looking for Richard Brennen."

"Brennen don't stay here. He don't even *come* here. Got the wrong place, dog."

"I'll have to expand my search."

"Don't expand it 'round here no more. Get the fuck on outta here!"

"You might want to work on your diplomacy, pal."

"I ain't your pal. Move your white ass off this property."

The phone on his hip rang. He picked it up and pressed a speaker button.

"Silo, where you at?" The voice was clipped. Spanish accent.

"Camp. We got us another trespasser."

"Who?"

"Dude who's been followin' me."

"Hold him till we get there."

TWENTY-SIX

An old school bus, painted army green, rolled to a stop at the far end of the camp. Dozens of men and women spilled out of the bus. Even from the distance, I could see the dirt and stains from the fields on their clothes. They seemed to creep through the camp like the walking dead, exhausted bodies and worn-out spirits.

A half dozen shuffled past me, avoiding Silas's eyes. Only one man, Hispanic, early twenties, yellow polo shirt, looked directly at me. He stopped for a moment. I could see him fidgeting.

"How are you?" I asked the man.

He shoved his hands into the pockets of his dirty jeans, looked at Silas and then at me.

"Go on, boy," said Silas. "He got nothin' to say. Don't speak no English nohow."

"I'll let him tell me that. Now, back away from my door."

Silas grinned, tossed his wet toothpick at my face, and held up both hands in mock surrender. He looked at an approaching vehicle and grinned wider. A new Ford Excursion, oversized tires, black, with darkened windows, eased around the migrant bus at the far end of the camp and started in my direction.

Silas waved the young man away, but he simply stood there for a long moment. He watched the SUV approach, looked at me, and began to walk toward a trailer next to where a small lamb stood. The animal was tied by a short piece of rope to a pine tree. The lamb bawled one time as the man passed by it.

Silas watched the approaching SUV and said, "You shoulda left when I told you."

"Maybe those folks know if Brennen is working the farm today."

"Maybe you can bet your ass on it."

The SUV pulled up on the opposite side of the Jeep. The window slowly lowered, and I could see two Hispanic men inside. Both were large, with bull necks, mirrored sunglasses, and baseball caps. The man closest to me wore a diamond stud in his left ear. "We help you?" The voice was more of a challenge than a question.

"Maybe," I said. "I'm trying to find Richard Brennen."

The man behind the wheel leaned forward. I could see the frosty mist from the air conditioner blowing his feathered, greasy black hair.

"Who are you?"

"Name's Sean O'Brien. And you?"

The man sitting in the passenger seat said, "Juan Gomez. This is my cousin Hector Ortega. That's Silas Davis. Sometimes we call him Silo, 'cause he's so big. Now that we all know each other, it's time to go our separate ways. No disrespect, but you're on private property."

"That's what I hear."

Silas pointed a broomstick-sized finger at my face. "Juan, the dude followed me from the store."

"I'm investigating the death of a young woman."

The man got out of the SUV and stood a few feet away from the

Jeep's passenger door. I didn't like the scene. I had a large African American man with a bad attitude at my door, and an even larger Mexican Goliath standing at the opposite side.

Juan Gomez looked at me like I was a roadside curiosity. "You a cop?"

"Used to be."

"If you're no cop, why you investigatin' some girl's killin'?" He stepped closer.

"I didn't say she was killed. I said I was investigating her death."

He grinned. "I figured you meant somebody killed her. Otherwise a person die, it's an accident, no?"

Another step closer.

"If I see Mr. Brennen, I will tell him you are looking for him. Where can he find you, Mr. O'Brien? Got a cell?"

He was close enough for me to see a black hair growing from a mole the size of a green pea on his cheek. His bulldog jaw popped as he chewed gum.

"I have a cell." I slowly lowered my hand to the pistol grip.

Gomez stopped, looked at my right hand, and locked eyes with Davis. Neither of the men standing seemed to be armed. I assumed the man in the SUV had a weapon. I said, "You two back away from the Jeep."

Gomez smiled. "Amigo, you have the wrong idea. We mean you no harm. I understand you have a job to do, no? You some kinda insurance investigator, right?"

"More like a private investigator. Now back off."

"You cain't take all of us," Davis mumbled.

"You're right, but I'll take you first."

Gomez gestured with both palms up. "Mr. O'Brien, relax. We just don't get many visitors down here. Sometimes Silo gets a little, how you say . . . agitated. Came back with somethin' from the Iraq war."

He glanced at my right hand and said, "Maybe you could write down your cell. If I see Mr. Brennen, I give it to him?"

"Don't have paper or pencil. Maybe your associate has some in your vehicle."

"Vehicle," he grinned. "You sound like a cop."

"I saw a bulletin board back at the convenience store. It has business cards on it. I'll leave my cell number there. I feel almost rude having to turn my back on one of you gentlemen as I talk. So if you don't mind, maybe you both could stand together."

Gomez smiled. "No problem. Silo, the man has a point. Come here so we can both speak with Mr. O'Brien." Silo shuffled around to where Gomez stood.

"Any of your female employees missing?" I asked.

"Missing?" Gomez shook his head. "No."

"Someone leave and not return? Did a girl walk away? Maybe she was kidnapped? About five-four, young, late teens or very early twenties?"

Gomez said, "You know workers come and go. When season's over, it's over."

"I understand that farm workers follow the seasons, usually with the same contractors, working various farms."

"Sometimes, that is so. People are free to go whenever they choose. But we have no missing women, right, Silo?"

"Right."

"We're very busy. I'll check for your number at the store in case we hear of anyone missing. Lot of camps through here, you know? If I see Mr. Brennen, I'll give your number to him. I hope you find your missing girl. Adios."

"Before you go, maybe you could help me with directions." I lifted my right hand off the pistol stock, opened the console, and pulled out the photograph of the dead girl. "Do you recognize her?"

Davis tried not to react, but the tightening of the neck muscles, touching the tip of his nose, and his diverted eyes gave him away.

Gomez's nostrils flared, like a giraffe that had just scented the presence of a lion. I held up the picture so the man in the SUV could see it. He pursed his lips, shrugged his shoulders, and looked away.

"I don't know this girl," Gomez said.

"Me neither," Davis mumbled.

I said, "Bet she was pretty before this. That's what happens to the human face when the cheekbone is crushed, the jaw is broken, and teeth are knocked out."

Gomez folded his thick forearms. Davis buried his hands in his pockets.

I said, "The man who did this left something."

"What?" Gomez asked.

"He left a trail."

"Trail?"

"A trail that led me here."

"Now you're fuckin' with me," Gomez said, in a voice that sounded like it came from a different man. "Ain't no trail bring you here. You ain't a real cop, so get the fuck off this land or somebody will find you on the side of the road. They'll believe you got hit by a truck and crawled in a ditch to die."

"I guess I wore out my welcome. *Hasta luego.*"

I saw the man in the SUV remove his sunglasses and reach for something under the seat. He slowly opened the door and slid to the ground, narrow-toed snakeskin boots easing onto the sand. He stood behind the false security a second too long. His right shoulder moved. I pulled the Glock up and leveled it at his head.

"Drop it!" I yelled. "Drop the gun!"

Both Gomez and Davis held up their hands. Ortega hesitated, looked at Gomez.

115

"Hector, drop the fuckin' gun," Gomez said.

The gun bounced a foot away from Ortega's left boot.

Gomez looked at me and gestured innocently. "A simple misunderstanding. My cousin had no intention of using the gun. He just wanted to make a point. We have a right to bear arms. This is America."

"I'll leave my number at the store. I know you have seen her. She had a name. Somebody here is going to tell me what it was."

I held the gun on them as I put the Jeep in gear and started to drive. I heard the cry of the lamb as I passed it. In the rearview mirror, I saw the young man come out of the trailer. He stood next to the lamb and watched me leave.

I drove slowly. A man sat on the edge of a tractor tire that was lying on its side, weeds growing through the center, rusted paint cans and beer bottles scattered around it. On the ground, between bare feet scarred and filthy with muck like dried cow manure, was a bottle of wine wrapped in a wrinkled brown paper bag.

Another man stood next to a mixed-breed yellow dog with the shape of a pit bull's square head. One ear was gone. Fight scars resembled barbwire tattoos on the dog's chest and neck. The man's dark face was the hue of a worn horse saddle. It was an emotionless face, hollow cheeks with smears of old dirt, unshaven and vacant as a field of weeds after a frost. His jeans were tucked into scuffed cowboy boots, hands shoved deep in his pockets, shoulders hunched. His eyes followed me, unblinking and lifeless as black marbles.

I felt like I was driving through the village of the damned.

TWENTY-SEVEN

The toothpick, wet with Davis's saliva, had hit me between the eyes and bounced onto my lap. I pulled over to the shoulder of the road and took the Jeep out of gear. Reaching in the console, I got one of the half dozen Ziploc bags, found the toothpick, and carefully lifted it up with a tissue by the end that wasn't chewed. I dropped it in the Ziploc and put the bag in the glove box.

The main gate to SunState Farms was open. I pulled in and followed signs to the office. The hard-packed dirt road wound around irrigation ditches, packinghouses, a machine shop, and trailers loaded with oranges.

The exterior of the office looked like the building might have originally been built as a small military base. All one story. Nondescript vanilla buildings and bungalows loosely joined. Citrus trees surrounded the entire fortress. I entered as a woman was picking her purse off the floor near a desk.

"You here to make a run to New Orleans?" she asked.

"No, but it's one of my favorite cities. Glad it's making a comeback."

I got the once-over curiosity look with glasses pushed up on the bridge of her nose. Early fifties. Hair pinned up. Sweatshirt and jeans. "Can I help you?" she asked, glancing at the digital clock near her desk.

"Is Mr. Brennen here?"

"Senior or junior?"

"Junior."

"And you are?"

I could detect that her guard dog training was about to come off the leash. I quickly said, "It's about the campaign. I'm trying to find the—"

"The fund-raiser?"

"Exactly."

"You're a little late, but not too late. The barbecue will be goin' on till about eight or nine, I suspect."

"That's what I assumed. Is it here?"

A smile. The guard was down. "Heavens no, it's at the ranch."

"Unfortunately, I didn't MapQuest the exact directions." I looked at the nameplate on her desk. "Carla, that's why I wound up lost. As a man, I have no problem asking for directions."

An eyebrow stencil arched. "Honey, you aren't alone. Been a half dozen people callin' the office, lost like sheep without a shepherd. You gotta be the last one . . . Mr. Hayes. Right? I'm glad you finally got here."

She started drawing a map. "Come here, darlin', I'll show you a shortcut."

THE BRENNEN PLACE WOULD HAVE been easy to find without the hand-drawn map. Simply follow the Mercedeses, Escalades, and Jaguars in a convoy. At least I'd washed the Jeep. I pulled in behind a dark Lincoln and waited my turn to go through the front gate. A rent-a-guard, starched white shirt, narrow pimply face, serious and unsmiling, held a clipboard and asked for names.

"Hayes," I said. His eyes scanned the list. He was starting to ask me something when a white limo pulled in close. The boy guard waved me onto the Brennen estate.

Farming had been good to the Brennens. I figured the winding driveway was a quarter mile long, bordered by freshly painted white fences that held prize cattle to the left and champion horses to the right. The house was the kind found on magazine covers or profiled on the Travel Channel. Its size and the Old South, antebellum feel made a statement. Members only.

Cars lined up in the large circular drive to be valet parked. I picked a spot between a Lexus and a Lincoln and backed in the Jeep. The smells of charcoal, burning hickory and mesquite wood, steaks, and barbecue ribs were mixed with the smells of manure and money.

As I stepped out, my cell rang. It was Leslie Moore. "Sean, there's some evidence missing in the case of the vic you found."

"What do you mean, missing?"

"Forensics has everything we initially found on the victim. It was the later evidence that you and the Indian, Joe Billie, found."

"What about it?"

"We'd already sent in the hair found on the duct tape for DNA analysis, but somehow the thread and shoe have been misplaced."

"Misplaced?"

"We had it sealed and kept with everything else. We were going to run the DNA tests on it first, but it was either misplaced or stolen."

"I'm betting on the latter. You don't often lose it."

"Unfortunately, it happens. I've never had it happen on my watch, though."

"Who has access to the forensics area?"

"The ME and all of her staff. Anyone working on the case, which is only a handful of people."

"Is Mitchell Slater one of them?"

"Yes, but why would he take it? It doesn't make sense."

"Yes it does."

"How?" she whispered.

"It makes sense if he's protecting someone."

"What do you mean?"

"What if Slater knows who killed the girl?"

"Why would he cover? Who would have that kind of power over Slater?"

"Powerful people, and I seem to have landed at ground zero."

TWENTY-EIGHT

I stood next to my Jeep for a moment to watch the money parade. Here were the millionaire migrants, the ones who followed the social seasons, an incestuous crossbreeding of old money, venture capital start-ups, bankers, lobbyists, politicians, and lawyers. The nip-tuck of Palm Beach mixed with cattle barons, horse breeders, and growers. They appointed golfing friends to environmental boards, water districts, zoning and public service commissions. Under their watch, Florida had turned into a land of tract houses, strip malls, a vanishing aquifer, a sickly Everglades, and condos lining the beaches like the Great Wall of China.

Maybe I could get a beer at the Brennens'.

Waitstaff stood smiling on either side of the entrance hall with trays of champagne and wines. The guests lifted the bubbly, chards, and cabs and followed white-gloved attendants toward the rear of the house. To get there, we passed a fifteen-foot-high waterfall cascading down a fieldstone wall. The water gently splashed down the stones in a dozen torrents, all spilling into an indoor koi pond.

We followed the hired catering staff and a cowboy, probably on the payroll, dressed in a denim sports coat, black silk European-cut T-shirt, and black pants. The boots were a dark ostrich skin. He looked at me as if trying to place my face.

Along with the real guests, I walked down a long corridor of powder blue Italian marble, descending three steps to emerge into what would be called a family room in an average house. The Brennens could have used it to hold conventions. Crown molding. Inlaid cherrywood floors. Expensive artwork with a Western flair.

Music came from the outdoor pool area. Dozens of guests sat or stood around the lushly landscaped gardens, bubbling spa, and resort-sized pool. In a corner, a three-piece band played a mix of modern country and oldies. A platoon of cooks turned thick-cut steaks and ribs on a river stone grill big enough for a resort.

"I noticed you didn't partake of wine or champagne when you got here." The voice came from behind me. The woman sipped chardonnay, leaving a lipstick kiss on the edge of the glass. She was blond and shapely, with a Jennifer Aniston smile and a diamond ring that didn't need a "point-something" to inflate the carat count. She extended her hand and said, "I'm Rene Roberts."

"Sean O'Brien."

"Nice to meet you, Sean." Her fingers slid over the wet glass. "I haven't seen you at a Brennen function before."

"Is that what this is, a function?"

"A barbecue. But it's a fund-raiser, sort of in disguise. Junior will say a few words. We'll all cheer and write checks. Not that the Brennens really need them, but the more contributions, the better it looks on the books, right?"

"Depends on who's looking," I said.

She smiled and sipped. "What are you drinking?"

"Think they have beer?"

"This is a barbecue." She lifted a perfectly manicured hand with a quick Saudi-princess-like beckon. She caught the eye of a young waiter.

"Yes, ma'am," he said

"Bring my friend a beer, and I'll take a vodka tonic."

"My pleasure. What kind of beer, sir?"

"Corona, if you have it."

He nodded and left. Rene Roberts turned to me, her lips wet with wine, her eyes playful. "Sean O'Brien sounds Irish. It doesn't look like you have a freckle or a red hair on your body. You look more like that actor, the James Bond guy."

"Sean Connery?"

"No . . . Pierce Brosnan, but taller. Wider shoulders. I think he's English."

The waiter brought the drinks and left. I took a full swallow from the bottle.

"My, aren't we thirsty," she said, with a smile that had less lipstick.

"Been a long day."

She sucked a piece of ice from her vodka. "How do you know the Brennens?"

"By reputation."

"So you don't do business with them?"

"Not yet. Maybe you can introduce me to the Brennens."

"Grace Brennen's in a wheelchair. You can't miss her, although I haven't seen her yet. Stroke. Poor thing. She was always the life of any party. Josh Brennen's rock. He's talking with Ron from the Arts Council. Never thought of ol' Josh as artsy fartsy."

Brennen was a large man, late sixties, handmade cowboy boots and top-of-the-line Western attire. He drank a dark whiskey from a crystal glass, resting his other hand on the shoulder of a smaller man about the same age.

I smiled. "You said Josh isn't the artsy type. How about his son, Richard? Dirt or oil paint under his fingernails?"

She looked around the party and lowered her voice. "Neither. He's about as nonfarmer as his Yale education could make him."

"How?"

"Pick a category."

"Let me guess, he can't drive a tractor, right?"

"Tractor! My dear new friend, Richard Brennen doesn't know an orange from a grapefruit. He's some kind of fruit himself. Handsome in a way that won't turn a real woman's head. Never married. Lives here on the estate. Can I be honest with you?"

"Why don't you lie to me?" I said, smiling.

Her laugh was like a cackle. She signaled for the waiter, who took her empty glass. "Same thing, please." He nodded and left. "Where was I?"

"You were offering a psychological profile of our hosts."

"I like you, Sean O'Brien. What do you do, by the way? And for godsakes, don't tell me you're a farmer or a plastic surgeon."

"I'm a sex therapist," I said, as straight-faced as I could.

Her laugh was now much louder. "You must come to the Brennens' barbecues more often. You're much cuter than Dr. Phil."

The waiter returned with her drink. She thanked him, waved him away, and again stirred the ice with a manicured fingernail. "Speak of the devil, Junior is making his first appearance."

As the band ended a song, Richard Brennen stepped from the dark into the light.

TWENTY-NINE

Richard Brennen's movements were measured, very controlled. The perfect smile. The perfect host. A wink, a squeeze on the shoulder, a sincere promise to look into something, and then off to the next huddled bunch. Simulated listening, teleprompter dialogue, and the feigned warmth of a TV game show host.

He stepped to the microphone. "I think we got us a record crowd for our first barbecue of the year. And I'm predicting this will be a great year." He paused while his friends applauded. "I want to thank y'all for coming out. We couldn't have asked for a prettier evening."

An older woman in a wheelchair was rolled from the great room out into the pool area. A nurse pushed the wheelchair, stopping it near where the senior Brennen stood.

Richard Brennen smiled and gestured toward the woman in the wheelchair. "Y'all be sure to say hello to Mama during the course of the evening." Brennen held his drink up in the direction of his mother. There was no response. I didn't know if it was because a stroke had paralyzed her facial muscles or because she found her son appalling, as did Rene Roberts, who stood with an empty glass and face.

Brennen beamed a shark's grin over his apostles. "I'm told the food's ready. Let's eat and drink like sailors on shore leave! Maybe the politically correct thing would be to say enjoy yourselves responsibly—but us Brennens, we've been known to be politically incorrect when it comes to throwing a great party. Have fun!"

There was a burst of applause as the band kicked in with a rendition of "Sweet Home Alabama." I watched Richard Brennen join his father at the bar farther away from the band. As I approached them, I could tell they were in a nearly whispered conversation, their backs toward me.

The bartender saw me coming. "What can I get you?" he asked.

Before I answered, I positioned myself on the opposite side of the bar, now facing them, ready for the reaction. "A Coke," I said, loud enough for the Brennens to overhear. "I know that's not the preferred drink of sailors, but I'm my own designated driver. So I have to deal with that whole issue of responsibility."

Richard Brennen seemed to appraise me the way a cat watches a bird just beyond the pane of glass. He cocked his head slightly, eyes unblinking, absorbed in the moment, showing no irritation, no threat. Nothing but a primal curiosity.

His father's face was reddish and a bit bloated. Tiny black veins could be seen just under the puffy skin on his cheeks. Eyes clouded with cataracts. He finished what remained of his whiskey and set his glass on the bar. "Ricardo, two fingers."

Richard Brennen flashed perfectly straight and whitened predator's teeth. He said, "Please forgive me, but I'm having a difficult time making the connection."

"Sean O'Brien."

Brennen extended his hand. As he shook mine, I could feel his powerful grip.

"Do you know my father, Josh?" The old man nodded at me.

Josh Brennen said, "Don't think I've had the pleasure. Any relation to the Ralph O'Brien in Sumter County?"

"No relation."

Richard Brennen's eyes opened wider, like a great cat following prey on the savanna. "What do you do?" he asked.

"I was brought out of retirement."

Josh Brennen sipped his Black Jack. A large diamond ring, in the shape of a horseshoe, caught the light. I thought of the bruise on the girl's cheek. I felt my pulse quicken.

He swallowed the whiskey and grinned. "Retired! Son, I'd like to have known how to retire at your age, when I was your age."

Richard smiled. "What brought you out of early retirement?"

"Death."

Josh Brennen made a slight grunt, like something was caught deep in his throat. He sipped the whiskey, the flush in his face darkening, his lower lip the shade of a beet.

But Richard Brennen was good. No involuntary movements. No tightening of the skin. No change in pupils. No visible response.

"Interesting," Richard mused.

"I'm investigating a murder."

His stare changed into something reptilian. It happened within the blink of an eye. A second later, he looked at nothing. *Maybe they're sharing some monstrous father-and-son killing game,* I thought.

"Please, tell us what happened," he said.

"What murder?" Josh Brennen asked.

"A young woman was killed. Raped, strangled, and finally stabbed to death. Her body was found near the St. Johns River."

"That's terrible news," Richard said, with the sincerity of a TV preacher. "What does that have to do with us or our ranch?"

"I think she was one of your employees."

"We don't employ any farm workers. We contract with others who do."

"Who owns the property south of SunState Farms off Highway 66?"

"Lot of land there. It depends. What are you getting at, sir?" Josh asked.

"I'd bet that SunState controls that land, and on it you have a migrant camp that makes third world slums look like the Ritz."

Richard Brennen said, "We lease property to a lot of people."

"I'm not here to make this a campaign issue, Mr. Brennen. I'm here to investigate a murder. Do you know if any of the women are missing?"

"With due respect for the deceased," Richard said, "we can't keep up with all of the farm workers. There are hundreds, maybe thousands, in Florida. A girl dying is tragic, but it's not something we would have a way of inventorying."

"Inventorying," I said. "That's an interesting word for the loss of human life. Sort of like losing a few bushels of tomatoes. It wasn't one girl. There are others. I happened to find this young woman as she lay dying."

"Why did you come here?" Josh Brennen asked, knocking back his Black Jack.

"To investigate the murder of an innocent girl. I thought you or someone here might have seen something."

"What are you drivin' at, partner?" The elder Brennen's clouded eyes glistened.

"I believe one of the victims, maybe two, came from this area. Probably one of your migrant camps. The girl was buried in a half-inch plywood box. Her headstone is a county ID number. She's lying in a convict cemetery, a place reserved for the kind of man who killed her."

"Are you a police officer?" Richard Brennen asked.

"No."

"It's really bad form to come here and impersonate an officer of the law."

"I'm not impersonating anyone. I told you my name and what I'm doing."

"You a private investigator?" Josh Brennen asked, his tone louder.

Richard held up his hand. "Daddy, let's not upset Mama." He smiled at the attentive nurse. "Maria, take Mrs. Brennen in to watch some TV."

The nurse smiled back and did as requested. Mrs. Brennen stared straight at her son. The facial muscles were locked in a cruel vise grip and the mouth curved in a theatrical mask of sadness or horror as she was wheeled around and rolled into the distant catacombs of the estate.

I saw the boy guard enter the great room and whisper something in the ear of the security cowboy. He pushed the Stetson higher on his round head, nodded, and marched toward the swimming pool. He came toward me.

"Excuse me, Mr. Brennen," Cowboy Guard said. "I believe there is a mistake on the guest list. Mr. Hayes just arrived. He's a little upset 'cause he had to show an ID at the gate. Unfortunately, new gate security didn't recognize him." Cowboy puffed up and turned toward me. "Mr. Brennen, is this man part of the guest list?"

"No, he's not." The voice wasn't from either of the Brennens. I knew who it was before I turned around and saw him.

Detective Mitchell Slater set a plate of half-eaten pork ribs on the bar and used a plastic cocktail toothpick to pry a piece of meat from between his teeth.

THIRTY

Josh Brennen swallowed the remains of his drink and wiped his dark lips with the back of his wide hand. "You know this man?" he asked.

"Yeah," Slater said. "Name's Sean O'Brien. He's a person of interest in a murder case my department is investigating."

"You mean he's a murder suspect?" Richard Brennen asked.

"He's about as suspect as you can get. Ex-cop with a drinking problem and a thing for rough sex. Maybe he got a little too rough with a young girl. He figures if he can stir up enough diversion, then the state attorney won't take it to a grand jury."

Josh Brennen's left jawbone moved as if his teeth had come unglued. "So what the hell are you doing in my house? Here with my friends?"

Slater said, "Probably followed me down, Josh."

I said, "Don't flatter yourself, Detective. But you did leave a trail."

Slater looked at Cowboy, then back at me. "What're you talking about?"

"You haven't investigated the obvious—where the victims lived. Who did they work for? Why were they killed? What's the motive, Detective? Of course, serial killers don't need a motive, do they? It's about the power and the urge to dominate and kill. I find it interesting that these two victims were most likely migrants. Both probably working on a farm like this one, and they died. No, they were murdered. Everything they dreamed about doing or becoming died in the hands of someone who enjoyed it. You're not looking for cockroaches, you're having drinks with them."

Josh Brennen barked, "You've got thirty seconds to get off my property!"

I looked at Josh Brennen. His eyes didn't break the stare, one lower lid drooping, runny with fluid. I said, "I can't imagine someone trafficking in human beings as easily as a rancher sells cattle. That seems profoundly evil to me."

"Daddy, don't let this intruder get you riled up. Mr. O'Brien, I'm going to have you escorted off this property immediately."

Slater said, "You're outta line, O'Brien, and you're about to be arrested."

"You're out of your jurisdiction both physically and socially. Break out the cuffs for me and the sound bite your candidate gives will be 'No comment.'"

Rene Roberts, now looking a little more drunk, sauntered right toward me, her face glowing, damp from the humidity, her mouth puckered and blood red with lipstick and barbecue sauce. "Can a lady get a drink here?" she asked.

As I started to walk around Cowboy, he stepped in my path. He stared straight at me, awaiting orders from either one of the Brennens.

"Excuse me," I said.

No effort to move. His breathing quickened, the gut moving as if he'd just finished running up a flight of steps. I could smell the mints on his breath.

Josh Brennen said, "Why don't you take our uninvited guest to pasture one? Show him the new stallion we bought."

Cowboy reached out with one thick hand and grabbed me under the arm like an angry father trying to forcefully pick up a child. He squeezed hard, fingers digging deep into my left upper arm. I said, "Cute hat. Bet your buddies with the spurs love you in it."

He took the bait and swung at my head. I leaned back, his knuckles missing my face. Using both hands, I held his fist and leveraged it down with his weight the same time I was bringing up my knee. I hit him hard in the jaw. The sound was like wind catching a plastic garbage bag. I grabbed him by the ponytail and the back of his belt, shoving him into the pool, the splash soaking a fat man holding a barbecue rib bone.

Cowboy's Stetson floated in the center of the pool while he thrashed like a drowning man to the far side. Josh Brennen let fly a drunken string of obscenities, and the band cranked up a rendition of "Proud Mary."

As I entered the cavernous great room, I heard Rene Roberts's crowing laugh. Mrs. Brennen sat in the dark, the light from the hall dissecting her face in shadow, the stiff skin frozen in a mold like a mask from a Greek tragedy. I nodded and continued moving down the hall, which now seemed like a maze. I felt a mist from the wall of water. Saw a half dozen koi breaking the surface, their mouths sucking in oxygen and bits of food like doughnuts bobbing in hot oil.

The night air was warm and smelled of fresh-cut hay and jasmine. The taste of rain was almost palatable in the thick air. A whippoorwill called out in the dark, its night song tranquil and beckoning. I didn't know where I'd be the rest of the night. At that moment, though, I felt like I'd just traveled back through the looking glass.

THIRTY-ONE

I saw a tall figure approaching. It wore a Mardi Gras mask and pushed a dressmaker's dummy in a wheelchair down a dark brick alley. Garbage spilled from cans picked over by homeless people and littered the path. Smoke drifted up from smoldering trash in a steel drum. Two homeless men stood by the open barrel, warming hands covered in street filth. I ran down the wet, timeworn bricks. Running toward a police car at the far end of the alley. The pulse of cherry red light bounced off a wall scrawled with graffiti and a body lying in the rain. I couldn't get my footing on the wet bricks. Slipping. Falling.

I sat straight up in the hard bed. My T-shirt was soaked in sweat. I looked around to gain my bearings. Sheets of rain drummed against the window, and the bluish light cast from the Lakeside Inn sign gave the room a surreal aura of calm, like being in the blue eye of a storm.

Earlier, around 10:00 P.M., I had to wake the desk clerk to get a room. It was now 3:37 A.M. The air conditioner rattled, blowing lukewarm air that smelled like it came from a blow-dryer with a burned hair trapped inside.

The thin blanket reeked of stale cigarette smoke and clothes that had been kept in the trunk of a car for weeks. I climbed out of the cot disguised as a bed and stood next to the window. The motel was circa 1950s. All twenty rooms faced the parking lot, a lot dotted with potholes and beer cans. Cigarette butts floated in holes filled with rainwater.

The taste in my mouth was like wet ashes. At that moment, I wanted two ounces of Irish whiskey. I watched the skinny fingers of rainwater roll down the glass. The letters in the Lakeside Inn sign pulsated VACANCY in a neon rain.

Dawn was still a few hours away, but I knew sleep wouldn't come again tonight. The funk of the room was oppressive with the yellow walls, the burnt orange carpet spotted with cigarette burns, and the smell of night sweats that Clorox couldn't erase.

I washed my face, brushed the taste of fungus out of my mouth, dressed, tucked my Glock under my shirt, and stepped out into the rainy indigo night.

TWENTY MINUTES LATER I was driving down a desolate country road, watching lightning rupture the dark, sending a strobe of light across the fields of tomatoes and cucumbers. I watched the windshield wipers for a moment, wondering where the killer was at that instant. I was now a bounty hunter with no contract except the one I made to the girl I'd found.

I drove toward the migrant camp. I didn't know why, but I just drove in that direction. Maybe the closer I got to where I thought the most recent victim came from, the more likely I'd find something that would fit in the puzzle. I felt that Gomez, Ortega, Davis, and the Brennens were part of the chain of events that caused the deaths.

I pulled the Jeep off the road, parked it behind a small clump of pines, and walked in the rain toward the camp. Even in the drizzle, I could smell the odor of burned garbage before I got to the migrant camp. I pushed my way through a perimeter of wet banana trees and scrub pines. All of the trailers, except the one I assumed was a store, were dark silhouettes.

As I started to cross the road, which was muddy and flowing in torrents of rainwater, I saw headlights coming. I ducked behind the Dumpster and waited. An old pickup truck lumbered into the camp, its tires splashing through the mud and water. The driver stopped in front of the camp store. When the passenger side door opened and the interior light turned on, I could see that three men were in the truck. One got out and unlocked the door to the store, entering and turning on the lights. The driver then drove toward the two converted school buses parked in a clearing between the rows of trailers.

A second pickup truck, a new model, drove into the camp. I could tell that Silas Davis was behind the wheel. A Lincoln Navigator, driven by Juan Gomez, followed his truck. He parked in front of the store and got out. His cousin, Hector Ortega, wasn't with him. Gomez entered the store while Davis went from trailer to trailer, unlocking each door. Even in the rain, I could hear him shout, "Let's go! People, get the fuck up!"

A minute or so later, weary farm workers, stiff and tired, spilled out of their housing, walking to the buses, the diesel engines idling, fumes belching an acrid odor.

The night was yielding to light in the eastern sky. I slipped into the tomato fields behind the trailers and went about fifty feet down one row. I wanted to retrieve a few soil samples to have them tested.

Just maybe I could prove the soil from the shoe Max found came from here. A remote chance, but worth trying.

I took a Ziploc bag from my pocket, knelt down, and used my fingers to scoop some of the soil into the bag. I moved a few rows over and scooped up a handful of soil into a second bag. The gray clouds moved like giant tumbleweeds rolling through the sky. The clouds opened to reveal a hint of sunrise, a ray illuminating rows of tomato plants that seemed to stretch to the ocean. Then the opening in the clouds closed and a gray descended on the field like a false dawn.

Some of the plants were heavy with green tomatoes. I saw areas where a few tomatoes had dropped from the plants, scattered down the long rows.

Something stood out among the green tomatoes on the ground. It was red. A woman's shoe. At that moment, it looked so small and so abandoned in this field of the rising sun.

THIRTY-TWO

I stood over the shoe for a closer look. Even though the rain had soaked it, turning it dark red, this shoe was identical to the one Max had found. Here it lay, dirty and wet. I used a small stick to lift the shoe out of its burial ground.

In the raw ugliness, I saw the hopes and dreams of a young woman left in a field. The glass slipper would never be returned and fitted on her petite foot, releasing her from bondage. That was the fairy tale. The reality was a horror story. I unfolded a paper sack from my back pocket and lowered the shoe into it.

As I entered the camp, Juan Gomez was coming out of the store. He held a foam cup of hot coffee in one hand and a doughnut in the other. He chewed and watched me walk up to him, holding the shoe in the bag behind my back. He was a bull chewing grass, staring at nothing beyond his limited vision.

My presence had a different effect on Silas Davis. He came out of the store, his eyes disbelieving and then glaring. His face snarled into a scowl. He bit into a strip of beef jerky, ground it hard in his teeth, and washed it down with a Mountain Dew.

Davis said, "You some kind of psycho ex-cop? Comin' in here all wet and lookin' like a crazy motherfucker." He crushed the can in his hand and tossed it into the mud. "Hector ain't here. So you lookin' for somebody else to draw down on, huh? That why you got your hand behind your back?"

Slowly I held up the bag. Gomez looked like the last bite of doughnut wouldn't go down his throat. "What's that?"

"The woman who wore the matching shoe was murdered. This one came from your field. Less than fifty yards from where you two are standing."

Gomez said, "We never seen it. Lots of red shoes. Lots of women. You won't find our fingerprints on that shoe."

"Maybe not, but this tells me she was here. It tells me you knew her. It tells me you both lied. I showed you a picture of her. How long did she work for you?"

"Did who work for us, man?"

"You tell me!"

Davis bit into the beefy jerky, chewed, and said nothing. Gomez said, "No, we don't know her. There are other camps besides this one. Many workers are women. Many could have red shoes."

"She didn't work the fields in a shoe like this. What kind of work did she do?"

Gomez said, "We don't know who you're talking about?"

"Yes you do! Her first name was Angela. I'm betting she was kept here against her will. What was her full name?"

Davis lifted a toothpick from his shirt pocket and began picking the meat out of his teeth. He said, "You can bet your white ass that my black ass would be burned if anybody tried to own anybody. Know where I'm comin' from, dog?"

A dozen farm workers, men and women, walked past us. Heading for the buses. I noticed one man limping. I almost didn't recognize him. He was the young man I'd seen yesterday, the one that stopped to speak with me but never got the chance. His face was swollen, bruised in shades of purple. He looked at me for a few seconds before limping toward the bus.

I said, "Silas, you asked me if I know where you're coming from. I think the image of that man tells me where you're coming from. He needs medical attention. What happened to him?"

Gomez shrugged. "Probably got in a fight with one of his amigos. It's something we have no control over. These men are highly competitive in the field. Each wants to be the next *tigre*. Sometimes they drink too much. Go crazy and start fighting."

"I'm going to do three things—"

Davis interrupted. "Whatcha gonna do, ex-cop? Who you gonna call?"

"I'm calling an ambulance for that man. I'm running a DNA check on the toothpick you threw at my face yesterday. And I'm going to prove that one or both of you killed Angela."

Silas Davis slowly removed the toothpick from one side of his mouth, looking at it as if it had a disease.

As I turned to walk to my car, I saw the second bus leave, filled with faces staring at the dawn. I heard Gomez open his cell phone. He spoke quickly in Spanish. The only words I could make out were something that sounded like "Santa Ana."

THIRTY-THREE

The cell phone seemed to ring for eternity. It was like an ambulance in the distance that never passed. The phone stopped ringing, and I opened my eyes, the sunlight pouring into *Jupiter*'s salon like a roving spotlight in sync with the boat's rise and fall in gentle wakes kicked up by boat traffic in the marina. I had a headache, but I felt better than when I'd arrived.

Earlier that morning, a little after nine, I'd made it back to *Jupiter*, poured myself a shot of brandy for breakfast, peeled off the wet clothes, and stretched out on the sofa in the salon. If I'd had dreams, I didn't remember them. I didn't want to. I rubbed my temples and looked at my watch. It was almost four in the afternoon.

I stood and picked the phone up from the table where I'd left it next to the bottle of brandy. Checking the caller ID, I didn't recognize the number. I played the messages back on speakerphone as I stepped into the galley and poured a glass of orange juice.

The first message was from Leslie Moore. "Sean, are you okay?

Please call me as soon as you get this message." The next two messages were from Leslie, too, essentially saying the same thing, but each time with more of an edge in her voice. It would have to wait. I needed a hot shower to cleanse dried sweat, dirt, and human misery out of my pores.

A HALF HOUR LATER I checked the pencil camera in the master salon. It was working flawlessly, the images being beamed to my laptop on Dave's boat. I would give Nick and Dave a lesson in video editing, should I need their help.

I fixed a turkey and hot mustard sandwich and took it topside. There were a few hours before sunset, and the first fishing boat in the fleet churned slowly back into the marina. From the fly bridge, I could see tourists' faces in various shades of sunburn.

I wanted to phone my neighbor to check on Max. I'd tell him when I thought I'd be home, but at that moment, I didn't know for sure.

"Hey, you don't invite me over for a beer. That's a violation of marina manners," I turned around to see Nick standing next to *Jupiter*'s cockpit with a beer in each fist. "So, I say to myself, self, you go on over to Sean's boat and show him what neighborhood watch means."

"Come on up."

Nick grinned and climbed the steps, making sure he didn't spill a drop of beer. He handed me a Corona and sat on the console. *"Salute!"* he said. After a long swallow, he wiped his mouth with the back of his hand. "Sean, how long you been on your boat?"

"Just got out of bed. Slept for the last seven hours."

"Sound like you got some kinda jet lag. You been out of the country?"

"You could say that."

"Better not be Greece!"

"No, it wasn't the ancient cradle of democracy. More like the dungeons."

"Yeah, where?"

"Not far from here. Felt like I'd spent a year in a third world country, and I was there for just two days." I told Nick the story while he sipped his beer and looked at me, shaking his head occasionally in disbelief.

"Where's the girl's shoe?"

"I gave it to Kim, and she hid it in the tiki bar. *Jupiter*'s not safe anymore."

"You gonna take the shoe to the police?"

"I have to deliver it to the right police."

"Yeah, man. I haven't seen Onion Head around."

"That's because he's too busy rubbing shoulders with his wealthy constituents."

"Yeah."

"He's on the take. Thinks he's one of them. They use him like toilet paper."

"That's no good. What will happen if—"

My phone rang, cutting Nick off as he looked at it with as much suspicion as I felt. Got to love caller ID. It was Leslie. "Hi there," I said.

"Where are you?"

"On the boat."

"What happened in your investigation? Uncover anything?"

"I need some time to explain things to you. I don't want to do it over the phone. I have some evidence for you to run tests on, and the sooner, the better."

"Whatever you have, hide it."

"Why?"

"Slater's supposed to announce his bid for the sheriff's job

Wednesday. He's looking for a splash, and you're it. He's on his way to find you with a search warrant. Sean, he's coming to arrest you."

"What's Slater's e-mail address?"

"Why?"

"He's got mail, and he doesn't know it's coming from me."

I jotted his address down, said good-bye to Leslie, and turned to Nick. "I'm going to give you a quick lesson in editing video. We'll go to Dave's boat, to my laptop. I'll give you both a lesson."

"Cool, man." His thick mustache lifted with his wide grin.

THIRTY-FOUR

It took me less than an hour to teach Dave and Nick how to edit a short scene, compress it, and e-mail the video. After the lesson, Dave stayed on *Gibraltar*, making sure the wireless signal remained intact, while Nick and I returned to *Jupiter*'s fly bridge to await Slater.

From the bridge, I could see Slater before he saw me. He pulled into the parking lot in an unmarked Ford, followed by a county sheriff's car. Slater and two deputies. The return of the posse. This time he had my walking papers. Maybe I'd record his.

Nick leaned closer to me from his chair, the afternoon light off the water dancing in his dark eyes. "You want me to stay?"

"Yeah, just follow my lead. It may sound a little crazy, but play along. Okay?"

"No problem, man. But it'd be my pleasure to toss Onion Head in the ocean. Let the sharks eat him as a cop salad." Nick laughed so hard I was sure Slater could hear it.

Slater got about halfway down the dock before he spotted us. He stopped and talked with the deputies. All three looked our way.

As I watched them come closer, I was glad I hadn't slept in the master bed. I'd left it exactly the way Slater saw it, with one exception. I had removed the long, dark hair that he'd so carefully placed near the pillow. Now, I would let him do his thing and capture whatever reaction he had through the camera I knew he would not find.

At the stern, he issued orders to the deputies, then turned to me. "O'Brien," Slater barked, like he was a drill sergeant and I was at his command.

"Good afternoon, Detective Slater."

"Come down, O'Brien. I have a search warrant. Who's with you?"

"This is my neighbor, Nick Cronus."

"Tell him to vacate the premises."

"Why don't you tell him? I haven't had my quota of rude pills this morning to match you." I climbed down to the cockpit with Nick right behind me.

Slater pointed to Nick and said, "You need to go back wherever it is you come from. Mr. O'Brien, stand on the dock with Deputy Myers, please. Deputy Morgan and I are coming aboard to search your boat." He handed me the search warrant.

"Search it for what? What's your probable cause? Maybe you don't need one."

Slater crossed his arms, glanced at one deputy, then looked at Nick and me. He said, "Get off the boat or my men will remove you."

"What's wrong with you?" Nick protested. "You think I look like a terrorist?"

"You can get off the boat or I call ICE," Slater said.

"And you can kiss my IC—"

"That's ludicrous, Detective," I said, jumping in before Nick lost his temper enough to get him arrested. "You talk about immigration and yet you party with people who exploit people because ICE doesn't interfere."

"You made quite an impression the other night, O'Brien. Pissed off a lot of people. The wrong people. Mr. Brennen didn't find any humor in your wrecking his party and breaking one of his employee's wrists. This, by the way, is one reason I'm here. Roger Burns has filed assault and battery charges against you. Deputy Morgan will be taking you in and booking you on that one. But before we all go down to the sheriff's office, we'd like to see what's on your boat."

"By all means, Detective. Nick and I'll just step aside and let the long arm of the law reach wherever it pleases." We got off *Jupiter* as Slater and his deputy boarded.

The deputy on the dock stood with his feet spread, arms folded across his chest.

Nick lowered his voice. "Sean, that dude definitely got a boner on to screw you, man. What the hell did you do to piss off the Onion?"

"I found a body, a body somehow connected to his wealthy friends, or at least their farming operation. His millionaire pals are no doubt funding his bid to become sheriff. If he gets it, I'll probably be in jail on some violation of the Patriot Act. Max will be tossed in the dog pound."

"Man, that's where they kill dogs."

I lowered my voice. "Dave ought to be watching the show live about now. After they take me, go to Dave's boat and play back the recorded images on the hard drive. When you edit the video, show a few seconds of the master cabin right before Slater enters, keep the video going as he searches, and then cut it right after he leaves."

"No problem."

"Here's the e-mail address."

"When you want me to send it?"

"I'll call you."

"Okay."

"Thanks, Nick."

"You be careful, man. That dick is crazy, and he's wearing a badge."

My cell rang. "Sean," Dave said, "you got him! He went ballistic searching your cabin. Caught on video! Body language really tells the story."

I watched Slater exit *Jupiter*. "Work with Nick on the editing," I said to Dave.

"Will do. Talk about reality television."

I closed the cell as Slater approached, the sunlight reflecting off his head, the sweat dripping from his face. "Pretty clean boat you keep, O'Brien. Guess you vacuum and scrub it down, that sort of thing, a lot."

"I like a clean boat."

"Then you won't like our county jail. Nasty place. Not nearly as clean as your boat." He turned to the deputy. "Book him. Bring Mr. O'Brien in on assault charges."

The deputy pulled the handcuffs off his belt and walked my way. "Hands behind your back," he said. Then he read my rights to me.

"Nick, don't forget to lock *Jupiter*."

The large deputy reached for my upper arm to lead me down the dock.

Slater and the second deputy followed. With my hands cuffed behind my back, I was marched by my marina neighbors. People paused from polishing or washing boats, turning my way to see the parade.

We had to walk right by the tiki bar on the way to the parking lot. A dozen locals stopped talking, put their beers down, and watched. One man, Big John, who lived on a twenty-year-old trawler called *Heaven's Gate,* held up his beer in a toast. He yelled, "Sean, you'd better be out before St. Paddy's Day! Ya hear me?"

Kim looked at me in disbelief, her mouth forming an O and her right hand touching a spot beneath her throat. As I was led to the patrol car, I heard a blackbird's cackling mixed with drunks laughing and Buffett on a CD singing, "Changes in Latitudes."

THIRTY-FIVE

Iwas booked and fingerprinted. They took my wallet, watch, clothes, and dignity. I was given an orange jailhouse jumpsuit that was three inches too short. Bond was set at two thousand. The flip-flops were worn down to cracker-thin soles. I had three minutes to make a call. I had two calls to make. The first was to an attorney friend in Miami, Carl Hoffman. He started the procedure to post bond. My second call was to Nick. "I have less than a minute. Tell me exactly what Slater did."

"Onion Head lost his cookies once he started searching your bed. At first he looked like a man who'd lost his key. Lookin' under the pillow. Feelin' the mattress, gettin' down and lookin' across the mattress and the pillow. He was cussin' your name the whole time. He said, 'Bastard's found it.' He started ripping the bed apart."

"Have you edited the video, the way you just described?"

"Dave and me. Finished!"

"Send it to the e-mail I gave you. Include 'warmest regards' and my name."

"Three clicks, and it's gone. Boom, boom, and boom. Gone!"

"Nick, I'll need you to come down here and make bail for me."

"I'm on my way."

"From my laptop, send the Slater video to Dave's e-mail for backup. If something happens to me in this jail, if I'm beaten up or killed, you and Dave e-mail the video to the media. Include CNN."

A deputy with a shaved head and a body built by a neighborhood gym and chemicals escorted me to the holding cell. The only time he made eye contact with me was when the cell door was slammed shut and locked. He simply nodded and walked away, the thud of his boots hollow, then faint as he marched down the corridor.

There is no sound on earth that rocks the cradle of your spirit quite like the finality of a cell door closing and locking in your freedom. Your mind paces the eight-by-six-foot cage like a wild animal searching for an exit that isn't there. You urinate in a hole in plain sight. You are stripped bare of the most precious of human rights— sovereignty. You are under the absolute authority of people who don't care what you did or didn't do, who you are, who you think you were, or what you want.

I stood in the center of the cell and listened to the sounds of despair. The sounds of madmen, the yelling, swearing, the never-ending noises coming from inmates who grunted, protested, and roared like zoo animals at feeding time.

There was graffiti scraped into the wall. The deadening effect of prison brought out jailhouse artists and poets that bordered somewhere on the fringe of genius and insanity.

I could smell the stench of urine and chemical bleach. I sat on the hard bed. I'd been standing so long that my legs felt rubbery, the muscles tight. I thought about how far I'd come in a half circle. I'd been responsible for putting hundreds of misfits in jails like this. Now I sat among them. Their catcalls, threats, and screams reverberated around my rectangle cage like heat lightning bouncing off steel. I felt like I did in the motel room, a smothering sense, like the air was poison. In the motel room, though, I could walk out in the chill of the rain to escape. In the cell, I had nowhere to hide from the torrent of misery that flowed down the long corridors searching for company.

I HEARD HIM BEFORE I saw him. The fast clip of the wing tips against the concrete, the strut, the sense of command and authority in his pace. Slater rounded the corner and stood in front of my cell. He stared, the eyes burning into me.

"Who the fuck do you think you are? Your little e-mail trick is horseshit. It shows nothing. Nothing! You hear me? Just a thorough search!"

"Go on and scream, Detective. Nobody will notice." I stood up from the cot and stepped to the bars. "But they will notice your reaction to not finding the hair you planted. I shot video when I found it; the date and time are displayed in the frame. I got a close-up where you'd left the victim's hair. That was exactly where you looked today trying to find something you'd left. Planting false evidence. Hope you have a hell of a good reason. Because right now it looks like you're the killer. The killer you're telling everyone you're looking for. You know, body language speaks volumes, Slater. We have your on-camera commentary. Let me see if I can quote you from memory, 'Bastard's found it.' You went berserk when you couldn't find the hair to frame me. Combine that with your comments and the fact that evidence acquired on your watch has come up missing. I smell an indictment."

"You're fuckin' nuts, you washed-up prick. I didn't murder anyone!"

"Then who did?"

"You're crazy, O'Brien."

"Maybe—but then jail does have a way of working on the psyche. You'll discover that when you spend the next twenty years in a place worse than this."

"What do you want?"

"You to come clean. Tell me what you know about the murder or murders. Tell me why you're so protective of the Brennens. Maybe Richard Brennen or his old man is a killer. They've got plenty of easy prey all around their ranch. You want to take the fall for a psychopath? Even you must have learned something in law enforcement before you got greedy. You know this guy won't stop. He's addicted to death. You want the blood of these girls on what's left of your conscience?"

He leaned forward on his big wing tips and made a slight snorting sound from the back of his throat. His eyes were slightly dilated; a nerve twitched under the right one. His breath smelled of Maalox. A tiny speck of antacid tablet dangled from the corner of his mouth. "Fuck you, O'Brien. You don't know a damn thing." He turned and left.

IT WAS AFTER MIDNIGHT and there was no sign of Nick. I was worried but didn't have any options. Now it would be too late to make bond. I stretched out on the hard cot and felt my heart beat in my temples. I could smell the stink of sweat on the thin mattress.

I closed my eyes, the fatigue and exhaustion flooding my mind. Somewhere in the twilight of my subconscious, the dream weaver entered my cell. I stood with my uncle on the wooden deck of my childhood home. He pointed to a pair of eagles starting their nest in the bald cypress tree near the end of our property.

I turned to open the sliding glass doors, but I couldn't push the latch free. As I struggled with the lock, I saw the silhouetted reflection of the eagles on the doors. I cupped my hands to the sides of my face and leaned into the glass to see if my father was in the kitchen. All I saw was darkness.

THIRTY-SIX

I awoke with a pounding headache and stiff back to a morning wake-up call from an inmate two cells down screaming that his ex-wife should have the lips on her vagina sewed together. He blamed his state of life on his wife's anatomy and his apparent inability to steer clear of her sexual pull. He yelled at the top of his lungs, "Bitch took my son, and she's fuckin' her probation officer. Y'all hear me! That's against the fuckin' law!"

Good morning, America, from the county jail.

TWO HOURS LATER I bonded out on my own recognizance. Although I told the presiding judge that I'd acted in self-defense, His Honor reminded me that I was formerly an officer of the law and should regulate my personal life accordingly. I paid two hundred dollars in court costs and promised to appear if the plaintiff pursued the assault charges.

As I was walking down the courthouse steps and wondering what had happened to Nick and how I was getting home, a black Ford pulled up to the curb. Detective Leslie Moore lowered the driver's window. "Looks like you could use a lift."

"I could use a drink. Bloody Mary, cold, very spicy, a scallion and celery."

"Get in," she said, with a smile that reminded me why I could never adjust to gender segregation in a cell.

I got in the unmarked police cruiser and could smell a trace of her perfume. Light and feminine. Her hair was pulled back, accentuating her striking profile. She looked at me, eyes falling somewhere on my face, before she adjusted the rearview mirror and merged in with the flow of traffic. She drove silently for a few seconds, giving me time to explain what happened. "Although I'm glad to see you, I'm concerned that Nick isn't here."

"Who?"

I told her who Nick was and what had happened.

She said, "Maybe he had a good reason. I read the arrest reports and decided to come here but didn't want Slater to see me."

"He wasn't around."

"That's odd."

"Not really," I said. "After our heart-to-heart chat last night, he's on the defensive at the moment."

"I know he's suspicious of me. He's popped some questions out of the blue."

"Such as?"

"He wanted to know if I'd questioned you at your home. Asked me things like whether I was withholding any evidence I might have on you. He actually said there was no place in his shop for cops, as he called them, who held press conferences. Now, this is coming from a man who just held a news conference announcing his bid for sheriff."

"Let's get that coffee. I have a lot to tell you and something to give you."

"What's that?"

"Drive to the marina and I'll show you."

A HALF HOUR LATER we were pulling into the parking lot at the marina, oyster shells popping beneath the tires, the smell of fish in the air. It was Monday morning, and there were only a few cars in the lot. Nick's motorcycle was gone. He usually parked near the wall between the tiki hut and the marina office.

I knelt down at the spot where I'd last seen the BMW motorcycle. Two imprints in the grass. Wide tires. A small shine on the grass between the tire marks. I touched the oil, rubbing the residue between my fingers and feeling the gumminess, and sniffed the burned deposit. Nick hadn't been gone too long.

As Leslie and I walked past the bar, Kim was filling a stainless steel bin with crushed ice. Big John was the only customer, sitting at the bar, sipping black coffee, nursing his head, and cursing events of the previous night.

"Good morning, Kim, John," I said. "Have either of you seen Nick?"

Big John looked over the lip of the coffee cup, his eyes red and soggy, a patch of white chest hair sticking though a black T-shirt that read SLOPPY JOES—KEY WEST. His voice sounded like he had gravel stuck somewhere in his larynx. "Nick pulled outta here last night. A few hours after they toted you off." He cut his bloodshot eyes over to Leslie and spoke out of one side of his mouth, like Popeye. "What did you do?"

"It was a little misunderstanding, that's all."

Kim dried her hands on a bar towel. "You okay, Sean?"

"I'm fine. If you see Nick, please tell him to stop by my boat."

Kim smiled. "I'll tell him. Would you two like some coffee?"

Leslie shook her head. I said, "No thanks. We might be back for lunch."

"Do that." Kim smiled and folded her arms across her breasts.

As we turned to leave, I heard Big John cough up something deep in his throat. His gravelly voice sounded like it was fighting a hair ball. He managed to say, "Sean O'Brien escorted outta here in handcuffs with three cops . . . back in the morning with a hot chick."

ON *JUPITER*, I put on a pot of coffee and hunted for some half-and-half that wasn't too far beyond its expiration date. "How do you like your coffee?" I asked.

"Fresh, brewed with cold water, and black."

"Then we're in luck. I have all those things."

"I like your boat."

"It's sort of my second home. Well, recently it's been more like my first home."

"I feel privileged. How many women get to see your bricks-and-mortar home and your boat home? Not many, I'd be willing to wager."

"My river home isn't bricks and mortar. All wood, except the fireplace, and that's river stone, not brick. Damn—"

"What?"

"I forgot Max! My poor neighbor has inherited Max. I'll call him after I bring you up to speed."

"She's adorable. I can't imagine her being much of a challenge."

"Oh, stick around a while, you'll see."

She smiled a radiant smile, eyes happy in the sunlight coming through the salon window and into the galley. I poured coffee into two large cups and led Leslie onto the cockpit and topside to the fly bridge.

"What a view!" she said, looking out over the marina. She held the mug with two hands and watched a sailboat head out to the channel. "This is really nice."

"I like it."

"What else do you like?"

"What do you mean?"

She sipped her coffee and said, "I think I know Sean O'Brien the detective—"

"Former detective."

"Yes, but now you're back in investigator mode, and I can tell you're good at it. What I don't know is anything about you. You know, what foods you like. Your tastes in music. Hobbies. Family. What do you enjoy doing?"

"Okay. I enjoy a good piece of fish. A steak cooked medium with a glass of dry cabernet. I appreciate good jazz. Blues when it's felt. I like a traditional Irish tune. I like fishing, boating. Used to like to sail, but I did that with Sherri. After her death, I sold our sailboat. As far as the rest of my family, my father was murdered when I was fifteen. My mother, a woman I learned was manic-depressive most of her life, committed suicide six months after my father's death. I lived with my uncle Bill for two years. In 1991, I spent a lifetime in the Gulf War and parts of Afghanistan. Sorry you asked?"

She didn't answer immediately, pausing to choose her words. "No, I'm not sorry. I am sorry these things happened to you. You're a good person, Sean. There are good people like you out there. I like to think I've helped a few on a professional level. Brought closure for a few folks. Put others in jail for a long time."

"But the system is a stacked deck with the wealthy turning the cards. The homicides that were the most satisfying to solve were the ones involving the people who thought they were untouchables. The rich who killed a spouse or a partner because they somehow got in the way. No matter how many layers of lawyers they hired, there was usually a chink in the armor somewhere. I'd try to find it."

Her eyes followed a charter boat leaving the marina. "Is that how you burned out? Dedicating whatever it took, maybe the quality time with your wife, to beat the stacked decks and to put these people in prison?"

"You pretty much summed it up."

"Now, by a twist of fate, you're back in the game."

"But things have changed."

"If you want to talk about it, I'm here."

"Thanks, Leslie—but my immediate concern is catching the killer. I believe the person we're chasing may be beyond bad."

"What do you mean, beyond bad?"

"He has no conscience. He's a predator. He's fearless. He thinks he's smarter than we are. And he'll kill until he's caught. One of the most prolific known serial killers was a guy named Dennis Nilsen. He was charged with a dozen murders. He said, 'A mind can be evil without being abnormal.' In other words, the serial killer can't be identified the way you'd easily spot a homeless person. To most people, this kind of psychopath is never obvious."

She was quiet a beat. "What's your instinct tell you?"

"I'm betting the killer is within the inner circle of the Brennens, knows them, or works on their ranch, or is somehow connected to them. The perp could be Richard or Josh. The old man wears a horse-shoe-shaped diamond ring on his right hand. The victim I found had a cut in the shape of a U on her face, her left side." I spent the next ten minutes telling Leslie everything that had occurred. Then I added, "I have the victim's other shoe here, hidden in the tiki bar. And I have a chewed toothpick that's oozing in DNA material. Let's see if anything matches what we have on my vic. Do you have something new on the Brevand victim?"

"No one has come forward to claim or even ID the body. We didn't find any foreign DNA on her. Everything clean. Under the nails, too."

I looked across the bay for a moment. A half dozen pelicans sailed over the mangroves. "As a detective, I always arrived at a crime scene after the body was cold, usually in rigor or beyond, and I always took death, at least murders, personal. The dead have no one left to speak for them unless we do it. I never had a victim die while I tried to help her until now. She looked me in the eye as I promised to save her, and she seemed to know that I couldn't. Her heart may have stopped beating at the hospital, but I believe she accepted death while I held her. That kind of death stays with you. Justice for them is your own life jacket."

I drained the remains of my coffee and started to back down the ladder leading to the cockpit. Leslie watched me for a moment. She pushed a loose strand of hair behind her left ear. "Any coffee left?"

"You bet. I'll bring up the pot."

"That's okay. I'll come down."

In the galley, I refilled our cups. "Are you hungry?" I asked.

"Do you cook, too?"

"I've managed to turn out a few edible meals. Nick, next door, is an excellent cook, at least when it comes to anything seafood. But right now, he's MIA."

"I can have an APB issued."

"It may come to that if I can't find him. Do you like omelets?"

"I love omelets, lots of cheese. Can I help?"

"Sure, reach down behind you and get that iron skillet out. It's the only one in there. Last time I made anything in that pan I tried to blacken some fish Nick gave me. The damn smoke set off the alarm."

When I glanced up at the smoke detector, my eyes locked on one small spot. A slight quarter circle of headliner was lighter than the surrounding area. The smoke detector had been moved. Just a quarter of an inch, but moved. Someone had taken it down and not replaced it exactly flush with the headliner.

I tapped Leslie on her shoulder, held one finger to my lips, pointed toward the smoke detector, and said, "I like a little onions and pepper in my omelet. Sound good?"

"Sure," she said, playing along, looking at the detector and then at me.

"I like music, too, when I cook. Helps with the rhythm." I turned on a radio and tuned in a station playing rock. I held a finger to my lips. Leslie nodded and followed me to the smoke detector. I gently twisted it out of the socket. Someone had replaced the battery with a bug, a small listening device that looked very sophisticated. I set the detector down on the wet bar and signaled Leslie to follow me outside. In the cockpit, I said, "I don't think they heard anything of consequence. Everything I told you, about what happened, I told you topside. I'll sweep up there for another bug. Before you leave, I'll give you the shoe and the toothpick. You think Slater planted the bug when he searched my boat?"

"I wish I could say yes. I'm familiar with the bugs our department uses. I've never seen one like that. Somebody wants to know what you know, Sean, and I think whoever it is doesn't work for the county sheriff's department. It's someone else."

"The question is, who?"

THIRTY-SEVEN

After Leslie left, it took me less than a half hour to sweep *Jupiter* for other bugs. Nothing. I sat in the helm and called my neighbor to check on Max. I was told she had made herself quite at home and displayed no signs of missing me.

I saw Dave Collins pop his head out of *Gibraltar*'s hatch and climb onto the cockpit. It looked like he'd spent the night on his boat. I caught his attention and signaled for him to walk over to *Jupiter*.

I climbed down from the bridge and stood next to Nick's boat as Dave approached. He said, "You either escaped or Nick made your bond. I'd say you have become one pain in the ass for Detective Slater. In that e-mail you sent, Slater looked like he was suffering from a stroke. He's adept at profanity."

"Thanks for helping Nick with the edit. He didn't make it to bail me out."

Dave seemed astounded. "After Nick sent the e-mail and copied me, I burned it to a DVD for safekeeping, and he left to make bond.

Odd. What charges did the detective throw at you to justify an arrest?"

"Trumped-up charges. I twisted a guy's wrist trying to keep my head from becoming a punching bag. He filed assault charges, or was told to file charges."

"What do you mean?"

I explained the course of events to Dave while he sipped from a large coffee mug. When I was finished, he nodded and said, "Hope your attorney's good. You're going against some big money. Tectonic plates are shifting, and you're on the fault line."

"You could say that. I feel like I'm in the middle of an earthquake. Come look at the bug I found on *Jupiter*."

"Did you call an exterminator?" he asked, grinning.

"It's a small one. Found it in my smoke detector. Thought you might have seen something like it before. Maybe you'd know who might use it."

"Let me take a look. It's been a while."

"I always heard you guys never really retire."

He took his sunglasses off as he stepped into *Jupiter*'s salon. The music from the radio filled the room. I pointed to the bug sitting in the spot where the smoke detector's battery used to be. Dave fished in his shirt pocket for a pair of bifocals. He studied the bug for a half minute before motioning for me to follow him to the cockpit.

He said, "It's new. Sensitive. Powerful. It'll pick up a fart."

"Would the sheriff's office have something like that?"

"Doubt it. Or they could be teaming up with the feds, using the feds' gear while trying to find whatever it is they think you can tell them."

"Could be. As rumors of a possible serial killer swirl, Kim says two agents from the FBI were asking questions about yours truly. It's all horseshit, Dave. I have a power-hungry detective who wants to become the next sheriff, and he knows I didn't kill the girl. Yet I think he's taking great pains to protect whoever did kill her."

Dave tossed the remains of his coffee over the side of *Jupiter.* "Let's take a walk."

I nodded, and we stepped out of the cockpit and started slowly down the dock.

"We need to put things in some kind of perspective," he said.

"I'm listening."

"The juggernaut in all of this is simply timing. You were in the right place at the right time to start a cataclysmic fall of the dominoes. A psychic told you the name of the woman you found, Angela. It could be accurate or not. We have no last name. We do have an Indian who was in the immediate vicinity of where you discovered the victim before you found her. You have the father-and-son symbiosis of Josh and Richard Brennen. Anyone else?"

"After I ruffled feathers last time in the migrant camp, when I stuck the vic's shoe in the faces of Juan Gomez and Silas Davis as I was leaving, I overheard Gomez call someone. The name sounded like 'Santa Ana.' It could be a place or their attorney."

"Or a hit man."

"That's comforting."

"The reality, Sean, is that you're shaking up the comfort level of a very powerful group and the businesses that the group represents. It doesn't mean that they are directly responsible for the deaths, but the killings are possibly linked to their business mode, their brand, agriculture. Some labor contractors are running modern-day indentured servant camps—profiting from human trafficking and forced prostitution. So a few of the girls run. They're getting caught and killed. Rather than take them back and beat them into submission, someone is killing them, which doesn't make sense because the women would be worth more alive than dead." He stopped walking and turned toward me. "The question is, why are they dying?"

"Because the perp knows they become numbers, not people, when they're killed. He's sadistic, and he's a chameleon. He can blend in anywhere—but when he's alone with his victim, the evil drips like hot candle wax. John Wayne Gacy used to ask his victims, 'How does it feel knowing you're going to die?'"

Dave scratched a three-day growth on his face. "We might have somebody on this Ferris wheel that finds sadistic sex, rape, and killing a sport. We have two recent bodies, no IDs, and no hard evidence to connect the dots. So the big wheel keeps turning under the control and *perhaps* for the amusement of a killer." Dave paused to watch a sailboat. "So what are we missing?"

"The thread that ties us to the killer. A strong clue is the DNA found in the hair stuck to the duct tape. I'll ask Leslie to get a DNA sample from the person who, at this point, might fit this pattern killer's profile."

"Who's that?" Dave asked.

"Richard Brennen."

THIRTY-EIGHT

When I got back to *Jupiter*, I could hear my cell phone on the table ringing as I stepped into the cockpit. I entered the salon, walked down to the galley, and saw it was Leslie's number.

"Hold a second," I said into the phone. I carried it fifty feet down the dock before I said, "I'm here, Leslie."

"There is a definite match with the victim's shoe. We photographed everything. It's the same size, color, style, fabric, and brand."

"What's the word on the toothpick?"

"That will take a few more hours. I've got a rush on it."

"Run a DNA test on Richard Brennen. Maybe his DNA will match the hair found on the duct tape."

Silence. Then she said, "That's going to make the six o'clock news if the media get wind of it. I may have to go around Slater for that one. I'll see if I can get Dan Grant working the legal end and logistics with some excuse so he doesn't tip off Slater. We'll catch Brennen with a court order for the DNA. Otherwise, the only time we'll see him open his mouth is at one of his fund-raisers. I'm lovin' it. Have you found Nick?"

"Not yet. He hasn't returned to his boat."

"I'll do a search. Maybe we picked him up for something."

"Can't imagine that."

There was a long silence. She cleared her throat and lowered her voice. "Are you doing anything tonight?"

"You never know. My plans have been rather interrupted lately. I want to do two things: find Nick and keep out of the county jail."

"I'll do what I can to help on both counts. Somewhere in there you have to eat. I make a pretty good steak. I probably can't compete with Nick's cooking talents when it comes to fish, but Dad did teach me how to grill a good steak."

"What time?"

"Around sevenish?"

"Okay," I heard myself say.

"I'll call you later today with directions. 'Bye."

After she hung up, I looked at my cell phone for a few seconds. I don't know why, but for some reason the phone seemed like an alien device in my hand. *Beam me up, Scotty, I have no idea where the hell I am on this planet at the moment.* I did know what I was going to say to whatever alien life-forms were listening in through the bug. I went back aboard *Jupiter*, lifted the bug off the table, picked up one of my deep-sea rods, walked to the bow, and stepped out on the long bowsprit.

A breeze came across the lagoon and tidal flats, bringing with it the smell of oyster bars and fish. I looked at the brackish water below me. The tide was incoming, traveling with the wind. A pelican sailed effortlessly by, cocking its head toward me. The bird seemed to know that I wasn't using shrimp or minnows for bait. It flapped its wings and flew over the mangroves.

I held the bug close to my mouth and whispered. "Listen closely, assholes. You're out of control, and I'm going to stop you. If you have Nick, let him go. You touch him and I'll come for you. I'll track you down. Then I'll hook you and reel you in. Remember this sound. It's what you'll hear in your head when I find you."

I took the large steel hook and pushed it into the center of the bug, cracking and breaking through the shiny metal like opening a tin can. I cast the line as hard as I could. The bug, with the hook and line attached to it, formed a high arc before plunging into the bay. It made a splash like a baseball hitting the water. I watched the ripples until they panned out, lost definition, and joined the rising tide coming toward me.

THIRTY-NINE

I hoped the gnawing in my gut would subside if I actually ate lunch. At the tiki bar, I ordered a blackened grouper sandwich. Kim brought my order, set the food down, and stared at me. "You okay?" I asked.

"I'm a little nervous because you haven't eaten here in a while. I just wanted to make sure your sandwich is okay before I serve the table behind you. Corona?"

I nodded and took a bite.

She opened a longneck Corona with specks of ice sliding down the sides of the bottle. "Enjoy, handsome."

"Kim."

"Yeah?"

"Food's great."

She smiled and left to wait on a table. I heard the sound of a motorcycle entering the parking lot. Within a few seconds, Nick pulled into his parking spot in the grass, killed the engine, and got off his bike. He looked toward the tiki bar, saw me, and shook his head with a look somewhere between a grin and a grimace. He walked up to the bar and flopped down on one of the bar stools.

"Sean, you're not gonna fuckin' believe where I've been."

"Try me."

Kim came around the bar, saw Nick, and said, "The prodigal mariner. Your pal here, O'Brien, has been pacing the restaurant trying to figure out if Martians captured you. Whatcha drinking, Nicky?"

"Bud."

Kim opened a bottle of Budweiser and pushed it in front of Nick. He took a quick sip, scratched at the stubble on his chin, and shook his head in a hound dog kind of resignation. "Man," he began, "I go to get you outta jail and I go to jail."

"What?"

"This cop, I swear he musta been waitin' for me. I get on my bike to go bail you out. I go about a half mile down the road, and all these blue lights start flashing. This cop pulls me over. Says my taillight is burned out. I say, no problem, thank you. I'll get it fixed. He asks me if I've been drinkin'. I told him only two beers. Then he tells me to touch my nose with this finger . . . then this finger. I do okay, but the cop, the same cop on your boat with Onion Head, he said I'm under arrest for DUI. I ask if he's kidding me. The next thing I know is I'm being handcuffed, read my rights, put in the back of the police car, and taken to the jail. They put me in a big cell with lots of people who were really drunk. The place smell like shit, man. Vomit on the floor. Blood on shirts from fights. And there I sit. No phone. No lawyer. No nothin'. I couldn't even tell you where I was, and I was probably not far from you. Come mornin', I explain to the judge, dude called Judge Pappas, what went down. 'Cause they didn't get a breath test, brother Pappas threw it out." Nick drained the can and got Kim's attention. "I'll have what Sean has. But bring me a hamburger instead of the fish."

"Okay, Nicky."

"Sean, what the hell's going on? These cops really think you're goin' around knockin' off farm girls?"

"Women who are held against their will, sexually exploited, and sometimes killed. I have a problem with that. And Onion Head, as you call him, has a problem with me."

"I say we go rearrange his face, 'cause now he's really pissin' me off."

"His fall is coming. I'm going to do everything I can to make it happen before any more women are killed."

"He's the killer?"

"Don't think so. Someone more cunning, smarter than Slater, is involved. Slater's role is probably public relations." I finished my beer and watched a seagull battle a blackbird for a piece of shrimp that had fallen from the table a teenager was busing.

"Nick, I found a bug on *Jupiter*, hidden in the smoke detector."

Kim brought Nick's food. He attacked it, taking two bites in a row out of the hamburger. Chewing, he managed to say, "What? Somebody spy on you? Listen to everything we talk about?"

"You got it."

"Everything? Even about women?"

"Probably."

"That's bullshit!"

"Either somebody really wants to pin all or some of this on me, or they think I know a lot more than I do. Whichever, I sent them a message."

"What do you mean?"

"I thought they'd picked you up. Maybe were holding you against your will."

"I was in jail. That's against my will."

"I know, but I thought it might be something worse."

"What's worse than being sober and spending a night with a dozen drunks vomiting on themselves? I coulda caught some disease in that place."

"I don't know how deep and far this thing is. I have a hunch there's sexual slavery here. There could be a lot of people involved at different levels. Underage women from anywhere in the world, forced to become prostitutes. Their johns are probably the people who bring or import them into the country. These girls are scared kids with nowhere to go. The customer base probably includes some pillars in their respective communities. Maybe a few politicians, cops, church-goers, men used to buying whatever they want: teenage girls, kinky sex, threesomes, toss a lawyer in because they're always involved in some level of corruption, and there you have a lot of powerful reasons for secrecy."

Nick shook his head and ran his tongue along the inside of his cheek. He sipped his beer and seemed to search for words. "What do we do?"

"You keep catching the big fish in the sea. I'll try to catch the land sharks."

"Man, I know I'm not a cop. I know you have all the professional training, but I'm strong, fast, don't take no shit from nobody. You need me, Sean."

"I need you to stay alive. To go fishing with me. To tell me about the Greek islands and why I need to live the rest of my life there."

Nick started to protest as my cell rang. It was Leslie. I thought she was calling to either cancel the dinner or give me directions to her place.

"Hi," I said on the second ring. "I forget to ask you what kind of wine you like. I'll pick up a bottle."

"Sean." Her tone was serious. "I got some early results on the toothpick. Jonathan, in the lab, busted his butt to get it done fast for us. No rush charges."

"What do you have?"

"DNA on the toothpick matches the DNA under the fingernail of your victim."

"Are you sure?"

"Ninety-nine-point-nine percent sure. We'll run the tests again, but it looks like Silas Davis, the jerk who tossed the toothpick in your face, beat up the face of your victim. I'd say you found the killer. Congratulations."

FORTY

It was a couple of hours before sunset, and I jogged toward the Ponce Inlet Lighthouse. I ran past tidal flats, dotted with small mangrove islands, past shallow pockets of brackish water, much of it no more than a foot deep at low tide. As my feet pounded the bike path, I could see Silas Davis's smirking face, a chewed toothpick in the corner of his mocking mouth, the smell of unwashed scalp, the odor of sweat and reefer clinging to dreadlocks like compost. Now I knew his skin cells were under the dead girl's fingernail. I ran harder.

A dozen cars were in the Ponce Inlet Lighthouse parking lot. Tourists snapped digital souvenirs of the old brick lighthouse that rises more than 175 feet above the surrounding land. I cut through the parking lot and jogged on the beach as I made my way back to the marina.

Except for the gentle roll of breakers, it was almost still and flat. I slipped off my sneakers, socks, and T-shirt and ran into the water. It was warm, and the water seemed to embrace every pore on my skin. I dove beneath a wave and swam underwater a half minute, feeling the coolness in the water the deeper I went. When my hand touched the sandy bottom, I headed back for the sun. When I broke through the surface, I inhaled a chestful of air and floated on my back.

I could only hear my breathing and the distant sound of the surf. I closed my eyes and simply listened. A gull called out. A small fish broke the surface near me. Beyond that, nothing. I laid my head farther back in the warm water, allowing it to cover my ears. Even the sound of a laughing gull faded away.

"Sean, find your peace." It was Sherri's voice. It came from the deepest reaches of the ocean. Soft, distant, and loving. Was it spoken between levels of my own consciousness, or did I really hear something? I opened my eyes and watched the lavender sky fill with warm hues of straw-tinted clouds.

I hadn't been out to sea since I had released Sherri's ashes. Now I floated alone on a desolate copper ocean. And I deeply missed my wife. I lifted my left hand and let the water run out of my palm. Somewhere in there, I thought, were traces of Sherri. Somewhere in there were traces of me.

I swam slowly to the shore. I could tell the tide was starting to rise, pushing the surf farther up the beach. I got my things and started across the sand to the path bordered by sea grape trees. I heard a wave crash, and I had an urge to turn and look at the ocean one last time. Instead, I walked toward the setting sun and followed long shadows all the way back to *Jupiter*.

As I shaved and showered, I thought of what lay ahead. I was going out, or staying in, with a woman. The first since Sherri's death. My emotions were like a tossed salad, lots of pieces in one ceramic bowl with a hairline crack in the center. I was starting with a woman who was in the same line of work that I'd left, sworn off.

For the first time in a long time, I made a conscious effort to think about what I'd wear. Clothes may make the man, but my choices on *Jupiter* were limited. I dressed in fresh jeans, polo shirt, and boat shoes without socks. Then I picked up a bottle of cabernet from *Jupiter*'s vast collection and headed out. I stood in the cockpit, locked the doors, set the paper-clip alarm, and suddenly sensed my own insecurity. I felt like a kid going on a first date. Maybe this was what I was supposed to expect. Since Sherri's death, I'd never rehearsed this moment.

Then why did I feel bad about trying to feel good? I started down the dock, wondering if I'd do well with the meaningless chatter that dating people often spew like bounced spam. I didn't want to go there. I didn't want to stay in emotional isolation, either. I liked Leslie. Liked her smile, her head, and her laugh. And I liked her body.

One foot in front of the other, I thought. But I didn't know if I was on the right path.

FORTY-ONE

When Leslie opened her front door, I wasn't prepared for what I saw. She looked stunning in a natural way. Her long brown hair was down, very little makeup, the skin on her face radiating a healthy glow, her eyes dancing in the light. She wore black designer jeans, three-quarter length, that fit her like paint.

"Hi," I said. *Nice open, pal.*

"Come in," she said, beaming.

"Hope you like this. The cab ought to go well with the steaks."

She took the bottle and glanced at the label. "Perfect. Let's open it. It can catch its breath and then we'll have a glass."

Her home was small, decorated in bright tones. Lots of green plants and furniture that Hemingway might have brought home from Burma or Africa. It had the look of an Asian-African fusion of the arts.

I said, "Looks like you have the Far East and the Dark Continent well represented. Sort of feel like I'm on safari here."

"That's the idea. I love Africa. Or maybe I love the idea of Africa, since I haven't been there. Friends who have been there told me you feel it's where life on the planet began. I'd like to touch the soil. There's something very old and earthy about the land."

"I felt that way in Texas trying to drive across it."

She smiled. "Never been to Texas. Think I'd like to see Africa first."

"I'd like to start in Ireland. Begin my trip in a pub, work my way over to Africa."

"You may not ever make it out of the pub."

"What's wrong with that?"

She laughed and went around the kitchen counter, handing me a corkscrew. "If you do the honors, I'll finish the salad. We can toast Ireland and Kenya and then put the steaks on the grill."

I poured the wine, handed her a glass, and said, "To the Dark Continent and to the place that makes the darkest beer, Dublin."

She closed her eyes, savoring the wine's aftertaste for a moment. "Very nice."

Her lips were full, wet with the taste of wine. She simply looked at me, waiting for me to respond, a subtle coyness in her expression.

"Glad you like it," I finally said. *Dumb.* "What can I do to help?"

"Salad's made. Steaks have been marinating in the fridge. I started the grill when I heard you drive up. Potatoes are in the oven." She opened the refrigerator and took the steaks out and removed the foil from the top of the glass dish. "Let's go tell stories around the fire."

"After you."

The outdoor table was set with plates and glasses. Two candles burning in the center of it all. Nice touch. I sipped my wine and watched Leslie turn the steaks on the grill. She was a pro, working the meat just close enough to the flames to sear it but not scorch it.

"I can tell you've done this."

"I like to cook, especially steaks. How do you like yours?"

"Medium."

"Me, too. Used to like them with a cool center. Then along came mad cow and I went to medium."

"Those cows weren't mad, just misunderstood."

Leslie laughed. Her smile was as warm as the fire. She sipped her wine, the flames playing in her eyes. She said, "I cook with hickory and mesquite."

"You sure you've never been to Texas?"

"Positive."

"That's where mesquite began."

"Really?"

"Absolutely. Cattle coming up from Mexico ate the mesquite bushes. They couldn't completely digest all the seeds, so on cattle drives across Texas, the seeds were scattered. Fertilized at the same time, too."

Leslie made a puckering motion with her mouth and cut her eyes up to me. "So that's where mesquite gets its rich flavor. Comes from a long line of cow pies across Texas. Or is this a little bit of O'Brien bullshit?"

"That's where it began, in bullshit. I'm sure today's mesquite harvest is a few generations removed."

"You're quite the historian."

"I'm full of needless information."

"Watch the steaks. I'll get the plates."

Even though the steaks didn't need turning, I yielded to the call of a hundred-thousand-year-old carnivore gene, speared the meat, and flipped the steaks.

We refilled our wineglasses and ate slowly, tasting, talking, and laughing. The more I got to know Leslie, the more I liked her. She told me about her childhood, the fights her mother and father had, especially as she was in her early teens. The battles escalated to the point that she saw her father draw back his fist to hit her mother, stopping before he did, but more angry with himself than her. The

179

next day, when Leslie got home from school, she found a note on the kitchen counter. It was a two-sentence good-bye he had written to Leslie's mother. Two years later her father had remarried and moved to Seattle, completely severing contact with Leslie.

She said, "Maybe it's why I got into criminal investigation. Learn how to track down my father to ask him why he never called me. Not even on my birthdays. Then I got to the point where I didn't care anymore." She sipped the wine, her voice disconnected, like it came from a documentary film flickering against her heart. "At least he's alive. When you told me the other day that your father had been murdered, I could feel your pain."

I was silent.

"Want to talk about it?" she asked.

"On routine patrol, he radioed in that he'd pulled over a car with a burned-out taillight. The driver opened fire on my father. Dad was shot in the stomach. He died trying to crawl back to the car to call for help."

"I'm so sorry. Was the perp caught?"

"He's doing life at Starke."

"Why'd he shoot? Couldn't have been the taillight."

"Investigators told my mother they found drugs, cocaine, and about a grand in loose bills near my father's body. Press had a field day. The next thing we knew was that people were not quite so sorry that a cop was killed in what some believed was a drug deal gone bad. Many officers in his department didn't attend his funeral."

"Dear God . . . and your mother was suffering from depression, and you became her caregiver. Your childhood—"

"More wine," I said, interrupting her.

She sipped the remaining bit of wine from her glass, closed her eyes for a long moment, and then looked straight into my eyes and said, "Sean, stay the night."

FORTY-TWO

I thought about my swim in the ocean earlier in the day. Thought about Sherri's voice in the soft roll of the breakers. *Sean, find your peace.*

Mesquite crackled in the grill. I said to Leslie, "A pop and a hiss, and you thought the mesquite cow-pie story was all bull."

We both laughed, and she sipped more wine. Then the look on her face became one of concern. Compassion. She swirled the wine in her glass, deep in thought. "Your childhood was stolen."

"Maybe."

"Things that happen to us as children, traumatic things, such as sexual abuse, the suicide of a parent, can be the stuff of nightmares for a long time."

"That's why the Irish invented whiskey."

"Want to talk about it?"

"About what?"

"About how all of that tragedy at such a young age can leave scars."

"When you bury something, it's not smart to keep digging it up."

"Maybe," she said softly, "but sometimes things just don't stay buried until you understand all the circumstances and come to terms with them. You were only a child, and there was absolutely nothing you could do."

"This isn't the time or place to resurrect old ghosts. My demons are my private demons. Just like the first Gulf War, did what I had to do. Not much of a topic for a dinner conversation, though."

Leslie smiled and inhaled deeply. She moistened her lower lip, searching for the right words. "As corny or presumptuous as this might sound, Sean, I only want you to know I'm a pretty darn good listener. I'm here if you ever feel like talking to someone . . . someone who cares." She looked at the coals glowing in the grill, the flames iridescent in her wide pupils. "Maybe, in an odd sort of way, your circumstances made you a good detective."

"I'm not sure how good a detective I really was."

"What do you mean?"

"The criminal mind is an insane place to enter. To hunt them, I had to program myself to become like them, at least in terms of motive. What is the line between justice and retribution? It was always clearly marked for me, until one night I'd tracked down a serial killer. The guy was a pedophile who started off by giving his oldest daughter a pair of high heels and lipstick when she was seven. She killed herself at age twelve when her father sold her a few times to pay for his gambling debts."

"Oh my God . . . where was her mother?"

"She was there, in denial. Her senses short-circuited on pills and cheap wine. The perp had gone way beyond his daughter and left a string of bodies. When I found him in an abandoned warehouse on

182

Miami's east side, he had just killed his seventh victim. A little nine-year-old girl he'd taken from her bedroom. Her bloody body lay there on the cold concrete floor of a former banana-import company. The perp got up and off her when he saw me approaching. I'll never forget his lurid face, the blood on his hands, his eyes mocking me like a hyena rocking its head above dead prey. 'You're not going to shoot me,' he yelled. I told him he was right. Then I charged, knocking him to the floor, and I beat his head senseless against the same concrete where the child lay dead. There was an open freight elevator shaft a few feet away. I dragged him to it and dropped him down the shaft. I don't know whether I beat him to death or he died when he hit the floor below. In the report, I wrote we'd fought, he lost his balance and fell."

Leslie was quiet, the pop of firewood the only sound. "Sean, you stopped a child killer. I'm not going to try to justify what you did. You've gone through that over and over in your mind. But anybody can understand it."

"Doesn't make it right. If every man has a breaking point, I'd reached mine, and I didn't like what I saw. I'd promised Sherri I would try to regain whatever it was in me she found and loved unconditionally. I'm still struggling with it. Now I'm chasing another serial killer. The question that haunts me is, what will I do when I find him?"

She touched my hand, eyes measuring her response. "You'll do what you have to do. You'll arrest him, and in a few years Florida will do the killing."

Over hot apple pie, vanilla ice cream, and coffee, the conversation turned to the murders and the DNA linked to Silas Davis. She said, "Although the DNA on the toothpick is a definite match for the traces found under the vic's fingernail, there's no DNA match between that and the hair on the duct tape you found. We didn't get a hit from CODIS on the duct tape hair. We'll pick up Silas Davis to-morrow."

"What kind of backup are you taking?"

"You worried?"

"Silas Davis, Juan Gomez, and Hector Ortega come from another planet. These are labor contractors who traffic in human beings. Worried? Nah, you can handle them."

"I believe Dan and I can handle the arrest, but we'll take backup." She paused, lightly tracing the tip of her spoon around the ice cream. "Dan's not a fan of Slater's, either. Slater's been watching me like a hawk. I was trained to work in forensic crime scene investigations, not to keep looking over my shoulder for a bad cop."

"That turns your job into a covert mission."

She smiled. "We'll question Davis tomorrow and see if we can get him to talk."

"Davis is big and cunning. Not a dumb guy. He abuses the work-ers because the system allows him to. He actually works for Juan Gomez and Hector Ortega, and they're as indifferent to farm work-ers as Davis, maybe more so. They speak the language, bring in the workers from other countries, slap false debt on them, and hold them. I believe Gomez, Ortega, and Davis are all involved in the killings in some capacity. Davis might have killed the girl I found and the other victim, but I'm not sure."

"What do you mean?"

"He doesn't fit the profile for the kind of killings. At least on the surface, he doesn't. He's no Scout leader. Mean as they come, but it doesn't make a lot of sense for him to kill these women. Plus you don't see many black serial killers."

"Maybe the victims were going to the police."

"That's possible, but doubtful. They don't trust a system that al-lows this to happen. Davis is a vile guy, a criminal, but even though

184

we got an exact DNA match, that doesn't make him the killer. That tells me she scratched him. Could have occurred the day of the murder. Maybe some time before it happened. Whoever is killing these women, and it may be Davis, is a psychopath of the worst kind. He can't feel guilt because he can't feel love."

"Can he feel hate?"

"His type can't form intimate relationships. He might not hate in the vengeful kind of way that most people understand. There is a banality to his killing. Which makes this guy the most frightening kind. You can't see him coming until he's there."

"And you believe these last two girls are not the first of his victims?"

"He's killed before. Could be responsible for the nine unsolved that fit the MO and profile. I bet there are more that we don't know exist."

She was silent, her thoughts somewhere else, and then she looked up at me, a smile as tender as the night.

"I really should be going," I heard myself say.

"Why?"

"I don't have a good answer, only an honest one, but not a good one."

"Then stay the night," she said again, reaching across the table and touching my hand.

FORTY-THREE

Leslie said, "I have some Grand Marnier a friend gave me, but I haven't had a reason to have an after-dinner drink. Now I do, because you're here. One nightcap?"

"Just one," I said.

She poured the Grand Marnier and raised her glass. "To the night. May this one be the first of many."

We toasted and sipped the liqueur. She set her glass down on the counter and touched my cheek with the tips of her fingers. She was trembling slightly, her eyes probing mine. She stepped closer, pressing her body gently against me. I could feel her warmth, smell the scent of her hair and a lingering perfume somewhere on her long neck.

"I don't think . . ." I heard myself say. Her lips seemed to move to mine with no measurement in space and time. They were just there.

The kiss was like a feather at first, gentle, searching. Her mouth was soft, tasting of the Grand Marnier, lipstick, and vanilla. In less than a half minute, the kiss became one of a buried passion erupting.

She was sensuous and receptive. I could feel a strong arousal, a heat building in my loins. I wanted to pick her up and take her into the bedroom, but I pulled back a moment, then kissed one of her closed eyes.

"I can't stay the night," I whispered.

"Then stay as long as you can," she said, rising to kiss me again.

IN THE BEDROOM, we undressed each other, eyes locking on eyes, hands discovering. I held her close, backing her onto the bed. The light from the patio broke through the partially opened blinds, illuminating Leslie's beauty. Her body was sculpted from good genes and exercise. I touched her hair and face. Our bodies moved in a rhythmic motion of discovery, and then moved as one. Our fingers locked, and I held her arms beside her head, the soft brown hair cascading on the pillow, her eyes searching, finding me. Within a few minutes, we both were climaxing, in long powerful couplings.

I leaned back, but Leslie's right hand stayed laced in my left as she held me, refusing to let me lean too far. She reached up and entwined her fingers in my other hand.

"Sean . . . just breathe . . . say nothing. You're here now. Nowhere else."

IT WAS AFTER 3:00 A.M. when I got back to *Jupiter*. The cockpit door showed no sign of entry. I unlocked it, got a beer from the galley, climbed up into the fly bridge, and sank into the captain's chair. A breeze stirred across the river and lagoon, bringing with it the damp smell of rain. It was the darkness before dawn. Fog drifted through glowing orbs of light cast from security lights down by the charter boats and at the end of the five long docks lined with boats.

The marina was eerily quiet, only an occasional strain from *Jupiter*'s bowline as the tide moved silently between the boats and pilings. I sipped the beer and turned my collar up in the cool of the morning. I was exhausted, but my thoughts bounced from Leslie to Sherri and then to the dead girl. But Sherri was dead. DEAD. As a former homicide detective, death was my shift. The eternal night shift. I had clocked in again.

I watched as the gray daybreak crept over the boats in a cloak of diffused light, enveloping the marina with the ethereal tint of an aged photograph. The dawn arrived unannounced, like the ghost of the Ancient Mariner. It was a black-and-white world, devoid of warmth and colors. A light rain began to fall, as soft as a whisper. Its gentle rhythm was the last thing I heard as my eyes closed. I wanted to dream in warm colors, to turn away the cold edge of shadows.

FORTY-FOUR

It was two days before I called Leslie. There was a pleasant smile in her voice, but more businesslike than I wanted. But then what did I want? I wanted to take her to lunch, to be with her, to meet and dine with her near the water. The way sun comes through a bent venetian blind, her light broke through the tiny slits in my armor even though I tried to shield my darkest corners from her.

Leslie met me at the Lighthouse Restaurant, a block from the Ponce Inlet Lighthouse and fifty feet from the Halifax River. A life-sized pirate, made from stone and painted in primary colors, stood next to a rusted galleon anchor in the parking lot. The restaurant was a blend of cracker Florida inlaid with Key West T-shirt tackiness.

Outside, a wooden deck was built around a large live oak tree. There were a dozen tables and chairs scattered across the deck. Some of the lunch crowd sat in a replica of a shrimp boat docked and attached to the deck.

Leslie and I took a table in a far corner of the deck with a nice view of the river. I watched a sailboat motor toward the pass. One man at the helm. I could see him opening the jib, a gust of wind pulling the bow in the direction of the sea.

Leslie said, "Nice spot. Do you bring guests here often?"

"Guests?" I asked.

"I thought I'd hear from you the next day. Then, when I didn't, I thought it was something I said."

"No, Leslie. It's not you. It's me. I have had a lot of closed curtains opened suddenly. It's just that this light pouring in has caught my house in kind of a mess."

"I don't want to change your world or redecorate your house. All I want is to feel comfortable when I'm in it. To feel welcome, maybe even special."

"You are."

She looked out across the water and was silent. Then she changed the direction of the conversation. "The DNA sample we got from Richard Brennen didn't match the hair from the duct tape. Got to be ice water in that man's veins."

"There's something cold-blooded in him."

"Okay, now to Silas Davis. Dan Grant and I grilled him at headquarters. Interrogated him for more than three hours."

"What'd you get?"

"Probably capable of murder, but I don't think he's the perp."

"Why?"

"You even said that his skin under her fingernail doesn't make him the killer."

"But I want to hear why you think he may not have killed her."

"Davis is cocky, but he's scared, too. We reminded him that his skin cells were under the vic's fingernail, which is enough hard, indisputable evidence to take it to the DA. Sean, the guy wouldn't crack. He insists that she slapped him, cut his face with her nails, and the

190

last time he saw her was when she got in a van to be driven to another work location."

"Talk with the other girls who were in the van that night. Who was driving?"

"Hector Ortega. Dan and I questioned him and Juan Gomez at that slum trailer park they run. Gomez said he pays his workers cash and doesn't know the vic's real name. Said he called her *pájaro*, Spanish for bird. Ortega says the last time he saw her was when she bolted from his parked van while he was urinating off the side of the road—and where he happened to make his unscheduled stop to pee is what turned your world around. He was less than a half mile from your home. The vic allegedly ran toward the river, where she was assaulted and left for dead. You stumbled onto her the morning after it happened. Ortega says some backwoods redneck probably did it."

"Maybe, but I doubt it. Did the pathologist find anything remotely similar on both victims?"

"Are you having short-term memory problems?" She laughed. "Remember, we couldn't find so much as a speck of hair, carpet fibers, blood, latent prints, semen, or anything physical that links the two. Although the second vic was raped, no foreign pubic hair, no sperm, and no condoms tossed in the bushes. Outside of the rape and their gender and ethnicity, the common link seems to be the way they were murdered, and the fact the bodies were found less than twenty miles from each other. Ortega and Gomez say they didn't know and had never seen the second vic."

"You believe them?"

"No, but then we don't have a lot to go on, either."

My mind raced down a long black tunnel, and an image flashed. It was a dead body. A girl. Broken. Beaten. Smashed like a bird that hit a car windshield. Legs spread. Bloody. Panties torn off. The headlights from a parked squad cruiser illuminated her face in a theatrical spotlight of white. I was kneeling by her body looking at her open eyes. Eyes locked on horror. Her nose was the only part of her face showing color. Tiny circles of blood were encrusted like rings on the outside of both nostrils.

"Sean, where were you? Your eyes were so intense."

Now I remembered what I'd seen on the girl I'd found. "The girl I found by the river was almost killed by strangulation and then stabbed. She had blood on her nostrils. If a guy hunting for frogs hadn't been shining a light near the area, I believe her neck would have been broken, too. The second girl also was strangled and found with a broken neck."

"Right. And your point?" Leslie asked.

"The coroner couldn't determine the exact cause of death, strangulation or a broken neck, right?"

"The psycho did both within seconds. ME's report said the second vic could have died from either. The perp probably strangled her, then broke her neck as a parting gift."

I looked at the bay and inlet for a long moment. "What if she didn't die from a broken neck or strangulation?"

"What do you mean?"

"What if she died from asphyxiation?"

"Sorry, I don't follow you, Sean."

"What if she wasn't strangled? What if she was asphyxiated? Toyed with . . . brought to the point of passing out. Brought to near death and then allowed to breathe again. Given mouth-to-mouth by her attacker until he tired of it and killed her."

"I don't know if a human can go to that level of cruelty," she said. "Almost kill a woman, resuscitate her only to kill her the next minute. I've never seen evil like that."

"I have."

FORTY-FIVE

Three bikers, straddling Harleys, roared into the oyster shell parking lot next to the deck. I watched them park their bikes, trudge into the restaurant, and sit at the bar.

Leslie reached across the table, softly touched my hand, and said, "Tell me about it. What happened?"

"Miami. About four years ago. It's one of the cases I still relive. You don't forget investigating a crime scene where women have been beaten, raped, and left with a plastic bag over their heads."

"What?"

"We never solved them. I never solved them, and I think about it often. For some reason, the killings stopped. My partner, Ron Hamilton, and I thought they'd stopped."

"What are you saying?"

"He killed at least seven women, probably more. He'd pick out vics that usually wouldn't be missed by family or friends. Prostitutes. Runaways. The killer would attack his victims, slap them into submission, place a clear plastic bag over their heads, and begin the asphyxiation. All the time raping them. When they'd lose consciousnesses, he'd push up the plastic bag and give them mouth-to-mouth. Once they regained consciousness, he'd do it again. He'd even kiss them through the plastic bag he'd pulled back over their faces. We believe he'd time his climax as they died looking at him."

Leslie touched her throat, her eyes looking toward the water.

"One woman managed to survive, barely. She was attacked in a park near South Beach at night. The perp was surprised by two high school kids making out in a car about two hundred feet away from where the assault happened. They turned on their headlights, and the perp got up and ran. They couldn't get a good look at his face."

"Could the vic ID him?"

"She said he was very strong. Dark features, but she was so traumatized, all she could remember was his eyes. Called them 'wildcat devil eyes.' Now I think those eyes could have resembled a jaguar's. After she recovered, at least recovered physically, she looked at hundreds of photos. Couldn't pick out one. Something inside her died. She left Miami and moved in with her mother. I think they're in Jacksonville."

Leslie pushed her plate away and wiped her hands a long time on a napkin. "Sick. Diabolical, evil bastard. You think these murders might be related?"

"Now I do."

"None of our vics were found with plastic bags over their heads."

"What did the pathologist's report say about the vics' noses?"

"Noses? Nothing. Their noses weren't beaten or broken."

"Inside their noses. The nostril cavities."

"I don't recall anything."

"Can you check?"

"Sure. I can call Dan, have him take a look."

"Do it."

"Now?"

"Now."

Leslie flipped open her cell and punched in the numbers. "Dan, are you at your desk?" She nodded. "Good, I need a quick favor. Look at the ME's report on the two vics and see if he found anything inside their nostrils."

She paused and nodded. "Yes, okay. Call me back. Thanks."

THE WAITRESS DELIVERED fresh coffee to our table and left as Leslie's cell rang. She flipped it open. "Whatcha got?" She pulled a pen from her purse and began writing on a napkin. She thanked Dan Grant, closed the phone, and looked across the table at me. Her eyes were distressed. "ME's report for both vics says—I'll read the exact words—'broken capillaries found inside the nasal cavities consistent with trauma . . . or pressure.' Why didn't I pick up on this before?"

"Because you weren't looking for it. With all of the other wounds on the bodies, combined with the rape, strangulation marks, broken neck, et cetera, a few broken vessels inside the nose normally wouldn't raise a red flag."

"What are you thinking?"

I sipped the coffee and watched a squirrel dart off with a piece of bread. "I'm thinking that the killer held his hand over the vics' mouths or used duct tape and then held their nostrils. When they passed out, he'd revive them. Then he'd cover their mouths, pinch their nostrils, and continue raping them as they died. In the case of the vic that I found, the duct tape may have been used to cover her mouth. Could have happened with the second vic, too. But the tape, evidence, wasn't found."

"I was hoping the feds would get a DNA hit on the hair from the duct tape, but nothing."

"No, because no one was ever charged, let alone convicted, in the Miami cases—but DNA was taken from the perp's saliva on the last plastic bag. It's been stored. It wouldn't have been included in the database because there's no ID attached to it. I'll call Ron. The three of us need to collaborate on this. You can send the DNA profile from the hair to him."

"And if we get a match . . ."

"We have the most prolific serial killer in Florida, maybe the entire nation, four years later. We just don't have a name."

FORTY-SIX

On the way back to the marina, I got Ron Hamilton on the phone and told him my theory about the Bagman resurfacing. "I believe he could be responsible for the fifteen cold case murders of women. He never retired, Ron, he just stopped killing Miami prostitutes and went inland. Made the farm country his killing fields. Or if the perp is Richard Brennen, he stopped going to Miami for weekend killing sprees and confined his evil closer to home."

"Is he leaving plastic bags on their heads?" Ron asked.

"No, but there are similarities. Duct tape instead of bags. Pinching the vic's nostrils."

"It's a long shot. Why not let the folks in homicide up there take it from here?"

"Because I think one of the 'folks' is part of this. I told you about Slater. He might not be the perp, but if it's Brennen, senior or junior, Slater is looking the other way. Detective Leslie Moore will be calling you. She's going to overnight a DNA sample we got at one of the crime scenes. I need a favor, Ron. Pull out the profile in storage from those plastic bags, the best we have from the Bagman murders. There is a good sample from the last body and a fairly good sample on the bag from the vic that lived. Have the lab start the process immediately. I'll give you Leslie's cell. Probably a good idea only to reach her on that number."

"No problem. Oh, almost forgot. Clayton Suskind, the anthropologist MIA, the guy who likes to rifle through Indian graves—"

"Did you find a body?" I pictured Joe Billie's face as he pulled the arrow out of the rattlesnake's head.

"Yeah, I found a body . . . alive. Suskind, who's unmarried, left Florida abruptly ten months ago for a teaching job at Arizona State University."

"Thanks. Ron, have you heard anything on the street as to whether the FBI is looking into these murders?"

"Haven't heard anything more. Why?"

"Someone placed a sophisticated bug on my boat."

"Why'd the feds do that?"

"Good question. Next question is, who's doing the killings?"

"If the perp's from Miami, you'll need help to pick him up, if we can find him."

"If it is the same guy, I think he has a connection to the farm labor camps. I'm not sure how or why."

"What do you mean by connection to the labor camps?"

"I know it sounds strange, but if it's the same killer, the same perp we tracked, how's he choosing the victims? Is he wandering the back roads, the farm country, picking up women randomly? Don't think so. The odds are he knows some of these people. Somehow, maybe, he's linked at the high end. The growers. Or he could be associated at the bottom rung, the labor contractors, worker bees who want to please a queen somewhere, or there may be no connection at all."

Ron snorted slightly. "For some Miami-based killer to leave his turf, sounds out of his MO."

"His MO lies in the dark. Anywhere he can prey on those weaker. The killings are increasing, so there's got to be a strong motive or urge. We need to start with the organized prostitution rings."

"Why?"

"I believe these women are being recruited, human trafficking, actually held as sex slaves and offered to johns all over the state. If it's happening, it seems too organized for a few labor contractors. Somebody is calling the shots, and I'm betting they're not the assholes rousting farm workers at the crack of dawn. They're probably right in Miami."

"You got about two dozen sleazebags, from mob to gangbangers, running prostitution between Miami and Daytona Beach. Where do I start?"

"I don't know. Maybe where we left off when we lost the perp's trail."

I heard Ron sigh and then heard him tap the keys on his computer. "If you don't have anything more to go on, what'll make this investigation any different? The perp dodged us four years ago. What's to keep him from doing it again?"

"Because this time he made a costly mistake."

"How so?"

"He left a young woman to die in my arms."

FORTY-SEVEN

I had agreed to meet Leslie at the tiki bar for coffee at 8:00 A.M. By 8:30, I was halfway through my second cup, and no Leslie. I tried her cell. After four rings it went to voice mail. There was no need to leave a message. She knew I was waiting for her, but she didn't know I was worrying for her.

I sat at the bar, sipped coffee, and checked my watch every five minutes. A morning newspaper was on the corner of the bar. I shook the bits of toast off it and opened the pages. I stopped reading, folded the paper, and slid it down the bar.

Kim looked up from slicing lemons. "No good news, eh?"

"I stopped reading newspapers after I left Miami. I should know better by now."

"I get most of my news online. More coffee?"

"Thanks."

"You okay? I don't mean to pry, but I know there's been a lot of stuff happening. It's a small marina. Word gets around. You're a suspect, or, as the papers have it, 'person of interest' in a killing, and you're trying to find the killer."

"Thought you didn't read the papers?" I drank coffee, glancing at the parking lot.

"I happened to see your picture in there after they found that poor girl. I'm sorry. I think you're a hell of a nice guy and you're getting the short end of the stick. The lady cop knows it. She likes you, Sean."

"It's her job to like people. To at least care about them and try to help them."

"She likes you beyond that. A woman can see it in another woman."

I saw Big John rounding the corner of the restaurant and entering the bar like John Wayne coming off a cattle drive looking for something to wash the dust out of his throat. He said, "Morning, Kimberly. Morning, Sean. Gonna be a hot one today."

Big John was already starting to sweat. He wiped his wide forehead with a bar napkin. Kim took his order and went over to the window to give it to Sam.

A charter boat captain I recognized came in and took a seat at the bar. He ordered a Bloody Mary and dry wheat toast. I was glad for the interruption.

Leslie was getting out of her car. Even from the distance, I could tell she was exhausted. She approached, nonsmiling.

"Sorry I'm late," she said.

"Want some coffee?" I asked. "Maybe we can sit at a table."

"Can we get the coffee to go?"

Kim overheard and said, "How would you like it?"

"Black, please."

"Make it two," I said.

Kim poured the coffee into two large foam cups. "On the house."

"Thanks." I handed one cup to Leslie.

She took it and turned to leave. I followed, and at the large open breezeway I asked, "You okay?"

"We have to go somewhere we can talk." Her eyes were red and tired. "This is getting much deeper, Sean—and I'm starting to get really scared."

FORTY-EIGHT

I pointed toward the south side of the marina. "Past the charter boats is another pier. It goes pretty far out into the marina and into the bay. There's a bench at the end of it. We can talk there."

Leslie was silent as we walked. A brown pelican sailed over us like a silent glider plane, its thick body casting a shadow across the moored boats.

Leslie looked out over the Halifax River and sipped the coffee. "Someone definitely has his claws into Mitchell Slater. First I assumed it was well-heeled old money backing him for sheriff. Now I'm not so sure."

I said nothing, letting Leslie gather her thoughts.

"About three months ago, Slater and I were on a drug trafficking stakeout. We were camped across from a Daytona strip joint called the Club Platinum. The guy who owned the place, a sleazebag named Tony Martin, was supposedly dealing in a lot more than skin."

"Prostitution?"

"That's a given. He fenced for the Colombian cartel. Martin was said to have been one of the main distributors on the east coast of Florida for cocaine. Supplied all the high rollers, lawyer bikers who wear leather during Bike Week and played hard, race fans with private suites at the track. You name it, whatever came into Daytona Beach on chrome wheels or private jets, Martin and his posse were the suppliers."

"Is this Tony Martin still the kingpin or is he now dealing behind bars?"

"Neither. He's dead."

"Double-cross one of his suppliers?"

"We don't know. He was found in the front seat of his new convertible Mercedes with half his head blown off. Whoever hit him did it in the very early morning. The ME put time of death at about 4:00 A.M. Martin's club closed at two in the morning. He'd just gotten in his car. He'd put the top down, and someone stepped up and killed him."

"No witnesses and probably no evidence, right?"

Leslie turned toward me. "It was one of the last cases I worked with Slater. He made the cursory calls. Asked all the whodunit questions from strippers to club deejays to busboys. No one had seen anything out of the ordinary that night."

"Then the question is, who wanted Martin dead?"

"He crossed swords with competition, dealers, you name it, but we had no hard evidence against anyone. When Slater and I were interviewing the club staff, I noticed that one girl was more emotional about Martin's death than the others. She got teary, admitted she'd been seeing Martin and said he'd treated her very well. I'd pressed Slater about a follow-up with the woman. Back in the office, he told me that strippers have, quote, shit for brains, that they're drugged half the time and aren't credible witnesses."

"What'd you do?"

"I went back without Slater. The girl had quit. No one knew where she'd gone. Seemed she'd vanished. Then three days ago I got a call, an anonymous tip. The caller said I could find her at a club called High Moon in Tampa."

"Any voice that you even remotely might recognize?"

"Female, and I didn't recognize it. Call came from a pay phone. I learned the girl we were trying to locate worked the day shift at the Tampa club. Yesterday I went there alone."

"What'd she tell you? Why'd she leave the Daytona club?"

"Afraid for her life."

"Why?"

"Because she *heard* a murder."

"Heard?"

"The girl's real name is Robin Eastman. She said she was at her apartment the night of the murder. She told me that Martin had called her to tell her he was on his way. His cell was built into his car, so he wasn't holding a phone to his ear when the hit went down. She said he was bringing a bottle of her favorite wine, a chardonnay made by Blackstone. Anyway, she said they were saying 'bye when she heard Martin say, 'Are you a cop? Show me some fucking ID.' She said there was a pause and then the other person, a man, said, 'Get out of the car and come with me.' She said Martin yelled, 'Hell no, I'm not going anywhere with you.' She said the next thing was a gunshot."

"Do you believe her?"

"We'd found a bottle of Blackstone chardonnay on the floorboard." Leslie paused and looked at me. "The stripper said something else."

"What?"

"She said the voice—the cop—sounded like Slater."

I looked down at one of the pilings covered with barnacles and

205

thought about what Leslie had told me. I watched the dark water escaping toward the estuary and river. Small crabs scaled the barnacles like old men climbing mountains.

Leslie said, "I think it's Slater. I believe he may be a hit man for organized crime. What if he's the one who killed the two women, our vics?"

"Is there a connection between the migrant murders and the killing of a strip club owner? What secret is so big a senior police detective would kill to protect it?"

"I wouldn't have made a connection before you told me about the Bagman and the possible MO link. Connect Slater's odd behavior to all this and suspicions arise. Phone company records indicate a call was made on Martin's cell at 4:07 A.M. near the time of death. Over a cell phone, Robin Eastman was a witness to murder. Sean, I did something really stupid."

"What?"

"I wanted to see how Slater would react when I told him I had found Martin's girlfriend. He was stone-faced until I said she was on the cell phone with Martin at the time of the murder."

"How'd he react?"

"I saw a look in his eyes I'd never seen before. Frightening. He composed himself. He said the DA may have a hard time if we tried to use Robin Eastman as a witness."

"Why would Slater kill Tony Martin?"

"I don't know, but at this point I'm glad the captain let me partner with Dan." Leslie's cell rang. "Speaking of Dan, it's him. I'd better take it."

I watched a tiny crab scale a wall of barnacles stuck to a piling. The barnacles are anchored for life but teased twice daily by waters that travel the world's oceans.

"For the love of God," I heard Leslie whisper into the phone.

"Yes, right away. Is Slater there? Okay, give me a half hour." She slowly closed the phone. "There's been another killing."

"Female?"

"Yes, but this time it's different. Horrible. The victim was found in a wildlife refuge. She was butchered."

FORTY-NINE

Each time I dialed Leslie's cell I got her voice mail. On the third call, I left a message telling her to contact me when she could.

I reached my neighbor to check on Max and to apologize for the delay in getting back home. I was assured that Max was a delight and had won over the visiting extended family. *Great*, I thought, *maybe she'll remember me*.

Dave was already one ahead of me when I approached *Gibraltar*. He grinned and waved me over to his boat. "Care for a libation?"

Dave listened as I brought him up to date on the latest killing. I told him about my suspicions concerning Slater and about his connection with the Brennens and their money and influence. I told him how an old case of mine, one I failed to solve, could be raising its ugly head again.

He said, "The latest victim may not be related to the first two killings."

"Why?"

"Completely different MO. The first victims were raped and strangled. We don't know right now if the third body had been sexually violated. Some of her organs were missing. Could be coincidental that all three were female and Hispanic."

"I don't believe in criminal coincidences."

Dave nodded and said, "Somewhere between the Brennens, the migrant labor contractors, Detective Slater, and a Miami murderer with a similar MO is the key. We just need to look at this from different angles."

"Right now it's missing a link."

"Slater could be working for organized crime or the Miami connection in some capacity. Maybe he's the front man for the Brennens. Sean, why would the Miami murderer, the man you called Bagman, leave his sphere in Miami to travel the inner circles of the farm camps?"

"Serial killers follow ties, patterns. They need easy prey. The sociopath blames the present on the past and tries to destroy the future for those he holds responsible."

Dave nodded. "It could be a deep-seated, vengeful motivation. Could go back to his childhood. This discussion warrants two more beers from the land of Montezuma. Where the hell does Corona find the good water? Ever wonder that?"

I was about to answer when my cell rang. I fished for it deep in the pocket of my khaki shorts as Dave went below for the beers.

Ron Hamilton was calling. "Sean, you nailed it! The stored DNA from the Bagman case involving the asphyxiation four years ago matches your killer. It's the same perp. Nice work, partner."

I felt my pulse rise. I was beginning to understand the complexity of the spider's web.

"Thanks, Ron. I'll get back to you."

Dave returned with two fresh Coronas. He set one down in front of me. "You all right? You look like someone just told you the Mexicans made this beer from recycled donkey piss. Sounds like that call wasn't good news."

"The Bagman is killing the women. We just matched his DNA."

Dave let out a low whistle and sat down. "Sounds like this guy never stopped killing. Just extended it into rural Florida. Perhaps he was driven to come here, or to come *back* here. Sean, you're tracking someone you hunted before—in the shadows. A killer with an enormous capacity for evil is lurking out there. Whoever is ultimately calling the shots fears nothing. He kills when he wants to. I bet he thinks he's smarter than anyone who would attempt to catch him. What if he knows you're tracking him? What if you chasing him again is part of what gives him his insane rush? Something that amplifies his kills even more."

FIFTY

Somewhere on the fringe of midnight, I felt *Jupiter* move. Slightly, but it was enough to pull me from the edge of sleep. I listened for the sound of a boat that had passed by in the night. Nothing. I was lying on the bed in the forward cabin, a little groggy but aware that something didn't feel right.

I heard the distinct sound of metal on metal. Someone was trying to turn the locked handle on the salon door. I reached under the pillow for my Glock. I slipped off the safety and stood. Pools of soft light poured in through *Jupiter*'s portholes. I had to walk through the light, past the galley, to get to the steps leading to the salon.

The noise stopped. The intruder wasn't gone. *Jupiter* didn't move. I ran beyond the light and stood on the first step. I leveled the Glock toward the salon doors. A silhouetted figure was on the other side, standing in the cockpit. Then hands came up to the glass on the doors and a face leaned forward to peer into the salon.

It was Leslie.

I put the pistol on the galley counter and opened the doors. I said, "I'd called you. Are you okay?"

"No, I'm not okay," she said, stepping into the salon. The light from a three-quarter moon seemed to trail her inside, settling on her face, revealing tired and reddened eyes. The usual glow had drained from them. We stood in silence. I heard the subtle groan of the stern lines against the tide and the drone of a small boat entering the pass.

"Can I get you something to eat or drink?"

"It was so horrific," she said softly. "She was so young. Maybe eighteen, nineteen."

"Let's sit down. Want a drink?"

"Do you have vodka?"

"Grey Goose."

"That's fine. Over ice, please."

I fixed the drinks and sat at the small bar with Leslie as she began to tell the story. She sipped the vodka and said, "The ME says the person that did it wasn't a hack. He or she knew what they were doing. Kidneys and heart removed with the skill of a surgeon. No sign of the organs with the body. We think that whoever dumped the body didn't plan on dumping it in the wildlife refuge. FHP was doing a spot sobriety check less than a mile away from where the body was found. The speculation is the perp or perps saw the checkpoint and then cut off the road and drove right through a chained entrance into the refuge. They drove a couple hundred feet in and dumped the body."

"Any tire tracks or shoe prints?"

"Too sandy. We saw a spot where they apparently got stuck. They used limbs and branches under the tires."

"Do you have an ID on the body?"

"No. She looked like the other girls, young. Dan and I will be going back to the camp at SunState Farms. I'm showing the latest vic's picture to every farm worker I can until somebody tells me who she was. If she wasn't from there, we'll keep going until we hit all the farm camps in Florida. Somebody knows these women."

Leslie released a pent-up sigh and swirled the vodka in her glass. "They traffic in human beings. They sell sex. Now they traffic in human organs."

"Was she raped?"

"Looks like it. Neck broken. Which is information we withheld from the media."

"Maybe she's the latest vic of the Miami perp," I said.

"Maybe none were killed by somebody who vanished four years ago."

"I wish that were true."

"Don't tell me it's the same perp, Sean." She took a long swallow from her drink.

"For the first two murders it's the same killer. Ron's sending everything to you. The DNA is a match, at least the sample from the victim I found. It matches with DNA from the Miami murderer, the one who mixed asphyxiation, rape, and death into each gruesome ten minutes."

Leslie finished the last of the vodka in her glass, closing her eyes as she swallowed. "Where does this take us?"

"It takes me back four years to a nightmare I didn't solve then. Now it's a lot nastier. We'll work with Ron and Miami PD. We'll find him."

"You don't sound like you even believe what you're saying. What's changed, Sean? The perp left a trail then. He went away, and now he's leaving a trail today."

"He never went away."

"What?"

"I think he simply changed playing fields."

"Why? He got away with it down there, why change?"

"Less chance of detection. Lots of prey. Maybe the stakes have changed, too. He simply stalks and kills when he feels the urge, but lately he's getting sloppy, reckless, or, as Dave said, bold. He's leaving his vics wherever he drops them, like trash on the side of the road. Like he's saying, 'Come get me if you can.'"

"Are you telling me the deaths we know about might be the tip of the iceberg?"

"Beginning to look that way. If he's responsible for the victim with her organs removed, we have a man who is playing the ultimate game of control."

"What do you mean?" Leslie looked at her empty glass.

"He may have gone on to something more sinister, more powerful, than resuscitating his rape victims just to kill them. What if he's deciding who he'll take a heart from to keep someone else alive through black market organ sales? There is a lot of money helping him make the decisions, but it's the ultimate deity complex. Who'll live and who'll be sacrificed."

"That makes me shudder. I'm still convinced that Slater is somehow mixed up in some of this. I know he's involved in the murder of the strip club owner. I couldn't locate Robin Eastman, the dancer in Tampa. The High Moon Club says she left after work one night and never came back."

"I caught the local news. Saw you and Slater for a few seconds in a wide shot at the crime scene. I could tell by the body language that you weren't in agreement."

"I guess I kinda flipped. It was after the body was tagged and bagged. Slater said he hoped the organs didn't go to waste, as he put it. Said maybe the heart would be keeping a CEO alive somewhere. I turned on him. No one else was directly by us and I asked him, 'Then why stop with trafficked women, why not move on to strippers?' At that point, he knew that I knew. He just grinned. Under his breath, he had the gall, the sanctimonious balls, to say that most strippers were so full of drugs their internal body parts weren't worth anything. I came close to slapping him across his arrogant face."

"So now he knows you've made him."

"No doubt."

"Leslie, now's the time to go to the sheriff with this."

"I need definitive proof, not supposition. I found Robin Eastman's mother. Name's Irena Cliff. She lives in a trailer park outside of Tampa in Ybor City. She didn't want to say much on the phone. I'm driving over there. She did tell me her daughter had worked for a strip club in Miami and was scared to death of her boss. She didn't say why, only that this man is some kind of power freak and Robin thought he might try to kill her."

"Did she give you the name of the Miami club?"

"Not yet."

Thunder rumbled out in the Atlantic. I stood and closed the salon door. Dark clouds tossed and turned in an acrobatic chase across the sky. The moonlight faded as if a wet rag had been tossed over a candle.

I turned back toward Leslie. "Rain's coming."

"Can I stay here? I don't want to go home right now. I know it sounds silly, but I don't want to be alone. Not tonight."

She stepped toward me and touched my chest with her hands, her eyes seeking something I didn't know if I could give. "Do you mind?" she whispered.

"Not at all. I'm glad you're here."

"Okay. Just hold me a second, Sean."

She felt small in my arms. Her head rested on my chest, and I held her for a long moment in silence. *Jupiter* swayed a little as the wind picked up and thunder rolled.

Leslie looked out the salon window and watched the lightning in the distance. She said, "I'd like a tiny bit more vodka. I usually don't react this way to a crime scene. This one was different, and with the stuff I'm finding out about Mitchell Slater, I guess I'm pretty stressed. I just need something to help me sleep."

I made fresh drinks. There was a loud clap of thunder, then the slight tap of rain against *Jupiter*'s exterior.

Leslie smiled. "I've never been on a boat in the rain. It's kind of like a barn, the sound of the rain on the tin roof."

"Maybe it'll help you sleep."

She hesitated. "Tonight, I need to sleep alone. Just knowing you're here, on the boat, will help. I'll sleep on the sofa."

"The bed in the main cabin is more comfortable. Please, take it."

"Are you sure?"

"I'm sure."

"Good night, Sean." She took her drink and disappeared into the main cabin.

Through the starboard window, I watched the lights of a shrimp boat tied across the marina. I got a spare pillow and blanket and stretched out on the salon sofa. The rain started to beat down with the deafening roar of a waterfall. A burst of thunder and lightning shattered in the heavens somewhere above *Jupiter*.

In my dreams I saw one of the young victims of the Bagman. She had been a prostitute. Too young, nineteen. Auburn hair, soft features, and porcelain skin. Lying on her back with her head covered in a clear plastic bag, rain splattering against the plastic, her eyes open and locked on the dark sky. I wanted to close her eyes, but the face floated away like a ghost ship on the horizon, a ship that carried the dead.

WHEN I AWOKE THE STORM was gone. I looked over to the glowing red numbers on the clock radio near the bar just as the time changed from 4:47 to 4:48. A cloud passed, and the moonlight spilled through the salon windows. It was a pale shade of white, a candle flame slow-dancing in a room of dead calm.

I got up and quietly went down the steps to check on Leslie. The cabin door was open, the room aglow with moonlight. The stress in her face was gone, replaced by calm serenity. Her breathing was soft and steady. A cloud enveloped the moon. The light in the cabin faded, and darkness pulled a blanket over Leslie.

I stepped out on the cockpit and climbed the steps to the bridge. The hour before dawn was cool and clean after the rain. I could smell the scent of the ocean in the air and hear the soft cadence of the waves in the distance breaking on the shore at high tide. I thought about Sherri and Max and the goodness found in the world, in the simple things. Then I thought about the mask of hate hiding the faces of bad men, about the indifference in their dull eyes and the wickedness permeating their souls.

I suddenly felt very alone, like my boat was floating in a vast sea without an anchor or a rudder to guide it, and I didn't know how to change the course.

FIFTY-ONE

I awoke on the bridge to the sound of laughing gulls flying by me and the noise of a charter boat leaving. The sun looked like it had been up at least an hour. I stood up from the captain's chair on legs that felt like I'd gone twelve rounds in the ring. My left leg was numb and tingling as the blood began to circulate through a cramped muscle. My joints were like spring flowers rigid from an unexpected chill.

I managed to climb down the steps to the cockpit without falling. Stepping inside the salon, I saw a note left on the couch next to my pillow.

Sean, had to run. Needed to get in early before Slater arrives. Call you later! You looked so sweet sleeping up top, didn't have the heart to wake you. Leslie.

I made coffee, headed for the shower, and planned to spend part of the day where the last victim was found.

. . .

ON THE DRIVE to the wildlife refuge, I called Ron Hamilton. "What's the last known address of the Bagman survivor, the last attack before the perp went underground? Didn't she move to Jacksonville?"

"Give me ten minutes and I'll see what I have."

"I'll be on my cell. If you can't reach me, leave a message."

"You gonna be unreachable by cell?"

"I'll be in a wildlife refuge."

"That where they found the last vic, the one who was opened up?"

"That'd be the place."

"Be careful, partner. The woods can be full of creeps."

THE PRIMITIVE ROAD into the St. Johns National Wildlife Refuge was narrow. Room for one vehicle to travel either way. As I entered the refuge, the sunlight was diminished by the tree line. I could smell blooming honeysuckle, pine straw, and thick grass still wet from last night's rain.

Within a ten-minute walk, I came to the crime scene tape that sectioned off the spot where the body was found. I began following the furrows, going deeper into the wildlife refuge. It was about eighty yards farther that I found the spot, I assumed, where the vehicle with the body had tried to turn around and got stuck in the mud. Even after the rain, ruts caused by the back tires spinning were deep. Rainwater had pooled in the bottom. I walked past the ruts, looking on both sides for broken limbs, bark, or logs.

I turned to head back toward the Jeep, but as I started to step over one of the ruts, the reflection of the tree line on the water caught my eye. A large sycamore tree stood less than twenty feet away. I reached into the dark water, my fingers feeling and sifting through small rocks, twigs, and sand. I pulled up three leaves and looked at the sycamore tree near me. In the dappled sunlight, I examined the leaves and wondered if there might be others, perhaps miles away, that were exact DNA matches to the muddy sycamore leaves in my hand. Was it possible? If so, and if I found leaves with the same plant DNA, it meant they could have come from only one place. The same tree.

FIFTY-TWO

In the Jeep I listened to the voice message Ron Hamilton had left on my cell.

"Hey, ol' buddy, as you're running around doing the fun stuff, I'm back here in database central. Got a last known address for Sandra Duperre. You might get lucky and find her in Jacksonville at 17352 Old Middleburg Road. Phone company has no records in her name. I figured that. Happy hunting."

As I drove to connect with I-95 north to Jacksonville, I tried Leslie's cell. No answer. Then I called her office.

A male voice answered. "Homicide, Grant speaking."

"Detective Grant, this is Sean O'Brien. Is Leslie around?"

"No, she came in and made a few calls and went right back out."

"Do you know where I can find her?"

"Tampa. Says she has an interview with an older woman who'll only open up woman to woman. Sort of a Barbara Walters interview. I'm getting used to it."

"Sometimes, when it comes to gender, especially if the interviewee is older, a one-on-one with the same sex causes a better dialogue flow."

"Yeah, I know. It just seems that Leslie's moving at such a fast pace that we're sharing more notes passing in the hall than we do in the field. She's been keen on your helping us in the Jane Doe cases."

"Now I could use some help."

"Does this mean I have a partner again?" He laughed. "Leslie has a lot of respect for you, but since she's my 'part-time' partner—whatcha need?"

"Can we meet?"

"When?"

"Now."

"Give me ten minutes. Where?"

"Parking lot of the Waffle House on Dominion."

IT TOOK DAN ALMOST a half hour to get there. He pulled up next to my Jeep, got out, and walked over to me. "Sorry about running late. Slater wanted to chat."

"And he's such a compelling conversationalist."

"In a monosyllabic four-letter-word kind of way. He wanted to know why I wasn't with Leslie."

"What'd you tell him?"

"Truth. Told him she had an interview and I was meeting with a source. The schedules conflicted, so she went to cover one and I did the other. I just didn't say she went to Tampa and I was meeting with you."

I reached into the glove box and took out the Ziploc bag with the tree leaves in it. "I need this tested."

He chuckled. "I see you didn't work narcotics."

"But can you tell me its genetic makeup?"

"Get outta here. You want the lab to do DNA analysis on some friggin' leaves?"

"You got it. If I'm lucky, I'll find some matching leaves. It'll be our job to find out how close they match."

THE HOME ON OLD MIDDLEBURG ROAD was mid-1960s, ranch style, in need of paint. The yard was brown from lack of rain or irrigation. Dandelions grew like lettuce in places. A seven-year-old Honda Civic sat in the open carport.

I turned off my cell phone and knocked. There was no sound. The second time I knocked louder. I heard a woman talking. To herself? I could tell someone was standing behind the door. I said, "Sandra, can I speak with you?"

Silence.

"Sandra, I hope you remember me. I drove up from—"

The door opened to the length of the chain lock. I could see a pasty face, cheeks sunken, dark circles under the eyes. I could smell the raw alcohol. In a tired voice, the woman said, "I remember you. Why are you here?"

"Just to talk a few minutes. May I come in?"

She said nothing for a beat, then slid the chain lock off and opened the door. The living room was dark. In one corner was a small television. It was turned on but the volume was off. The house smelled of Scotchgard and cigarettes.

I sat on the sofa, and Sandra sat in a worn chair opposite me. Her hair was dull, the brown now peppered with streaks of gray, deep-set creases around the edge of her downturned mouth. "How have you been?" I asked.

"Like anybody, I've had ups and downs."

"I remember your mother during the investigation. How is she?"

"Mother's dead, Detective O'Brien. Cancer. Started in her ovaries and moved like wildfire. Nothing they could do. This is Mama's house. I lived here as a kid. Moved back in for a while after the . . . after the rape. I was actually married for two years. I had good and bad days. After a miscarriage, what was left sort of fell apart." She inhaled deeply, and I could hear a slight rasp in her lungs. "Why are you here? Did you finally catch him or did somebody kill him?"

"Neither."

She glanced away, her attention now somewhere else, maybe four years ago, but gone from the room. "Sandra, I think he's back."

She looked at me as if she had noticed a painting on the wall was a little off center. I almost expected her to reach out to touch my face. "Why are you telling me this?"

"Because you are the only person who can identify him."

"I've tried for years not to remember him."

"He's never stopped killing. Went from Miami to rural farms. Killing young women. And he'll keep on until he's caught or stopped."

"If you find him, Detective O'Brien, are you going to arrest him or kill him?"

"I have to find him first."

"That's not a good answer."

"I can't arrest him."

"Why?"

"I'm not a detective anymore."

"Then why are you here?"

"Because I made someone a promise, and I'm trying to stop what I couldn't stop four years ago. What can you remember about him?"

"Nothing more than what I told you then."

"Sometimes people remember things that were buried."

She looked at the silent glow from the TV. "His eyes were different. Strange eyes. Almost like a cat, but I told you that. I was so glad when Mama's cat finally died. I couldn't look the damn cat in the eye."

"What color were the cat's eyes?"

"Mustard-yellowish gold, a greenish tint and little flecks of brown in them. Kind of a wild hazel." She got up and took a photograph off the bookshelf. "Here." She handed the picture to me. "That's the color."

The photo had been taken close-up with a good camera and lens. It was a picture of Sandra's mother holding a large cat in her lap. I looked into the mesmerizing eyes of a cat that seemed to stare back at me.

"Thanks for your time, Sandra." I got up to leave.

"Detective . . ."

I turned around and she said, "His voice . . ."

"What about it?"

"He spoke in a monotone kind of whisper. Never shouted. Just total control. His voice made you listen to it. Sometimes I still hear it."

FIFTY-THREE

More than two hours into the drive back to the marina, I remembered that I'd shut off my cell phone before I met with Sandra. I saw that I had three missed calls. The first two were from Leslie. I didn't recognize the third number. I played my voice mail.

"Sean, I talked with Irena Cliff," Leslie began. "The poor woman called Robin a sweet child, her 'happy baby.' She asked me to bring her back home. Then she spoke about her in the past tense, like she suspects her daughter isn't coming back. Said Robin stopped calling, which is a red flag because she always called, at least twice a week."

I punched the phone's speaker button, glanced in my rearview mirror, and continued listening to Leslie's message.

"No other immediate family. Father dead. No siblings." She paused and sighed. "We, of course, have no body. If it's Slater, he knows damn well how to cover his tracks. The club in Miami where Robin worked before coming to Daytona, it's called Xanadu. Irena said her daughter was terrified of her ex-boss, guy named Santana, Miguel Santana.

Robin told her mother this guy raped her the day he fired her. She got out of town and took a job far enough away that she felt like she was out of this Santana's business circle. Robin told her mother that she was scared. When she was with Tony Martin, one night when he had too much to drink, he'd confided in her, telling her that Santana was trying to cut in on Martin's action. Said this Santana even wanted to buy Club Platinum. Martin refused. Robin was afraid Santana would retaliate for something she did while working for him. She wasn't specific with her mother, but she did tell her that she thought Santana was dealing in everything from drugs to prostitution at a high level. Santana and Xanadu sound like real winners. Later, Sean, 'bye."

I remembered the club. Catered to high rollers, sports figures, rock stars, B-list actors, and businessmen with nondisclosure expense accounts. I hit the speed dial, and Ron answered on the first ring. I filled him in on my interview with Sandra Duperre.

He said, "You'd think, after all this time, she'd reclaim a life."

"She did, for a while, but these wounds seem to get the stitches popped at all the wrong times. What can you tell me about Club Xanadu and a guy that runs the place, Miguel Santana?"

"One of the managers and a bartender were busted for trafficking in cocaine and prostitution. These guys are like cockroaches. I heard the owner, Santana, is mostly an absentee proprietor. Doesn't get his hands dirty."

"Maybe he's got a speck of dirt under his fingernails that he just can't wash away."

"Sounds like you're back, pal."

"No, but I'll be back in Miami." I heard the beep of an incoming call. "Ron, I need to take this. See you in a couple of days." I pressed the button and said, "Hi, I got your voice mail. It looks like the mother's instinct is corroborating your gut feeling."

Leslie said, "Unfortunately, but without a body we only have a missing person, although this missing person was involved with a club owner who was murdered."

I told Leslie about the sycamore leaves I'd left with Dan for testing, my Jacksonville trip, and my pending Miami trip.

She said, "I got a voice mail from the ME. He has a prelim tox report waiting for me on the latest vic's hair. He found blood, a trace amount, on a single strand from the back of the head. His message said the blood didn't come from the vic."

THE SUN WAS SETTING when I pulled the Jeep into the marina parking lot. I unloaded groceries and started for *Jupiter*. Nick's boat was back in the slip. I could see him using a hose with a high-pressure nozzle to wash down the *St. Michaels*. As I approached, he looked my way and grinned. "Got some beer in those bags?"

"I do."

Inside the cockpit I switched on the air conditioner and tossed the perishables into the refrigerator while Nick plopped down at the bar. I opened two beers, found a lime, sliced it, put a slice inside each bottle, and set one in front of Nick. "Welcome back. How'd you do?"

"We did good, man. Mackerel were running. Sold three hundred pounds. I'll keep back some for the grill."

"Good to see you, Nick. It's been a little tense here."

"I heard on the TV about this last dead girl. That part of the crazy shit you're in?"

"It looks that way."

Nick tilted up the bottle and took three long swallows. "You don't need that. Somebody needs to feed this crazy fuck to the crabs."

"Let's hope you get called for jury duty."

"They don't want me on the jury. I find them all guilty. Where's hot dog?"

"Home, back on the river. My neighbor is watching her and the place. I've got to go to Miami for a couple of days. Could you keep an eye on my boat?"

"Sure, man. Anybody come near it, I'll shoot 'em!" He laughed.

"Be careful. These people shoot back."

AN HOUR AND A SIX-PACK LATER, Nick had gone back to his boat to shower and get ready to meet his latest girlfriend. I'd stripped down to my shorts and was about to climb in the shower when Leslie called. "Are you ready for this?"

I never like conversations that start that way. "What do you have?"

"The tox report on the blood has me scratching my head."

"What's it say?"

"Says the blood came from an alligator. An alligator certainly didn't slice her up, unless the gator had training in surgery. So where would the vic have been to get alligator blood in her hair?"

"Could be a wild card, but I have a possibility."

"Can you tell me about it over dinner, maybe in an hour? I'd like to rinse some of the past twelve hours off me."

"See you then."

I was about to hang up when I heard her say, "I missed you today. And please don't take that the wrong way. I just really enjoy your company."

"Then your expectations aren't very high."

I could almost see her smile through the phone. She laughed. "When this whole thing is over, maybe we can go away together for a long weekend. Let's find a place where there are lots of tropical flowers, a turquoise sea, and gentle people with genuine smiles. Do you know a place like that?"

"I know a place like that."

FIFTY-FOUR

At eight o'clock I called the Blue Heron to cancel the dinner reservation. I was told that I wouldn't need reservations after nine and they served until ten.

I tried Leslie's cell for the third time in two hours. The first two times I got her voice mail. The last try, there was a clicking noise like the phone had been disconnected.

I locked *Jupiter* and started walking to my Jeep. The tiki bar was filled with people and song. As I walked by, I could see the sole entertainer, dressed in white island cottons and wearing a hat that looked like a mix between a fedora and an Australian bush hat. He was crooning the Jack Johnson song "Crying Shame."

Nick was at the bar with a woman. He got off his stool and waved me inside. "Sean, this is Margarita."

She smiled and said, "Nice to meet you." She looked like she was imported from Colombia. Dark skin, exotic features, high cheekbones, and full lips.

"Good to meet you, too."

"Sean, I drank all your beer today. Let me repay you." He turned toward a bartender. "Corona for my friend."

"Nick, I can't stay. I want to give you a number." I wrote Dan Grant's name and phone number down on a bar napkin. "Call him if I don't make it back tonight. He's a detective with the Volusia County Sheriff's Office."

"Man, you need some help? What's going on?"

"If my Jeep's gone all night. Call him. Tell him I went to Leslie's house, I left at 10:30 tonight, and tell him to go there."

As I walked toward the door, Dave Collins entered. He grinned and said, "Care to join me for coffee? I've been thinking about your predicament, your quest, perhaps."

"I'm meeting Leslie for dinner."

"It's getting a little late for dinner."

"I know. She's not answering her cell, which is not like her."

"I've been thinking." Dave's voice had a sense of urgency I hadn't heard in a while. "If the same guy is now killing people for organs, maybe this is part of a larger, much more frightening enterprise that is far beyond the scope of your average serial killer, beyond your talk-show tabloid murderer. He's got issues that will add a chapter to psychology books."

"Maybe we're coming to the same conclusion."

"What would poison a human mind so much it would make a man rape, kill, and then butcher?"

I said nothing, thinking about Leslie.

Dave continued. "Someone is having his way with a frightened group of people with little or no voice, but it seems deeper than that—like he's flaunting the killings in someone's face. Why? If Richard Brennen is a serial killer, is it because he hates a larger-than-life domineering father so much he's killing their workers?"

"You're giving me something to think about as I hunt for Leslie."

"I'm sure she's fine."

I wanted very much to believe him.

I DROVE UP A1A, past Daytona Beach Shores and the high-rise condos. My Jeep was engulfed in the roar of a dozen bikers passing me on both sides. I turned left on Main Street and drove past Boothill Saloon and a dozen other biker bars and strip joints. As I passed the Club Platinum, I thought about what Robin Eastman's mother had told Leslie. *She was my happy baby.*

As I drove west toward Leslie's subdivision, half a dozen emergency vehicles passed me, including two Volusia County sheriff's cars, a Daytona Beach police cruiser, a fire department EMT ambulance, and another county ambulance. I was hoping I wouldn't drive up into the chaos of a multicar accident scattered across an intersection.

I was still a couple of miles away from Leslie's house when an uneasy feeling hit my stomach, like I'd gone over a hill too fast. What if she was in a car accident?

Maybe she'd left the ME's office, stopped by her office, and left her phone in the car. What if the emergency vehicles were rushing to her house?

I tried her cell again. Nothing but a disconnect sound. It was the most desolate sound I'd heard in a long time. I drove faster. Sped in the direction of sirens. It was the direction that sounded alarm bells in my head. It congealed fear in my heart, knocking on the door of a dark place I was afraid to open again.

FIFTY-FIVE

As I turned the corner, I could see the hue of pulsating blue lights above the tree line. *Bastard!*

I raced down Leslie's street, taking out a large plastic garbage can near the curb. At the end of the cul-de-sac, all hell was breaking loose. Dozens of police and emergency vehicles were parked. Blue, white, and red emergency lights whirled and flashed, sending an eerie color spectrum across yards, houses, and trees. The blur of lights and wide-eyed stares was like a slow-motion parade of the arcane.

Neighbors, some in bathrobes, stood in the shadows pointing and whispering. I gunned the Jeep and pulled to a stop on the sidewalk near Leslie's front yard. I jumped out and ran through the bystanders, the emergency crews, the crackle of police radios, TV reporters rehearsing lines before live shots, finally reaching the crime scene tape like a marathon runner.

A uniform stopped talking into the radio microphone on his shoulder and barked, "You can't go in there!"

I ignored him and ran to the front porch just as the body was coming out. Two grim-faced members of the coroner's staff pushed a gurney with a white sheet over it. I could see a bloodstain about the size of a quarter on the sheet in the head area.

"Leslie!" I shouted, my voice sounding strange, like a foreign language coming out of my throat. Please God . . .

"Stand back, sir!" an EMT ordered. "Out of the way!"

Two strong hands clamped down on my shoulders, pulling me backward.

"This is a crime scene! Stay outta the house!" one square-jawed officer yelled.

"Take your hands off me!" Blue uniforms charging.

"Put the cuffs on him!" ordered an officer.

Dan Grant stepped from inside the house. "It's all right! Let him go."

The officers released my arms. Dan frowned and motioned for me to follow him. We walked a few feet away from the porch, near a flower garden Leslie had planted. Dan's eyes were wet, tearing. "Sean . . . she's gone."

My stomach burned, the taste of rage raising though my esophagus like a sulfurous gas as I stared at the roses in her garden. I pictured her face, heard her laugh, and felt my eyes moisten. "What happened?"

"Shot once in the head. Professional hit. No sign of entry anywhere. Nothing broken. Looks like she was going out the door and was surprised. Somebody was waiting in the bushes for her. Probably stuck the gun in her face and backed her into the foyer. That's where the body was found. She had her car keys in her hand."

"She was coming to meet me for dinner. No answer on her cell."

"Whoever killed her stomped on her cell. Crushed it right next to the body."

I said nothing.

Dan looked toward the coroner's van. "Can't believe she's gone . . ." He paused to compose himself. "I was just talking with her earlier. She told me a joke she heard on talk radio. She filled me in on the questioning of the mother in Tampa. She told me about your trip to Jacksonville and the Miami connection, this guy called Santana who may have put out a hit on club owner Tony Martin." He exhaled pent-up air. "Who'd do this, Sean? Hit Leslie? Why? The perp didn't even take the time or initiative to make it look like a forced burglary. Nothing seems out of place."

"Any idea what caliber of bullet?"

"Not yet."

"See if it matches ballistics in the Martin shooting. Who reported Leslie's death?"

"A neighbor. Man two doors down. Out walking his dog. Said he saw someone running down the road." Guy slipped on a sprinkler head. The neighbor tried to see if he was okay, but he just took off running. Neighbor walked his dog a little farther. When he came to Leslie's house, he noticed that the light was on in her car. He was worried that the car battery would be dead in the morning, so he went up to Leslie's door. He said when no one came to the door, he stuck his head in and called out to Leslie. Saw the body in the foyer."

"Where's this neighbor?"

Dan pointed toward an elderly man standing behind the yellow tape with two dozen other onlookers. I approached him. "I understand you saw a man leaving the area."

He pushed black-frame glasses up on his nose and said, "Yes, sir, he took off running after he tripped on a sprinkler head."

"Whose lawn?"

"Leslie's yard. She has the sprinklers come on the same time every night in the summer, eight o'clock sharp. I felt bad for the feller. He took a nasty spill. Hit the grass and the sidewalk. Had to hurt like the dickens. He comes up all wet, probably grass in his mouth and he starts running."

"Running or jogging?"

"He was running. Coming around third and heading for home."

"Could you identify him?"

"Not his face." He nodded toward a utility pole. "That streetlamp isn't working. Told the county about it. They can't be bothered. Meantime, poor Leslie is killed."

"You said you wouldn't know his face. Can you identify anything else? His build? Clothes?"

"I'd just started walking my dog toward Leslie's when I saw a man trip and fall. The sound was like what I'd hear when I used to play football. He fell right near the sidewalk toward the front of Leslie's yard."

"Can you show me where?"

"Sure," he said, walking to the sidewalk. "Right there." He pointed to a spot where there were a few pieces of grass on the concrete. "The feller tripped on the irrigation head. He was running across Leslie's yard. Looks like he got a good soakin' before he could run off. He dressed a little funny. Had a hooded sweatshirt. Didn't have the hood on his head, but as he ran the opposite direction from me, I could see it bouncing around his shoulders. You know how a woman's ponytail bounces?"

I knelt down and looked at the sidewalk. "Are you on county water out here?"

He laughed. "Hell no. We're on well water. I spend a lot of my pension just putting salt and chemicals in the tanks to keep the rust outta the water."

"Thank you."

"Is that all? Think he did it?"

Dan said, "Thank you, Mr. Boone. We'll probably talk with you again."

I walked toward the house with Dan and said, "Put the tape up immediately around the spot where he tripped and fell. Keep people off the sidewalk!"

"Okay." Dan turned to a uniform and ordered the crime scene tape around the sidewalk. Then he turned to me. "I wish I could let you in Leslie's house to go over the place. Slater's in there. Probably wouldn't appreciate my inviting you in."

"Maybe I'll just go in, crash his party."

"He'll have you thrown in jail."

"He's done it before."

"Yeah, but why play his game? He'll mess up, and when he does, we'll be there."

"Because the bodies keep piling up. As a cop, Slater has the perfect alibi, the perfect cover, and the perfect opportunity to take people out. Even cops."

"He's coming out of the house right now. Maybe you ought to go back home. I'll keep you posted."

"Can't do it on this watch," I said, walking up to Leslie's house.

FIFTY-SIX

I saw a TV news reporter and his cameraman slip under the crime scene tape.

Dan said, "O'Brien! Wait a damn minute!"

It was too late for Dan to pull me back or have an officer tackle me. Slater saw me coming. There was a mixture of nervousness and contrived arrogance in his eyes.

"What are you doing here, O'Brien? Might have known you'd be here. Anytime there's a body, there's O'Brien. Why's that?"

"I know you killed her."

"I'm having you committed. We'll Baker Act you for your own protection."

"How is it investigating your own crime, Slater? Which do you like best, the killing part or coming back as the actor, acting like you're investigating a crime when you're covering up one? Doing your best to make it a cold case."

The pupils in his eyes became tiny enraged dots.

"Fuck you!" He raised his right hand, and I grabbed his wrist, turning his hand over, exposing a fresh scrape on his palm. The portable lights from a TV news crew turned on, freezing an image of Slater as I gripped his wrist. He drew back his left fist to connect just above my eye. I felt my skin split and the blood flow.

Two uniforms pulled me back as a reporter yelled, "Get a close-up!"

"Get them back behind the tape!" Slater bellowed. "This is a crime scene!"

Dan ran up. "All right, gentlemen, behind the line, you know the rules."

"What's the argument about?" asked a reporter holding a microphone.

"Just a little misunderstanding in the middle of a crime scene investigation. The gentleman was overcome with grief and struck out at Detective Slater. I'm sure there is nothing intentional. Emotions are a little frayed at a time like this."

Dan was good. He turned toward Slater, the cameras still rolling, and said, "I'm sure if the gentleman volunteers to leave the property peacefully, we won't have a need to file charges under these trying circumstances. Don't you agree, Detective Slater?"

Slater didn't know how to react. His mouth was opening and closing, trying to form the right words. He said, "I'm sure it was just an overreaction, but this is one reason why we can't allow anyone to cross into a working crime scene."

"How was the victim killed?" asked another reporter.

Slater stepped closer to the TV camera, his composure regained. "This has been one of the toughest nights in my life. We've lost one of the finest members of the Volusia County Sheriff's Department . . ."

Dan motioned for me to follow him to one side. Under the seclusion of a tall tree he said, "That was fucking dumb! What were you trying to prove? You take a swing at the chief of fucking detectives while TV news crews are camped out to record it. And I know you saw them coming!"

"Let's hope they got their close-ups."

"What are you saying? You know, Leslie had her doubts about you. At first, she didn't know if you were really good or just plain lucky. She felt you were good. Maybe the best. Why'd you go off like a nut? Slater can have you committed—and he can get a court order tonight! This the kinda shit you did at Miami PD?"

I looked at my watch. "Call your office and record the eleven o'clock news. You have twenty minutes."

"Why?"

"I want to see if they got a close-up of Slater's hand."

"Why?"

"Because it was scraped and bloody, just like he slid into home plate."

"You saw it?"

"Yes, and if the cameras saw it, you have visible proof."

"A scrape on the palm of his hand won't get a conviction."

"It will if you can get some skin samples off the sidewalk. The sprinklers didn't hit the sidewalk. The sample might be still there. Right where the old man pointed."

"Maybe."

"Use sheets of clear adhesive plastic to lift anything if something's there. Bring in klieg lights and shine them at a low angle across the sidewalk. Look for fibers, grass, blood, anything. Find the hooded sweatshirt he wore. Analyze it for the grass and water stains. Do a chemical analysis on the grass. Her yard is St. Augustine. The grass leaves a distinct stain. The well water will be like nature's fingerprint swirling with good stuff like iron and sulfur. Take a sample from Leslie's well. Compare that with what's in Slater's sweatshirt. If the stuff matches, book the bastard, Dan."

I started toward the Jeep.

Dan said, "Sean, wait a sec." I turned to face him. "Leslie was right about you."

"He's not convicted yet. And he's not in this alone. Find that sweatshirt. Get a court order, knock down his door, do whatever it takes. Find it tonight while he's here."

"Where are you going?"

"To be with a friend."

I SAT WITH MAX on my screened porch and watched the fireflies play tag in the dark down by the river. Heat lightning danced in the sky. I stretched out in my rocking chair, my feet up on the cypress table, Max curled in my lap. The cicadas and the crickets seemed to alternate their chanting. A bullfrog droned across the river.

I sipped three fingers' worth of Jameson over ice and thought about Leslie, thought about the last thing she'd said to me, *Let's find a place where there are lots of tropical flowers, a turquoise sea, and gentle people with genuine smiles.* My chest felt like a vise was compressing it.

The temperature started dropping, and the wind picked up and pushed the air across the river. I could smell rain coming. I scratched Max behind her ears. She didn't even open her eyes. "Max, let's go to bed."

I finished the Irish whiskey, picked up Max, and started for the bedroom. As I walked past Sherri's framed picture, I stopped, my eyes falling on hers. "Good night," I said. Max licked my chin, and we went to bed.

I lay there in the dark for more than an hour, the events of the day playing back in my mind, scenes in slow motion, intercut with my own public service messages about how I could have prevented Leslie's death.

Max sensed my restlessness. She inched up beside me and laid her head on my chest. I rubbed her neck for a few minutes, my eyes heavy, my mind drifting to the sea. Then darkness descended like a high tide at midnight and carried everything away.

They had no faces. I felt myself reaching out to catch one. All I wanted to do was get my hands around a neck. They were dark figures at the foot of the bed. Faceless apparitions. Standing, staring, appearing on the threshold between madness and dreams.

In the white flash of a lightning bolt, I sat straight up in the bed. I tossed the sheet off, sweat dripping through my chest hair and down my sides. My heart pounded, and my lungs seemed to ache for more air than the bedroom could provide. Distant thunder rumbled downriver. Through the windows, I could see the live oaks swaying in the wind.

Max stuck her head up like a prairie dog coming out of her den. She looked at me through sleepy eyes, her tail wagging. She crawled into my lap and licked my hand. She gave one of her yawns that seemed to be a whinny at the same instant.

"Want some fresh air, Max?"

I opened my back door and stepped out into the night air. It was after 3:00 A.M. As I stood on my porch, I thought about Joe Billie and the native people that once populated the river basin. Maybe some of my night stalkers were spirits of these long-forgotten people. Maybe they were angry that I was here. I couldn't fault them. After we annihilated their race, they had a right to be pissed off.

The cool breeze brought the promise of rain and the scent of blooming night jasmine. Within a minute, the first large drops began plopping, almost one at a time, on the tin roof. They were soft tears from heaven, and then the gentle weeping turned into frenzied sobbing.

Thunder hit on top of us with the percussion of mortars as lightning sliced through the black sky, striking a large oak at the river's edge. The light was a searing explosion of white heat, shearing a thick limb in a split-second freeze frame of rain and raging wind.

The air smelled of sulfur, burned oak, and wet Spanish moss. I sat down in the porch rocker and put Max on my lap. Within a few minutes she fell asleep. I listened to the rhythm of rain beating the tin roof, the palm fronds scraping the screened porch, and the frogs singing like a chorus of thousands. Long rolls of thunder seemed far away now.

The storm passed, and the night shadows became gray ghosts that faded into trees in the dawn light. A mist rose from the river's surface. Soon the sun, like a glowing coal, cleared the tree line and backlit the mist, as ruddy spirits emerged from the water.

The elusive dream weaver finally came. I was a young boy again, walking through an orange grove on our farm. I stood on my tiptoes to pick one of the ripe oranges. I jumped and snatched the orange like a shortstop grabbing a fly ball barehanded. With my pocketknife, I sliced the orange in half. The juice dripped down my hands and wrists. The sun was warm on my face. I bit into the orange, and the sweet liquid quenched a thirst deep in the back of my throat.

FIFTY-SEVEN

The next morning I left the house early. I was beginning to feel very guilty about handing off little Max to my kind neighbors. First, I felt like I was taking advantage of their generosity, even though they insisted I wasn't, and second, Max genuinely seemed sad when I left her.

I thought about that as I looked in my rearview mirror on my way to SunState Farms and realized I was being followed.

The driver was good. I hit my brakes for five seconds, and my pursuer or pursuers backed way off, almost out of sight. I sped up. The car followed, then made an abrupt turn off the road, vanishing on a country road. He or she or they knew I had made them.

I slowed down to less than twenty miles per hour and watched my rearview mirror. Nothing. No pursuit. Only the flat topography of the rolling Florida landscapes.

I turned off the state road and began driving down a county road. The land was a mix of cattle pasture, scrub oak, and lakes. As I rounded a curve, I slammed on the brakes. Just ahead, a farmer was driving a tractor at a speed of less than ten miles an hour. It was an old green John Deere, puffing diesel fumes and taking up most of the lane.

As I checked my rearview mirror, pulling out into the passing lane, I noticed a car far off in the distance. It was the same car that had been tailing me. Nobody was that good.

I passed the farmer and brought the Jeep up to more than ninety miles an hour. I wanted to put a lot of real estate between the posse and me. I swerved off the paved road and took a bouncy ride down a dirt road. I intentionally kicked up dust. *Come get me, assholes!* I found a wooded area, parked the Jeep, left the motor running, and ran to wait behind the natural cover.

The dark blue Ford sedan rolled quietly down the road. They were in no hurry, and I knew why. There was nowhere I could run where they wouldn't find me. I knew they'd been tracking me by satellite.

There were two people in the car. A man and a woman. The man drove slowly, and I could see the woman pointing toward my Jeep. As they stopped, I chambered a round in my Glock and waited. Less than fifty feet from my Jeep, they got out of the car. Both of them had drawn their weapons. The man approached the Jeep from the driver's side. The woman covered him.

I crouched behind the palmettos, lifted my cell phone, and started recording video.

"Out of the car!" ordered the man, pointing the pistol directly into the empty passenger seat. "He's not here!" he said, about to turn my way.

"I have a gun aimed at the back of your head!" I yelled. "Drop your weapons! Turn around slowly!" They hesitated. "You've got two seconds! One of you will have a bullet in your leg. Drop the guns and hold your hands in the air." They both did as ordered and turned to face me.

The man was in his midthirties. Teeth gnashing. Disbelieving face that looked pained. He sported government-issued attitude and a crew cut. The woman was striking, even from a distance. Brunette. Nice legs. Hair pinned up. Eyes testing. I recognized her.

The man said, "You just committed a felony."

I said, "And I may commit a few more."

"You drew a gun on federal agents," he said. "You could be spending the next twenty years of your life in a federal prison."

"You look more like a travel agent than a federal agent."

He started to lower his hand. "Hold 'em high, pal, and let's get something straight real fast. You and your girlfriend drew on me first. Got it all right here on cell phone video. The video these phones record is good enough to use on TV news. I have a permit to carry this gun. I'm holding you at bay in self-defense."

I touched a nerve in the woman. She spoke up. "I'm not his girlfriend. I'm FBI Special Agent Lauren Miles, and this is Special Agent Mark Helmer. We didn't come here to harm or arrest you, Mr. O'Brien."

"Could have fooled me."

"My apologies. We actually wanted to talk with you."

"There are simpler ways than using GPS tracking to stalk me. Maybe at Quantico they didn't teach you to use the telephone. I'm sure you have my number. I know you visited my boat and my marina friends. If you needed to know anything about me that you don't already know, Special Agent Miles, all you had to do was ask, especially after I fed your bug to the crabs."

"Would you please lower your gun and your voice?" she asked.

"Show me some ID," I said, approaching them. They produced their federal IDs, and I shoved the Glock behind my belt.

"Thank you," Miles said. Agent Helmer seemed as warm as a Little League coach who'd just lost three in a row.

I said, "Before we get cozy, where'd you put the transmitter?"

"It's inside the right front bumper," Miles said, looking at the Jeep.

"Then let's have Special Agent Helmer get it out of the special hiding place."

"Find it yourself," he said.

Miles said, "Mark, get it, okay?"

GI Joe's nose wrinkled like a spanked puppy.

"Please," Miles said, "just get the damn thing."

Helmer pulled out a small penknife and worked the GPS tracker from under the Jeep's bumper and set it on the hood.

I said, "All right, what's on your mind? I'll assume at least one of you is wired."

"We're not," she said. "We know you're investigating the murder of the girl found not far from your home. We believe her death and others involving farm workers are related."

"Now that's damn good police work."

"Please, Mr. O'Brien. Give us a few minutes to explain. These deaths are part of a bigger picture."

"Let me guess, you thought I was part of that big picture. Maybe doing a little international export business out of my old home city of Miami. Probably tipped off by a trusted detective with Volusia County SO. You followed me via satellite to see if my path crosses paths with the vics'. Even for you guys, it'd be easy to calculate location and time of deaths. Then, bingo!"

"You're a first-class asshole," the Little Leaguer yelled.

"Orwellian tactics before old-fashioned communications happen to rub me the wrong way."

"It's not surveillance," Miles said.

"Maybe that's not what the FBI calls it."

She stepped forward, sighed deeply, crossed her arms over her breasts, and said, "Mr. O'Brien, I knew of you from Miami homicide. I also know you had one of the best conviction records, actually the

247

best in your department. We were hoping you could lead us to the perp or perps doing these serial killings. It's that simple."

"Either that's the worst compliment I've ever received or the FBI is just plain lazy. You're looking for an ex-cop to help you do your jobs? What's the real reason?"

Little Leaguer shoved his hands in his pockets and said to Miles, "Let's just get the hell out of here. Last thing we need is a burned-out cop with an attitude."

"And the last thing I need is two wannabes using me to help them do their jobs. Go back to Miami and put your transmitters on ships. Catch some terrorists."

I turned to leave, and Miles said, "Now you wait just a minute, Mr. O'Brien!"

"Or you'll do what, bug my bedroom this time?"

"We're short staffed. The Miami office is in charge of keeping all the South American sleaze in check. We do have more ports and open coastline to secure than any other state. There are more drugs, international gangs, and criminals filtering through Miami than any city in the nation."

"I served my time in Miami."

"We're aware you took early retirement after the death of your wife. We know you've moved on but wound up in the middle of this. Can we work together?"

"Not interested in government work."

"We're not offering you a job. We're asking for some cooperation."

"Why? Why and how has this evolved to get you guys out of your offices?"

She was hesitant, choosing her words carefully. "You're involved because you care about innocent people. We don't have the means or manpower to check the tidal flow of human trafficking into America. We know there's sexual abuse, sexual slavery, beatings, and murders.

No one will talk because everyone's scared to death. It makes it very easy for a serial killer to penetrate because these people are afraid of the government, afraid they'll be deported, and they're afraid of the contractors they work for. In the last few months, the prostitution ring escalated from serial murder to the sale of human organs."

"So it takes the sale of hearts to get to the heart of the FBI? Is that when you finally send in your troops? Or is it because it's six months to the primaries and this wouldn't look good to the incumbent? Unsolved serial killings, human trafficking, sexual slavery. *So* not politically correct."

Her nostrils flared, pupils at pinpoints, the carotid artery pounding in her neck. "What is your problem? Why won't you cooperate?"

"Problem? The problem is it takes the media, the reports of human organs cut out of victims, to get the FBI moving. It's not enough for these people to be held as sex slaves, beaten, and killed. They've got to be sold like a side of beef to raise some red federal flags."

She started to speak, then abruptly stopped. I said, "A friend of mine was just murdered. It's because of what's happening in these sex slavery circles that she was killed. For me, it started when I found a young woman dying near my home. Now a woman I cared about has been shot in her home as she was coming to have dinner with me. This is personal."

"I'm sorry this has happened to these people. The point is we're trying to do something, to find the person or persons responsible. You've made inroads in this case. You've penetrated the inner circles. We know a lot of the abuse is coming from contractors working for SunState Farms, but we don't know who their upscale clients are and who's killing these women."

I said, "In other words, as my best buddy in Special Forces used to say, you don't know shit."

Junior said, "That's fucking enough—"

"Mark! Please! Mr. O'Brien's right. We don't know shit. But we will, and we'll do it with or without you, Mr. O'Brien. If you become a problem, it's obstruction of justice. If you work with us—"

"It's what? Cooperation? Save your threats for someone you can scare. They mean nothing to me. What does mean something is catching a man who'll look you in the eye, Special Agent Miles, while he's shutting off the air to your lungs, while he's raping you. Right before you pass out, he'll place his lips on yours and blow the kiss of life into your lungs—just to do it again. The second time he won't bring you back. He'll literally suck the life out of you. And after your heart stops, he'll remove it."

She lowered her arms and stepped closer to me, her hazel eyes exploring mine. She said, "Will you partner with us?"

"Under one condition," I said.

"What?"

"Never do I find one hint of bugging or surveillance of any kind from you. That includes my boat, my car, and any of my or my friends' property. If and when I do find who's doing this, you'll arrest and prosecute vigorously. No politics. No bullshit."

"A deal," she said.

"I'll call you. Don't call me. And I'll work only with you, Special Agent Miles. Send Junior back to the farm."

She nodded. Agent Little League's face turned crimson with anger. He cocked his hands on his hips and watched me walk to my Jeep. I picked up the GPS transmitter, and tossed it to Agent Little League. "You can stick that where the sun doesn't shine."

FIFTY-EIGHT

It was after midnight when I parked my Jeep about a half mile away from the migrant camp. I left the Jeep on the side of a dirt farm road, sprayed on mosquito repellent, and began hiking through the palmettos and Australian pines, dodging an occasional car headlight and gaining ground. It was a long shot but one worth taking.

As I moved stealthily, I could hear Latin music and cursing coming from one of the trailers. A chained dog howled. A man swore at another in Spanish. The odor of burning garbage lingered in the night air. Two pickup trucks were parked in front of the last trailer at the end of the dirt road. A man came out of the trailer, turned, and said something to a woman. He swore, shook his head, and drove off in one of the trucks.

I almost didn't see it. To the far left of the last trailer was a dark-colored van. I crouched down near the front of it. I could smell human urine, a sickly smell that was produced from cheap wine passing through a diseased bladder.

I crept to the rear of the van, turned over on my back, and wedged beneath the undercarriage. Using the small flashlight I had with me, I looked up into the wheel area and around the straps that secured the exhaust system. There was nothing but mud. I crawled over to the other rear tire and began the same examination. Just as I was about to chalk it up to a good effort, I saw it.

Wedged in fresh mud was a small piece of green. I used my penknife to scrape the mud away and removed the leaf from the undercarriage. The tire had tossed mud over the leaf and sealed most of it like a caterpillar in a cocoon. The leaf looked identical to the leaves I'd found at the bottom of the rut in the wildlife refuge. I cradled it in my hand like a tiny broken wing of a butterfly.

I slipped a Ziploc bag from my shirt pocket and placed the leaf inside. After I closed the seal, I started to shimmy out from underneath the van.

The van rocked.

The door opened and slammed too fast. Someone had seen me. The driver knew I was under the van when he started the motor. I had maybe five seconds. I lay as flat on the ground as possible. I turned my head and body away from the transmission gearbox. The driver gunned the engine. Tires spun and the van lurched forward. Part of the undercarriage raked across my chest and tore through the skin.

As soon as the van cleared over me, I rolled to one side, grabbing the Glock and springing to my feet. I leveled the pistol at Juan Gomez's face just as he was pulling a gun from his belt.

"Drop it!" I yelled.

Gomez held on to the pistol and slowly lowered it to his side. He said, "You're one dumb motherfucker!"

"Toss the gun! Now!"

Gomez grinned and threw the gun a few feet away from him.

"You're trespassing again, ex-cop. Thought someone was stealin' the van. Lucky we just didn't shoot you."

I pointed the Glock straight at his head. "It's over! Murder. Black market sales of human organs. You've got a date with a lethal injection."

The driver in the van turned around and hit his high beams. Gomez was between the van and me. He was a silhouette, the high beams blinding. I yelled, "You move, you die!" The driver fired a shot from the van. The round hit a tree directly behind me.

The van gunned toward me. The instant I saw the muzzle flash, I heard the bullet whirr less than an inch from my left ear. I fired one round into the van's front windshield. I rolled out of the way, scooping up Gomez's pistol as the van came straight for me. It missed my leg by inches and crashed hard into the tree.

When I jumped up, Gomez had vanished. In the red glare from the van's taillights there was no one. The van's engine raced. Throttle stuck. A loud hiss coming from under the hood. I could smell coolant, oil, and raw gasoline.

I pointed the Glock at the driver's window as I approached the van. The driver slumped over the wheel. I opened the door and held two fingers against Silas Davis's wrist. He was bleeding from his mouth, but his heart was still beating. I put the pistol under my belt and pulled Davis from the van, sliding him at least fifty feet through the dirt. The smell of gasoline was strong. I turned and started running toward the county road as the van's engine exploded. I looked over my shoulder to see flames half as high as the pine tree.

Through the roar of the flames, I could hear the chained dog howling like a lone wolf in the night.

FIFTY-NINE

The next morning, Dan Grant met me at the Boston Coffeehouse in DeLand. I said, "Davis was still breathing when I left and called 911. Gomez and his cousin, Hector Ortega, weren't anywhere to be seen. I don't know if the fire did any damage to the interior cargo area of the van."

"I checked with the ER. Davis is alive. Bullet grazed his shoulder. The force of the crash knocked him out cold. You saved his sorry-ass life."

I reached into my pocket and handed him the leaf in the Ziploc bag. "This, most likely, will be an exact genetic match with the other leaves I gave you. Match the plant DNA and you'll place their van at the crime scene where the last body was dumped. Use luminol inside the van. If the fire didn't engulf the cargo floor, you'll probably find traces of blood there. I'll bet you that it matches the blood from the last victim."

"We'll test the van for a blood match," he said, sipping the coffee.

"Speaking of blood, I'll give you directions to a place. A cinder-block building, about twelve hundred square feet, that sits close to the St. Johns River."

"Now why would I want to go there?"

"You wouldn't. Meet me there. Bring some of your best forensics guys. Keep it from Slater." I sipped my coffee.

"Okay, why am I going there?"

"The place has been used for years as a tanning house. It's got a cooler, running water, and drains. A licensed gator hunter, guy by the name of Floyd Powell, told me he sold it. He sold it and six adjoining acres for top dollar to a consortium, a group of fishermen, to use as a retreat. Floyd kept gators he killed in there until he had time to skin and dress them. Leslie said the ME found alligator blood on the last vic's hair. The property isn't that far from the wildlife refuge."

"You think these freaks are using a former gator-processing shop to remove the organs from these women?"

"It might not be only women victims, and that's exactly what I think." I drew on the back of a napkin. "Here's a rough map to the place. When can you get there?"

Dan looked at his watch. "Give me a few hours to pull everyone together. Let's meet at two thirty. I can't imagine what we'll find."

"I can."

SIXTY

I drove down State Road 40, south of the bridge near Astor, and looked for the high-tension power lines. I turned off the road and onto a dirt drive almost hidden by scrub oaks. I stopped the Jeep, shoved the Glock into my pants, got out, and walked a few yards down the dirt drive. There were fresh tire tracks. Wide tires. Probably from an SUV or something like a Mercedes.

There, in a clearing, was the concrete block building. It was about the size of a small home. The cinder blocks were painted white and had baked to a dull yellow under the Florida sun. There was a detached awning that would shade a car. A cast net hung from one of the four wooden posts that supported the awning.

I parked the Jeep under the cover of a cabbage palm and then approached the building, circling around the rear before going to the front. There was a low droning noise coming from inside. It sounded like a refrigerator or freezer motor.

I heard a rustling sound from behind me. I raised the Glock toward the noise. A long blacksnake scurried through the dried palmettos and slid into a hole beneath the cinder-block foundation.

I holstered the gun in my belt, put on plastic gloves, and tried to turn the handle on the rear door. Locked. I walked to the front door and picked the lock in less than a minute. I held the Glock, took a deep breath, and jerked the door open.

The hinges squeaked, and a two-inch cockroach ran from between the joints toward my shoes. I stepped over the roach and entered the room. The light switch was to my immediate left. Fluorescents flickered and illuminated the room. The wall was solid concrete. A stainless steel table stood near the center of the room. There was a single light on a large-wheeled gooseneck stand in the corner. On one wall was a double stainless steel sink. A pair of folded rubber gloves hung over the faucet. The concrete floor was sloped to a large drain in the center. The air in the room smelled musty, like a biology lab with a mixture of bleach, formaldehyde, and sulfur gas.

I turned the handle on another door, and it opened to an office that seemed to be a storage and shipping area. There were two folding chairs next to a long table. On the shelves were dozens of small foam coolers. A dry-ice machine sat in the back of the room, the motor barely audible.

I walked back out into the concrete processing room and approached a large stainless steel door in the rear. I pulled the handle and the door opened toward me, the blast of cold air hitting my face. The air was stale and had the odor of death. I turned on the light and stepped into the cooler. There was a clear, icy liquid in a large stainless steel vat, a frostlike effervescence on the outer rim.

A pool of blood, the color of dark plums, coagulated on the floor in a near frozen state. I didn't want to breathe that air into my lungs. I stepped out of the cooler.

A gun barrel was shoved between my eyes.

"You're next," Juan Gomez said.

SIXTY-ONE

I could smell stale beer and decaying beef jerky between his teeth. Gomez pressed the barrel against my forehead and said, "Drop the fuckin' gun!"

Silas Davis, fresh stitches across his forehead, stood behind him, a pistol in his hand, his lips parting in a grin. I dropped the Glock.

"Step out of the cooler, asshole," Gomez said. "You'll be in there soon enough. Silo, bring a chair."

Gomez backed up, and I stepped out of the cooler. Davis returned with one of the folding chairs from the other room. Gomez said, "Sit, asshole cop. Sit right there next to the drain. It'll make cleanup a lot faster." He pushed me toward the chair.

Both men had their guns pointed at my head as I sat. Gomez said, "Tie him up. There's some rope next to the storage shelves."

"Why waste time?" Davis asked.

"'Cause we got to call Santana. He has to make the arrangements. Everything has to be timed perfectly."

Santana, I thought. Now I knew that the phone call Gomez made wasn't to Santa Ana. It was Santana. Maybe Dave Collins was prophetic. Santana, as a serial killer, would be the ultimate hit man.

The Bagman had a name, and it was a name that I might carry to my grave. I looked at Gomez and Davis and said, "Why do you do it?"

"Shut the fuck up!" Davis said.

"You let Santana turn the clock back before the Civil War to enslave people? How can you play a part in slavery, the same thing that enslaved your ancestors?"

"You!" shouted Davis. "Shut your fuckin' mouth!"

I had to stall them. "Why do you take advantage of these people? The physical and sexual abuse is bad enough—but murder? Why do Santana's bidding?"

Gomez said, "Forget you ever heard the name Santana!"

"Why are you working for him? You're businessmen. He's a psychopath. What's his hold, money? How many have you killed?"

"We don't do the killin'. We started doin' the packaging and the disposal. Cops wouldn't have found the last girl if they hadn't been stoppin' traffic at the crossroads, lookin' for DUI drivers. Had to dump the body in a place where animals and shit can get at it. Hate doin' that. Disrespectful to the dead."

"If you aren't killing these people, who is? Santana? Does he call you to tell you where to find the bodies for organ removal after he's had his fun? And you go from harvesting crops to humans?"

Gomez said, "Shut the fuck up!"

"Santana's got you, doesn't he?"

"Fuck you, O'Brien!" Gomez said. "You know nothin' about Santana. The man's a lot smarter than you and the rest of your cop friends. He's a genius!"

"He's smart enough to get you to do all the grunt work while he calls the shots from the sidelines. What's his hold on you, Gomez? Why partner with Santana?"

"Because he's one of us! He's powerful! El Diablo! The man knows and sees things. He knows who we're seein', what we're doin', what women are in our trucks. How many, and even what they look like." Gomez pulled a pint of Jack Daniel's from his pocket and took a long pull, then passed the bottle to Davis.

I said, "That's because he controls it. What if he has people to handpick the women from third world countries? What if he knows what's happening in your migrant camp because he has spies there? Can you trust Silas?"

Davis sipped the whiskey, pumped up his chest, and glared at me.

"Or can you trust Ortega, or any of the farm workers who might be on Santana's payroll? If the Brennens are on his payroll, if he's got a detective in his pocket, don't you think he can buy Silas?"

"Shut up, fool!" barked Davis

"The Brennens on his payroll?" Gomez asked, his eyes wide.

"Shut the fuck up, cop!" Davis yelled. He turned to Gomez. "Don't believe a fuckin' word this asshole says. I ain't never even seen Santana. For all the fuck I know, there ain't no Santana. Could be something you and Hector invented to cut me out later."

"I might cut you out now!" Gomez said. "How about last month when you were gone to Miami for three days? Maybe you were meeting with Santana up in his penthouse. Santana is a Santeria master! He can control our souls."

"Juan, listen to yourself!" Davis said. "You sound like some fuckin' voodoo nut!"

Gomez cut his eyes over to Davis and said, "Get that rope from the other room."

Davis went into the adjoining office.

"Shut up about Santana." Gomez's voice was flat. Something

drained from his eyes, replaced by half-closed slits of hate. "You had to keep stickin' your nose where it don't belong, amigo. Now you're a dead man. The good thing is this—you'll be keepin' somebody else alive. Part of the great cop lives on!"

Davis brought the rope. Gomez said, "Tie his hands behind the chair."

Davis yanked my hands behind the chair and began tying the rope tightly around them. I could feel the circulation being cut off.

To Davis, Gomez said, "I'm callin' Santana. He can get Doc out here quick. Soon as Doc arrives, we'll pop him. Until then we'll make him pray he's dead."

Gomez drove his fist squarely into my jaw, almost turning over the chair. The force caused a white explosion in my brain. I was back in a dank interrogation room in Afghanistan, the slap of a 9 mm across my jaw, the surge of electricity through my body. The whirl of chopper blades fading.

I spat blood and heard Davis laugh. It sounded like a laugh track playing a second behind another one. Through blurred vision, I could see Gomez stepping to the open door to use his cell phone. "We got O'Brien . . . at the gator shack. Send Doc with all his tools . . . Sure, Santana . . . No problem . . . Got it, yeah . . . Okay man."

He closed the cell phone and stood in front of me. I looked up at him, blood dripping from my crushed lip and gums.

Gomez rubbed his knuckles and hooked his thumbs in his wide belt. He rocked on the balls of his ostrich-skin cowboy boots. "We got a little while to kill before you go under the knife. What can we do to pass the time?"

Davis said, "We can cut his balls off. Toss 'em in the river for the baby gators to chew on. Don't think nobody wants recycled cop's balls."

My right eye was swelling shut. Through my left, I watched him take the pistol out of his pocket. I said, "Why are you two going down for Santana? Do you think I came here alone? Santana is calling the shots from his hideaway in Miami while you two are about to be arrested. If you cooperate—"

"Shut up!" Gomez bellowed. He stepped closer, held out the pistol, and said, "I had a feelin', sooner or later I'd take you out. You're one tough dude, O'Brien, but every man's luck runs out if he keeps on rollin' the dice."

Davis stood to my left, his arms folded, a smirk working on his face. "Before you waste him, I need to pee real bad. Always wanted to piss on a cop."

"You piss on him and Doc would be pissed. He don't have that kind of time."

Both men laughed. Davis said, "I think Doc left one of his scalpels in the drawer. We can use it to scalp him. Maybe that's where they got the name scalpel. Got it from cuttin' people's scalps off." He laughed and said, "Mexicans learned the art from the Southwest Indians. Shit, man, we probably taught them how to do it, you know?"

Gomez's cell rang. He answered it, stepping to the door for a better signal. "Yeah. Where you at?" He listened, then said, "If you're a few minutes away, we can go on and take care of him. We know you don't like that part, Doc."

He disconnected and turned back toward me. "Crazy fuckin' Doc. He can fillet a man faster than I can cut on a steak, but he don't like the part when the lights go out."

Davis gripped my hair in one hand and jerked my head back. His breath was sour, smelling like vomit and marijuana. His T-shirt stank of chicken grease. He stuck the index finger of his other hand into the blood pouring from my mouth and drew a line in blood across the top of my forehead. "We could start the cut here, go down to the bone, and end over here. It's like pullin' the skin off a catfish. Hand me the scalpel, Juan."

Davis stood in front of me, legs slightly spread, a sneer on his face. I waited for just the right second. I brought my left foot up hard between his legs, burying my shoe deep in his groin. His face seemed to detonate in pain.

He hit me in the ribs, causing the air to rush out of my lungs.

Gomez said, "Stand back, Silo! 'Less you want O'Brien's blood spray on you. Head shot sprays like a melon dropped from a movin' truck." He pointed the pistol directly between my eyes, a grin working at the corners of his mouth. "Now's the time to kiss my brown ass, O'Brien."

I saw a shadow move. Between Gomez and Davis, in the doorway. I looked at Gomez, his eyes wide with delight. I said, "If you drop the gun, you and Davis walk out of here. If you don't, they'll carry you out in a body bag."

He laughed and brought his left hand up to his right, holding the pistol with both hands, the barrel less than three feet from my face.

"Beg, motherfucker!" Gomez yelled.

I said nothing.

"Waste him!" Davis said, stepping back.

"I want to hear O'Brien beg! Beg, cop!" Gomez shouted. "Lemme hear what you're gonna tell the Virgin Mary! O'Brien, you ain't gonna go to heaven. You're gonna see the devil. What you gonna say to him, huh?"

I looked deep into Gomez's eyes and said, "Fuck you."

He stopped grinning. His face went blank. "You really aren't afraid to die! You got balls, O'Brien. Now they're dead balls!"

I could see the index finger on his right hand slowly start to move against the trigger. He grinned just as a hole the size of an orange exploded in his throat. Blood sprayed across my chest and face. Gomez fell like a giant at my feet.

"Put your hands up!" It was Dan's voice. He had his arms extended and a pistol pointed at Silas Davis's head. Dan and two uniforms stepped into the room. They threw Davis up against the wall and cuffed him.

I said, "There's another one coming."

"He's the first we got," Dan said. "Cuffed. Scared. Sitting on the grass crying like a baby. Says he didn't kill anyone, only did the organ removal after death."

"What a Boy Scout," I mumbled as my head entered a vertigo spin.

Dan knelt down. He used both hands to hold my head as he examined my face. He turned to one of his men and said, "Call for an ambulance. Tell them to step on it."

SIXTY-TWO

It took about five days before Max could look at me without quickly turning her head. I don't think my swollen face scared her. She seemed to be more uncomfortable than afraid. She still slept at the foot of my bed. The dark is often the great equalizer.

On my sixth day of convalescence, I left the river house with Max and took her to the beach. She played in the small breakers while I floated on my back, tilted my face into the sea, and let the sun and saltwater gods heal my cuts and bruises.

From the beach I decided to head over to Ponce Marina to pay the boat-slip rent. My cell rang. It was Dan Grant.

"Sean, the guy you said Davis and Gomez referred to as Doc, is a real doctor. His name is Jude Walberg, an oncologist. He says he didn't kill anyone. He was being blackmailed by someone he never met. Walberg says one day he received an e-mail with a video attachment. Showed him having sex with underage girls. Swears he was told they were all over eighteen. He met them through an escort service that specializes in Central American women. Said he was given directions to meet the women at a posh condo. Camera must have been hidden there. The good doc is married with two kids. He cried straight through the entire hour we questioned him."

"Who's blackmailing him? What's the escort service called?"

"He didn't know the guy's name. Service is called Exotic Escorts. Because all their biz is done online, who the hell knows where they're located. Probably some pimp's house. Walberg would get a call a few hours before he was supposed to drive to the processing shack near the river. Vics would be on ice. He removed a heart or kidneys and left them in Styrofoam cartons with that clear liquid in the tanks."

"Did he say what the caller sounded like? Any accent, speech pattern?"

"He said the guy talked in a soft monotone. Like he was in total control."

At that moment, I wanted to hear Santana's voice. I knew how Richard Brennen spoke. Measured. Complete control. Richard Brennen had brown eyes, though, unlike those of a jaguar.

I PARKED IN THE MARINA LOT and walked to the office. The door was locked. I had forgotten that it was Sunday. The office was only open from 8:00 A.M. to noon on Sundays. I checked my watch: 2:45 P.M. I wrote a check and slipped it under the door.

Turning to leave, I almost ran into Dave Collins.

"Sean, what the hell happened to you? Don't tell me I should see the other guy."

"He's dead."

"What?"

"Worse shape than me."

"Did you—"

"I didn't kill him. I would like to have, though."

"What happened?"

We sat on the aft deck of the *Gibraltar*. I told him everything that had happened. I concluded by saying, "Not only is Santana a serial killer, he's figured out a way to make a huge profit from his spoils. Dave, this perp is the most sadistic and smartest criminal mind I've ever come up against. I might have to set a trap to draw him out."

"What kind of trap?"

"Not sure. It has to be one that he can't resist. I need to dig as far into his mind as I can. I have to get as close to his way of thinking as I can consciously permit myself to travel. Evil is a dark destination."

"Maybe if you knew Santana's past, you could predict his future. If you could open his mind, a psychopath who kills the way he does—the asphyxiation—what would you see? I'll make drinks. Maybe it'll take away some of the pain in your wounds."

Dave served Grey Goose martinis with slivers of ice bobbing on the surface.

I said, "In the processing shack, the liquid in the vat looked like this martini. I didn't see any ice in it, but it was cold. Not a subzero cold, but kind of a chilled syrupy liquid."

He listened intently, brow wrinkled, eyes trained on me, and then he glanced to the side as if what I said brought back some distant connection. "Santana has a pipeline for quick distribution," he said. "Maybe some hospital is turning a blind eye and accepting the organs. He might have a network getting them to recipients far away."

Dave sipped his martini and continued. "I remember a study done on the wood frog. The frog is found as far north as Alaska. They survive severe winters by increasing the glucose stored in their cell fluids. This acts as a kind of antifreeze providing the tissue, membranes, and internal organs with a greater freeze threshold. Gives the frog the ability to withstand temperatures minus twenty degrees Fahrenheit.

What if Santana had some type of agent, antifreeze if you will, that allowed them to cool down organs without damaging the cells and tissue, essentially providing greater latitude from the time the organ leaves the victim to the time it enters the receiver's body? Makes it easier to ship from point A to B."

I watched Dave scratch Max behind the ears. She was asleep in his lap. I said, "Thanks for the martini. I can't finish it. A little sore. Can you watch Max for a few hours tomorrow? I have her food on *Jupiter*."

"I'd love spending some time with the lass. Where're you going?"

"To point A."

SIXTY-THREE

On the drive to SunState Farms migrant camp, I called Special Agent Lauren Miles. It had been ten days since I had last spoken to her. After the shootout at the processing house, I'd asked Dan to fill her in on the details. Between the soreness in my mouth and my cracked ribs, I had been in no mood to deliver a dossier for the FBI.

She had news for me. "We have a little more on Santana, but it's not much. Nothing from DMV. Can't find photos. There is no record of his birth in America. He's said to speak three languages. Owns or has partial ownership in an upscale strip joint called Xanadu. He's also said to have ties to some of the new hotel-casino combos and some coming up in Florida. His Xanadu Web site mixes pictures, video, and pay-per-view porno. We found a connection to an Internet escort site, Exotic Escorts."

"I bet the guy has a few degrees of separation between himself and his businesses. He's smart, ruthless, and well connected and manages to buy people or trap them like a spider, and that's when he uses them."

"As in Jude Walberg, the good doctor?"

"The same. One of Santana's former strippers is missing, probably dead. Name's Robin Eastman. Ring a bell?"

"No, it doesn't. You think Santana did it?"

"Or he had it done. May have been a cop who did the killing, a Detective Mitchell Slater, Volusia County. See what you can find on Slater. For some reason he's connected. The guy who owned Club Platinum in Daytona, Tony Martin, was killed after he left the club. Martin had just got into his car and was talking on his cell with his girlfriend, Robin Eastman, when he was killed. Eastman told her mother that Martin had said, 'You're supposed to be a cop,' right before she heard gunshots."

Lauren was quiet a moment. "If it was a rogue cop playing hit man, Santana's either paying him many times his pension or he has something on him."

"Slater has political aspirations. He was at the Brennens' for a fund-raising, and my questioning them pissed him off. He knew Leslie was about to implicate him. I'm convinced he killed her. I think he's a guy paid to look the other way, and when the stuff really hits the fan, then he's a triggerman behind a badge. Your people are good at surveillance. See if you can follow Santana."

She was silent for a long beat. "We have followed him, but we can't seem to get close enough to catch him in anything."

"What do you mean?"

"That's where your skills have helped greatly. You're closer, at least you're coming closer than anyone else. You're beginning to directly link him to things. Our profilers say Santana's one of the worst of the worst, if these creeps can get any worse. So, although we've managed to profile him, we haven't caught him."

"Your profilers? You've known about Santana all along, but you recruited me to hunt him down for you!"

"It's not that simple," Lauren said. "Our information corroborates everything you've said, but you actually have more than we do."

"Were you planning on sharing what you knew, or was I always the only one to sift through clues and hand it to the feds?" I felt my anger boiling up.

"Sean, it's not like that."

"Bullshit! Keep me in the dark and let me hunt for a jaguar that knows I'm walking under his tree. Thanks, Lauren."

"We're not using you, we need you." Her voice dropped. "We need your help. I'm sorry."

I said nothing.

"Sean, Santana is an easy guy to despise, but he's a hard person to catch because he has everyone else doing his dirty work. No one's talking because he seems to have some frightening power, absolute control over those who work for him. We believe he's joined at the hip with one of the most ruthless human-trafficking rings in the world."

"One of the most ruthless? What do you call harvesting human organs? Does it get any more ruthless than that?"

Lauren sighed. "I haven't held information back from you that would help solve this or find Santana. He's a terrorist of a different breed. Intelligent. Fearless. And he enjoys killing—personally. We're running out of time."

"That's insightful," I said. "He's probably two moves ahead of anything we can do right now. We need to get a DNA sample from him. Gomez is dead. Davis isn't talking. He says he doesn't know where to find Hector Ortega."

"What about this doctor, Jude Walberg? Can he identify Santana?"

"He says he never saw Santana. Only took orders on the phone. He insists the vics were dead before he got there. He says Gomez and Ortega were the ones who packaged and delivered the organs. Walberg said he didn't know how the distribution worked. Said as soon as he was done they told him to leave. Gomez is dead, Silas Davis is in custody, Hector Ortega is MIA, and Santana remains a phantom."

Lauren was silent.

I said, "Detective Dan Grant questioned the girls in the van that night, the same van transporting the vic I found by the river. Dan said the girls didn't want to talk. One finally did say that when the vic ran from the van, Ortega chased her for a few minutes but came back to the van and said she deserved what she was going to get."

"How many victims?" Lauren asked.

"Walberg says at least six. At first it was one a month. Then business picked up and the slaughters became more frequent. Because the doctor only identified Ortega and Gomez, they must have picked up the bodies and took them to the shack after they got a call from Santana. I was convinced that Richard Brennen fit the profile, but the hair on the duct tape didn't match his DNA. It did match the killer known as the Bagman. I bet the Bagman and Santana are one and the same."

"We've got to bring Santana down immediately."

I looked at my watch. "We need a positive DNA match. Follow him."

"What are you going to do?"

"I'm going to try to find the bodies. Maybe I'll run into Ortega along the way."

"Do you need backup?"

"I need to find Ortega. Then I think I'll find a real body count."

"If Ortega's fled to Mexico, what's left?"

"I hope the FBI has some good bloodhounds."

"To track him to Mexico?"

"No, to find the bodies here."

SIXTY-FOUR

It was late afternoon when I drove into the migrant camp. Some of the buses had returned with exhausted workers. I parked the Jeep under two Australian pines and tried to blend in with the farm workers as they shuffled to the store or in and out of the trailers.

Out of the corner of my eye, I felt someone staring at me. I turned and recognized the man. He was the young man I had seen earlier, the man who'd been beaten. He looked the other way and started walking. "Wait!" I shouted. He kept going. I ran toward him. He darted between two trailers, limping on his right leg. I caught him easily, put my hand on his shoulder, and turned him around.

"It's okay! I'm not here to hurt you. *Comprende?* I'm here to help. Please—put the knife away."

"I understand English, some."

"Good. What's your name?"

"Manny Lopez."

"Manny, listen to me. I know what's happening here. I don't care what they say, you're a free man. They can't hold you or the others against your will."

"I try to leave . . . to run . . . they find me . . . hurt me . . . say they kill me next time. Others try . . . try to run . . . they no come back. I think they killed."

"Who do you think was killed?"

"Some workers . . . I don't know all names. They take people from camps . . . you know . . . some in Immokalee . . . Lake Placid . . . Palatka. Some no come back."

"Is it men and women—or mostly women?"

He gestured with his palms up. "The womens." He glanced away, his eyes looking over the dark tomato fields.

I described the woman I had found, and he slowly turned his face back to me, his eyes heavy.

"She wear a small gold . . . how you say?"

"Crucifix."

"*Sí.*"

"Tell me, what's her name?"

"Angela . . . Angela Ramirez."

I could see her face as clearly as the morning I found her. Now she had a name. Angela Ramirez. "Is her family in Mexico?"

"No. Honduras."

"How can I find them?"

"I know the *casa* . . . where Angela's family live. I can show to you on map."

"Thank you."

"Angela dead?"

"Yes. I'm sorry."

"How she die?"

"She was murdered."

"Gomez . . . he kill her?"

"I don't think so. I think it's a man in Miami who's connected to Gomez, Ortega, Davis, and maybe even the Brennens. Do you know where I can find Ortega?"

"I no see him for six days."

"Where does Ortega usually work? Where might he be hiding?"

He shrugged his shoulders. "I not sure. He sometimes with Gomez. Sometimes he with the *grande* black man name Mr. Silo. Sometimes he take the womens in the . . ."

"The van," I said.

He nodded.

"Where does he keep the women?"

He pointed to the double-wide trailer at the end of the road.

"The largest one?" I asked.

Manny nodded. "That's where they take Angela. She no go . . . they not break her . . ." He pointed toward his heart.

"Spirit," I said.

"*Sí.*"

"Manny, I think even more people have been killed. Is there any place on this farm where someone might be burying bodies? An area difficult to find them?"

"Many places. Some fields have no fruits . . . no tomatoes. Somebody could make graves out there." He looked down the hard-packed dirt road and pointed to a backhoe near a tall Australian pine. "That machine . . . sometime I see them take it out at night." He paused, licked his dry lips, and asked, "Angela in a cemetery?"

"Yes. I will take you there."

"*Gracias.*" He made the sign of the cross.

I thanked him. Then I headed for the trailer at the end of the dusty road.

SIXTY-FIVE

I walked behind the double-wide trailer. A rusted air conditioner, braced by a sawed-off two-by-four, hung from a window, rattling and dripping water into the sand. There was one rear entrance or exit. To reach the door I had to step up on a large paint can. The door was locked. As I worked my way around the back of the trailer, heading for the front, I stepped over dozens of used condoms.

I saw the sun wink from something shiny behind a clump of trees to the far right end of the trailer. I recognized the SUV. It was the Escalade that Ortega drove. I could hear the engine ticking from heat. I felt the hood. The motor was warm. The vehicle was unlocked, and keys hung from the ignition.

I could feel Ortega was close. Maybe watching my every move.

I opened the front door of the trailer. The recycled air smelled of cheap perfume, sweat-soaked sheets, and nail polish remover.

Six women, all looking terrified, sat on tattered furniture. The couch was the shade of a UPS truck, frayed and faded. The floor was linoleum, stained yellow, dirty and buckling in places. Latin music played from an area that looked like a kitchen. I stepped in from the heat and closed the door.

One girl, no more than seventeen, sat with her arms wrapped around her bent legs, her small body rocking back and forth. She didn't look up at me; her eyes were wide and not looking at anything in the physical sense. I could see cigarette burns on her arms, between the scars from what looked like self-cutting. There was a handprint bruise on her thigh, fresh bloodstains on her yellow shorts.

The other women simply stared at me. Expressionless. They were all so young, ranging in age from about sixteen to early twenties. I said, "*Buenas tardes. Habla inglés?*"

"*Sí,*" said one of the youngest girls.

"What is your name?" I asked.

She said nothing, looking at the other women. I said, "It's okay. No one is going to hurt you. I'm not a policeman, and I'm not with the Border Patrol or Immigration. My name is Sean O'Brien. I'm here to help you. Are you being held?"

The girl stared at me, not sure what to say. I asked her to repeat, in Spanish, what I said so the others could understand. She did, and none of the women spoke.

The youngest girl said, "My name is Maria." She was fearful, eyes wide.

"How old are you?"

"Sixteen," she said in a voice just above a whisper.

I could see dread in her eyes, and I felt it wasn't because she was afraid of me. She licked her dry lips, her eyes darting around the room.

"I know you're being forced to have sex. People can't be made slaves—sex slaves. Do you understand?"

The women each offered the slightest nod. I looked at the youngest girl. "How do they pay you?"

She reached into her jeans pocket and pulled out a condom wrapper. "We give these when the week is done. All five dollar."

"Five dollars?"

She nodded.

"How much do they charge the men?"

"Farm workers, twenty dollars. The mens we meet in the hotels and houses and condo . . . maybe five hundred dollar."

"And you get five dollars for that?"

"Sometimes more."

"Where is the condo?"

"I don't know. They take us there."

"Who takes you there? Is it Hector Ortega?"

Her eyes found mine, the whites showing. She looked at the other women. They sat straight. Too straight. I knew Ortega was in the trailer.

"I'll write my number down," I said, just as loud and with the same inflection. "You'll call me. We'll file a lawsuit against the people that run this outfit."

I gestured for one girl to come forward. She did, and I leaned in and whispered in her ear, "Where in the trailer is Ortega?"

She looked over her shoulders, bit her bottom lip, pointed toward the back, and whispered, "Last room."

SIXTY-SIX

I pulled out the Glock, motioned for the women to leave the trailer, and started down the hall. The interior had been divided into at least a dozen small rooms. Most of the doors were open. I could see the same sized small beds in each room. The farther into the trailer I got, the stronger the odor became of sheets and mattresses soaked in perspiration and body fluids. I could hear the air conditioner straining in the hot sun.

I also heard a sound behind me.

I whirled around and pointed the Glock at the terrified face of a farm worker. He looked like he'd just come back from the fields, a John Deere hat on backward, ruby red FSU T-shirt, filthy jeans smelling of green tomatoes and pesticides. He stuck his hands straight up.

I lowered the Glock. He looked over my right shoulder for a half second. It was all I needed. I dropped to the floor just as the gunfire roared in the trailer. The bullet hit the farm worker in the chest. I came up firing a shot at Ortega as he unloaded two rounds at my head. Both bullets missed my left ear and slammed into the flimsy trailer wall.

Ortega ran down the hall and out the front door. I followed. I saw other drops of blood past the fallen man. I had hit Ortega.

I ran around the side of the trailer where I knew Ortega had parked the SUV. I could see him searching frantically for the keys. I crept up behind the SUV and pointed the Glock in the window. "Hands on the wheel!"

"You shot me, motherfucker!" he screamed.

"That's the appetizer. Drop the gun and put your hands on the wheel. Now!"

He dropped his gun in his lap and slapped his hands on the steering wheel. I held the Glock in his face, reached though the open window, and lifted up his gun.

"I need a doctor!"

I looked at the gunshot wound in his right arm. "Get out of the car!"

"You're trying to kill me!"

"I will kill you if you don't get out of the car!"

He got out and stood in front of me holding one hand against his bleeding arm.

"Start walking!" I said.

"Where? Man, I need a doctor!"

I pushed him toward the dirt road in front of the trailers. He gripped his upper left arm and walked, the blood seeping through his fingers, running down his bare arm. Farm workers watched from the edges of the road. The dog tied to a backhoe began barking.

"Shut up, shithead!" Ortega yelled at the dog.

That machine . . . sometime I see them take it out at night, I remembered Manny saying.

"Stop!" I said. I pushed Ortega toward the dog, a mixed breed with more Lab than anything else. I kept the gun on Ortega as I rubbed the dog's head. I looked up to where the rope was tied to the backhoe. It was then, in the late afternoon sun, that I saw it.

A long blond hair, catching the afternoon light, seemed to glisten as it hung motionless from one of the teeth on the backhoe claw.

SIXTY-SEVEN

The strand of hair was caught in dried dirt in the tip of one dull metal tooth. "Well, what do we have here, Ortega?"

He swallowed and licked his thin lips. "I need an ambulance!"

"That *is* a lot of blood pouring down your arm. Must be the heart beating faster to compensate for the loss of blood already. I'd say you're down to about five, maybe seven minutes before your heart starts pumping air."

"Call 911, asshole!"

"Tell me where the bodies are buried and I'll call an ambulance. If you don't, we'll have to follow the backhoe tracks, could take a while. You and me tromping all over the south forty. I know the backhoe was used to dig graves. Where are they?"

He looked at the hair and looked back at me. The color drained from his face. Sweat beaded on his forehead. He blurted, "A half mile down the easement, past the packing house, follow a dried-up canal to Farm Thirteen. There's fresh earth there. We don't use that field. They're buried there."

"How many?"

"I don't know exactly."

"You don't know exactly? I ought to let you die! You bastard!"

I saw Manny Lopez standing near one trailer. "Manny, take off your belt and tie it around his upper arm, right above the wound."

Manny started the tourniquet as I held the gun on Ortega and dialed my cell with one hand. I called Dan Grant and told him what had happened and added, "Send an ambulance. Bring in forensics, the whole team, and a lot of body bags."

I hung up and called Lauren Miles. "This will be one your folks in Quantico will talk about in classes for years to come. Bring your camera guys. That way your instructors will have illustrations when they teach the chapter on the real killing fields."

"We'll take choppers and be there in an hour," she said.

TWO SHERIFF'S DEPUTIES held Ortega under armed guard as he and the farm worker he shot were taken to the hospital in an ambulance.

A small army of investigators and forensics people assembled at Farm Thirteen. The former tomato field looked like it hadn't been farmed in years. Weeds and Brazilian pepper trees sprouted over the 150 acres of sandy soil. It was easy to see where the backhoe had been. A strip of land about fifty feet long was disturbed, fresh-turned soil.

It was here where men in white jumpsuits with masks over their mouths and noses descended with shovels. The first body was found within five minutes. County and federal law enforcement people stood in a rough circle as the forensics investigators began uncovering the rest of the bodies. The dead were lined in a shallow mass grave, almost shoulder to shoulder. There were seven women and two men.

"Internal organs missing," the ME said, looking up from the mass grave.

I stepped closer. The victims looked to have dark hair and features except for one, whose matted hair was blond. I had a feeling I was looking at the partially decomposed body of Robin Eastman. The sad life of a young stripper, caught in a maniacal turf war, ended like a gutted fish.

Lauren and Dan stood next to me and watched the proceedings. Both the FBI and the county investigators were doing a good job documenting with video and numerous digital cameras.

Lauren looked to the west and pointed. "Chopper isn't ours. Media are coming."

Dan said, "We've got to keep them back a good fifty yards!"

The senior ME came up out of the ditch of the dead, removed his mask, and said, "In thirty-three years, I've never seen anything like this."

"Any idea of the time line from the first killing to the latest?" I asked.

"That'll take some lab work, but I'd estimate the one at the far end has been in the ground about five months. The last one down, a few days."

Dan shook his head. "How do you even try a case like this?"

"What do you mean?" Lauren asked.

"Quantity of bodies. Death penalty isn't enough."

I said, "Lauren, maybe you can take your FBI team and pay Josh and Richard Brennen a little visit. Their neglect, the abuse they handed out, and indifference allowed it to exist in the first place. That's a crime in my book."

Dan looked over and held his hand up. To four deputies he yelled,

"There's a bunch of media people coming. I see the satellite trucks. Make sure nobody gets on this side of the tape. Nobody!"

I said, "The last puzzle piece has to be found. I need to get on the road to find it."

"Where're you going?" Lauren asked.

"Xanadu."

AS I APPROACHED MY JEEP, Manny Lopez was standing near it. "You found bodies?"

"Yes. Too many."

"I never think this would happen when I come to this country."

He held out his hand. I saw the keys from the Escalade in his dirty fingers. He said, "I took these so Ortega could not go. You take them."

He smiled and handed me the keys.

I cranked the Jeep and started down the dirt road. I looked in my rearview mirror and saw Manny petting the dog I'd freed from the leash. Both the dog and Manny seemed to be grinning.

SIXTY-EIGHT

The Club Xanadu was posh in a tacky kind of way. It was a cavernous club with plenty of seating in dark recessed areas away from the stage. A small chain hung across a flight of steps leading to a second floor. The sign in the middle of the chain read VIP ONLY. On the stage, one dancer played to an audience of a dozen or so men. Her boredom was the only thing she was hiding.

Half a dozen women worked the room offering conversation and lap dances for hire. Ron Hamilton and I sat at a table away from the stage. His tie was loose, hair grayer than I remembered, dark circles under his eyes. He said, "This definitely isn't your run-of-the-mill strip joint. The women all have the same type bodies and looks. Handpicked from somewhere."

"I always appreciated your powers of observation. Can you see what I see?"

"What's that?"

286

"Lots of small cameras all over the room. If Santana is here today, he's seen us."

"We don't look any different from the rest of the guys in here."

"Maybe—but I'm thinking that if he's the same perp from four years ago, he might recognize me. Remember the media frenzy? I hated to see my face in the papers."

"Sean, you've changed. Job does that to us."

A cocktail waitress approached our table. She said, "Hi, gentlemen. What can I get you?"

"Corona," I said.

"Same thing," Ron said.

She flashed a real smile and took an order from another table before going to the bar. The first dancer left the stage, slipped into a low-cut dress, and began working the room. She walked over to our table. Dark hair, black eyes, and a smile that seemed as manufactured as her breasts. She said, "How about a dance?"

"Maybe later," I said. "I'd like to get to know you first."

"Lot of guys just want somebody to talk to. My name's Alicia."

I said, "Sean and Ron."

"Hi, Sean and Ron. Buy me a drink?"

"Just don't order champagne," Ron said.

"Gotcha."

The cocktail waitress brought our beers, and Alicia ordered a glass of white wine. She said, "I haven't seen you fellas in here before. First time?"

Ron said, "Yeah, kinda hard to get out much anymore."

"I understand. The wife factor, huh?"

"Something like that," I said.

The cocktail waitress brought the glass of wine, set it in front of Alicia, and said, "Gentlemen, you want to run a tab?"

I handed her a twenty. "Keep the change."

Alicia sipped from her glass. "I know all about the wife factor. This club is like a big ol' group-therapy place for men. Women got Oprah. Men got nobody."

"Alicia," I said, "where's Santana?"

She looked like she couldn't swallow the sip of wine. She inhaled through flared nostrils. "I don't know. I don't see him."

I saw her glance up at one of the hidden cameras. She positioned the wineglass in front of her lips. "Y'all cops? I haven't done nothing."

Ron said, "We didn't say you did. All we want is a little information about—"

I cut Ron off, lifted my beer glass to my mouth, and said, "He reads lips, doesn't he?"

She smiled and nodded with her eyes. "You got it, big guy."

"He's watching us now, isn't he?"

"Maybe."

"Alicia, what do you want to do when you move on from this profession?"

"I want to be an actress. Always wanted to since I was a little girl. First time I saw Sarah Michelle Gellar in *Buffy the Vampire Slayer,* I knew I wanted to act."

"Okay," I said, pulling out a hundred-dollar bill, folding it quickly, but giving her enough time to see the denomination. "This is your chance to act. I'll take that lap dance, but what I really want is for you to whisper in my ear. Act like you're telling me all the fantasies you think I want to hear, but you're really responding to my questions. Okay?"

"I can do that."

She stood and slipped off her dress. She wore nothing but a G-string. As the music started, she sat in my lap and whispered in my ear, "What do you want to know?"

I could see the flash of glitter body makeup, smell her perfume, and feel the heat of her body against me. "Tell me everything you know about the person I mentioned."

In a soft whisper she said, "He's weird. Sort of a Michael Jackson weird, I guess. Real choosy about the girls he sleeps with. I've never done him. I wouldn't. One of the girls, she doesn't work here anymore, told me about him."

"What was her name?"

"She goes by the name Tabitha, but her real name is Robin Eastman. Anyway, she told me he showers before and after sex, and he shaves his body. Everywhere, even his friggin' balls. No hair anywhere."

"Where's Robin?"

"She left a while back. Nobody's seen or heard from her since."

"Did she quit?"

"Don't know. She would have told us 'bye if she quit. He probably had one of his managers fire her. Makes my skin crawl, the way he looks at you."

"What color are his eyes?"

"Greenish, but I try not to look at his eyes."

"Does he keep an office here?"

"I heard there's an office above the VIP area, but I can't say for sure it's his."

"How would you know if he's here?"

"I've only seen him twice in the nine months I've worked here. There's a private entrance on the other side of the building."

The music ended, and I handed her the money and closed her hand around it. "Good luck in your acting."

"Thanks," she said, zipping up the dress.

SIXTY-NINE

Ron and I lifted the chain from one of the stanchions on the steps and walked up to the VIP area. It was darker than the main part of the club. There was a second bar with overstuffed chairs and a small stage on a Plexiglas floor. An NBA game was on one of the four large plasma screens. Two men sat at the bar, nursed drinks, and seemed to be reading some kind of contract.

I said, "Let's see what the private office looks like."

At the door marked PRIVATE, Ron turned the handle. "Locked."

A man large enough to be a pro linebacker came up behind us. He was dressed in a white tuxedo shirt, a bow tie, and dark pants. "That's private." His hair was regulation boot camp, face angular, blue eyes hard. "I'm the manager. Nobody goes in there."

Ron reached into his pocket and pulled out his badge and search warrant. "This tells me we do have a right to go in there. You have a problem with it, go discuss it with Circuit Court Judge Healy. Now open the door before we kick it down."

The manager's face was flushed. "I'll have to get the keys."

"Where are they?" I asked.

"Downstairs."

Ron said, "You wouldn't tip off Santana while you're down there, would you?"

"Who?" He turned and left.

It took me less than thirty seconds to pick the simple lock and open the door.

"Sean, I see you haven't lost your touch."

We followed a hall covered with red carpet to another door. There was only one office, and now we stood in front of Miguel Santana's door. My heart was pounding. Palms sweaty. I tried it. Locked. Pulling out my Glock, I whispered, "It's showtime . . ." I kicked hard, the heel on my shoe connecting to the left of the lock. The door popped open like a jack-in-the-box.

We entered the office, pistols extended.

There was a soft whirr from an ornate paddle fan in the plush office. The desk was clean. I noticed a speck of white on the ridge of a leather coach. I bent down and lifted a sliver of fingernail and said, "Let's see if we can match this." I dropped the fingernail into a Ziploc and slowly opened the door leading to an adjacent bathroom. It was spotless, the shower dry. I knelt down and looked at the white tile floor. In the sand-colored grout, I saw what looked like a tiny crack. I pressed it with the tip of my finger and it disappeared. On the end of my finger was an eyelash.

"Gotcha," I said.

"What'd you find?"

"An eyelash."

As I put the eyelash in a Ziploc, Ron looked in the open toilet. "What do we have here?" He pulled a pencil out of his coat pocket and used the tip of the eraser to lift something floating in the toilet water.

"Maybe the reason Santana lost an eyelash is because he took out disposable contacts and flushed them down the drain. This one didn't go all the way down." He held it in the light and uttered a slow whistle. "The stripper said he had green eyes. This contact is blue."

"He really has eyes more on the yellowish gold side, like a cat. If you cover yellow eyes with a blue contact, what do you get?"

"Green."

I heard a noise at the door. Ron and I both spun around at the same instant, guns extended. The GI Joe manager stood at the door. He raised his hands up. "Don't fuckin' shoot! You two crazy or what?"

I smiled, lowered my Glock, and walked over to him. "I guess we did get off on the wrong foot earlier."

"Fuckin' A. I see cops in here all the time. You guys are some of the worst womanizers." He grinned and glanced toward Ron. It was all the time I needed. I wedged the Glock under his chin and shoved him over to the couch. "Listen very carefully, pal. You work for the world's worst womanizer. Want to know why?"

"Huh?"

"What makes Miguel Santana the worst womanizer is that he destroys the woman. First he destroys her dignity by beating and raping her. Then he begins with the mind and tries to end with the soul. He asphyxiates her. Want to know how she feels?" I pushed the barrel onto his lips and continued, "Of course, Santana pinches the nostrils so hard she can't breathe as he continues raping her while she's dying beneath him. Ron, hand me the portable phone on the desk."

I stood and kept the gun aimed at the bouncer's round head. "You're calling Santana. Which line on this phone is private?"

"Line six," he coughed, the words thick.

"What's Santana's cell?"

"I don't know."

"Want to know what it's like when the air passages from the nose are closed? Worst than drowning. What's the number? I won't ask you again."

"He's got a dozen."

"The one you know he'll answer." I tossed him the phone. "Dial it. When Santana answers, tell him it's urgent and you need him here. There's been an emergency at the club. One of the girls has been shot in the parking lot. You got it?"

He nodded and started dialing. I said, "As you dial, speak the number you're dialing. Ron will write it down."

"And put it on speakerphone," Ron said.

There was one ring. "Yes?" The voice was somewhere above a whisper.

"Mr. Santana, this is Rob at the club. There's been an emergency down here."

"We employ managers like you to handle emergencies. What emergency?"

"A shooting, sir. Crazy ex-boyfriend shot one of the girls. We need you here."

"That's very odd, Rob. Because I'm watching the club online. Everything appears very normal, inside and outside. And why am I on speakerphone? I will assume it is because of the two detectives I saw in there earlier. I recognized one. Hello, Sean O'Brien. It's been a few years. I'd heard you retired."

The bouncer's eyes went wide. I grabbed the phone and said, "Santana, you recognized me, and I recognize your signature murders. So much so that I made a promise to one of the girls you killed. I told her I'd hunt you down."

Santana chuckled. "Detective, if I ever should resort to violence and have to kill someone, perhaps it would be you."

Then he was gone.

SEVENTY

After Ron had gone home for the night, I agreed to meet Special Agent Lauren Miles for a late bite and a drink. She had picked the place, Reflections on the Bay. It was too trendy and pricey for my tastes, but I was hungry, and the government was buying. Earlier I'd filled her in on the events at Club Xanadu and my conversation with Santana. I had given her Santana's cell number, and she was working with the phone company for GPS coordinates or cell tower pings.

Lauren said, "No chip and no usage. Looks like it was a throwaway phone. Nice move using the bouncer to get Santana on the phone."

"Did you find anything else on him?"

"We don't know the depth of his involvement in Club Xanadu, but it's owned, or partly owned, by a holding company called ShowBiz Productions. They own a half dozen clubs in Florida, one in Atlanta, and one in Dallas. Looks like ShowBiz is tied to Exotic Escorts, the online escort service I mentioned. It, of course, is a front for prostitution. All the women go by aliases."

"That doesn't surprise me. What'd you find on the sale of human organs?"

"We believe Santana heads an international export company, Orion BioLife LLC. It offers human organs for sale online. Web site says they're in the business of connecting human 'donor' organs with those 'in need.' Except there is a price. The prices aren't listed. The buyer bids on whatever he or she needs, such as a heart or kidney. If the bid is 'acceptable,' the organ is shipped, counter to counter, usually overseas. A Japanese CEO could have a new kidney in forty-eight hours."

"The whole concept of 'donor' gets blurred when these organs are auctioned to the highest bidder," I said.

"Exactly, but Orion BioLife says the costs are to cover administrative fees, logistics, and travel arrangements. They say the organs are received from the family of the deceased. The dead person was allegedly someone who wanted his or her organs sold after death to help defray funeral costs and help the surviving members of the family. It's illegal, but so is prostitution. Both are selling body parts."

"BioLife is probably charging a half million in shipping and handling charges."

"Something like that," Lauren said.

"Can you find a location, assuming they have a brick and mortar address?"

"Online you have little to go on. You try to follow cyber tracks to someplace that will ultimately unveil the identity of the criminal or criminals. Although there's a demand and the Internet makes it easier to connect, it's harder to track."

I sat back in the chair and watched a palm frond sway in the warm Miami night air. I could smell the ocean. In a dark corner of the restaurant, I saw the manager, a middle-aged man, rest his arm on the shoulders of a college-aged waitress. He rubbed her back, his gold wedding band winking in the dark of the alcove.

Lauren said, "What are you thinking about?"

"You don't want to hear. I'm thinking about how too many people with wealth and power abuse those without it."

Lauren traced her index finger across the lip of her wineglass. "I guess I'll think twice before I ever ask you what you're thinking," she said with a smile. "Thanks for agreeing to meet me tonight."

My cell rang. "Ought to grab this. Probably Ron, or maybe Dan." I could see there was no caller ID in the display. "This is O'Brien," I said into the phone.

"I know who it is."

I immediately recognized the voice. It was calm, total control, a subtle mocking undertone. I said, "Santana. How'd you get my number?"

"Where you left it, in a convenience store, right there for the world to see. Convenient for me. Inconvenient for you. It was pleasant chatting with you earlier today, Detective O'Brien. Oh, I know you're not with the Miami Police anymore, but you're still a detective. It's in your blood. Sort of like what I do is in my blood. We're blood brothers, O'Brien. I can't change it any more than you can change what you do. Took you years to find me, but you finally got there. I'm glad it was you."

"And I'll get to you, Santana." Lauren's eyes were popping.

"You can call me Miguel. You failed to find me because I didn't want to be found, but I didn't go away completely, Detective O'Brien. I realigned my operations farther inland from Miami. Nobody seems to notice when a few stray sheep are missing. Then you stumble along, years later, and start causing roadblocks. If you didn't cost me money, I would actually enjoy the irony. After I read about your early retirement, I wondered if it was because of me, or am I indulging in self-gratification? Now here we are again."

"I'll find you."

"But I'll find you first, because I already know where you are. This is the last time we'll chat, Detective. Cat-and-mouse games bore me. I can't make money doing it. I can't fuck it. I can't consume it, I can't sell it, so what's the use? The next time we speak, it will be your final words on earth. Have you ever wondered what you'd say?"

"Listen to these words: I'll be there when they inject you."

Santana laughed. "O'Brien, the woman you're sitting next to, the one sitting up so perfectly straight, love her posture, she might be next. Very erotic and so stimulating when they fight hard. After I'm done with her, I'll sell her piece by piece. Maybe I'll keep the edible parts for myself." He laughed and disconnected.

I held the phone, my pulse hammering, hand shaking, sounds of the traffic on Collins echoing like tanks reverberating and coming toward me. I stared at the small screen on the phone, not sure whether to toss Lauren to the floor. Shooting wasn't his style. Too impersonal.

Lauren leaned closer to me. "I'll start a trace on your phone now! Maybe there's a chip in this phone. If not, we'll find the tower closest to wherever he placed the call."

"He's watching us now."

"Oh shit! Is he watching through a rifle scope?"

I stood. "Don't think so. He likes death up close." I looked through the bougainvillea. A Ferrari was purring at an intersection, the driver waiting for a traffic light to change. A stretch limo drove slowly by the restaurant. The reflection of neon rolled off the black windows like rainbows.

Across the street were opulent high-rise condos glowing from the polish of money. Outdoor lighting showcased manicured landscaping that was imported from the islands. Canary date palms swayed in the warm sea breeze.

"Lauren, we're sitting on an outdoor patio enclosed by a six-foot wooden trellis covered with bougainvillea."

"What are you saying?"

"The only way Santana could see us sitting here is from a high elevation."

I looked at the highest oceanfront condo across the street, slowly scanning from the palms to the balconies overlooking the dark Atlantic. I could see muted shapes drinking and lounging in the million-dollar cages. "We have three high-rise condos you could easily see this restaurant from, especially from the top half dozen floors."

Lauren stood from the table. "You think that Santana is on one of those balconies watching us?"

"Yes. And right now you'd better triangulate the cell call to one of those buildings, because if he's there—he won't wait for us to find him. Let's move!"

SEVENTY-ONE

It took Lauren less than thirty minutes to find out that one of the $2.8 million condos was owned by ShowBiz Productions. We had a search warrant thirty minutes after that and began our approach.

One middle-aged FBI agent, a guy who looked like he'd been called while he was eating, joined Lauren and me in the condo parking lot. His name was Phil Barfield. Stocky, thick wrists, a small scar over his left eyebrow. The scar was more evident when he concentrated, as he did listening to Lauren. He asked the right questions. I could tell he'd been there and done it, but I'd bet his federal pension that he'd never been in the presence of a psychopath like Santana.

Ten minutes later, Ron rolled up in an unmarked cruiser, followed by four Miami PD patrol cars with two uniforms in each. Ron had made sure there would be no announcement of their arrival. No sirens and no lights.

I could see the condo manager pacing in the lobby, waiting for us, passkeys clutched in his hand. We huddled in a corner of the lot near the entrance. I said, "We'll need backup at the rear, in the underground parking lot, on the roof next door, and at the front and back exits." The officers nodded.

Ron said, "Jim, you and Ralph take the back, Carlos out front, Bob and Tyler in the garage, and Jackson on the roof of the Miami Towers next door."

I said, "Security is waiting to escort you up. Everybody be careful. This guy's smart and insane. Probably has no fear of death. Let's go."

"Got a rush back on the eyelash," Ron said, almost as an afterthought.

"And?" I said.

"Bingo. It's a match with your victim's hair found on the duct tape. It's Santana's DNA. He killed her. And the piece of fingernail found on the couch matches with the hair you found on the backhoe, probably from Robin Eastman. Santana can run, but he can't hide anymore."

"Be careful," I said. "He didn't call me to just chat. Could be a trap."

We got the passkeys from a portly man with thick eyebrows flaking dandruff. He looked over the tops of his brown glasses, a tic pulsating under his left eye. "This can't get in the news. We're selling the building."

I said, "Stay here. Where's the service elevator?"

"Beyond the alcove, where those plants hang from the second floor."

It took us two minutes to ride the service elevator to the top floor, forty-six floors above the Atlantic Ocean. We walked down the polished marble hall, though pods of soft light, past ornate original oil paintings of the sea, and around marble columns.

We stopped at condo number 1619. Each person on our team held a pistol. I slid the passkey through the electronic detector. There was a click, like a wooden spoon against a wooden table, subtle.

"Freeze! Police!" Ron yelled as we burst into the condo.

The lights were on. A sea breeze teased at the curtains near the balcony. The place seemed vacant. We fanned out into each room, pistol arms extended.

The condo was large. Professionally decorated. Artwork collected from around the world hung on the walls. The face of a sun god in a composite of gold, silver, and rubies looked out from one wall. Classical music played softly throughout the penthouse.

"All clear!" Ron yelled.

Nothing. No sign of anyone. In the master bedroom, I looked in the closet. A bright blue silk shirt was in the center of the expensive clothes. I took it off the rack. It was the same color as the thread Joe Billie found at the crime scene. Sleeve was torn.

"Sean!" Lauren yelled. "Take a look at this."

We all stepped out onto the large balcony. A candle burned on an end table next to a recliner. On the wet bar was a bottle of champagne half submerged in a bucket of fresh ice. There were four glasses next to the champagne. In the center of the glasses was a piece of paper with my name on it. It read:

O'Brien and company, you're to be congratulated. Pour yourself some champagne and toast each other—because tonight you almost caught Miguel Santana.

"Who the fuck is this guy?" asked Agent Barfield.

Ron opened the radio microphone. "He's slipped us! Everyone come back!"

The radio crackled. "This is Jim."

"Carlos here."

"Tyler on the roof."

"Ralph at the rear emergency exit."

Ron said, "Bob! Can you read me? Bob!"

Silence.

SEVENTY-TWO

The elevator to the basement couldn't move fast enough. On the way down, Ron radioed for more backup and an ambulance. He watched the digital lights change as the elevator descended from the penthouse. Forty-six floors to the garage. Ron said, "He's one of our best. Did a stint in Iraq. Special Forces. Volunteered to help stop the anarchy in New Orleans after Hurricane Katrina. He's got three kids, all small."

Floor twenty. Seventeen. Fourteen.

"Move, elevator!" Ron shouted. His jawline could crack stones.

Lauren said, "Lots of concrete and steel in the basement. Could block the radio."

"That's a possibility," said Agent Barfield. "Since the hurricanes of '04, builders have been sinking the footing for these new condos very deep."

When the doors opened, we stepped into the parking garage, handguns drawn.

"Oh shit!" Ron said, stopping like an animal frozen in a car's headlights.

"Try to reach the paramedics!" Lauren ordered. "Tell them where we are!" She ran toward Bob.

He was slumped against a wall between a Mercedes and a Jaguar. It looked like he was sitting, resting after jogging. The closer I got, the more I knew it wouldn't make any difference how fast the paramedics arrived. He was beginning to turn bluish. His head was resting against the concrete block wall. Blood trickled out of the right side of his open mouth, soaking into his uniform. His eyes were open, like a camera shutter that had jammed, exposing the film to the image of horror. Blood settling in the retinas.

Agent Barfield crouched beside the body and did a perfunctory reading of the pulse. He shook his head. "No sign of a bullet or stab wound. From the position of the body in relation to the head, looks like his neck was broken. Snapped like a tree branch."

I said, "Let's search the garage. Stay within sight of each other."

I could hear the wail of sirens growing louder as we looked for Santana. I knew he had escaped. He was probably in the backseat of a cab en route to the airport, or he might be strolling along Ocean Boulevard, stopping to consider a Versace window display. He'd blend in, like an international tourist. Blasé as the police cavalry roared by in a blur of chrome, their red, blue, and white lights enveloping the condos in the moving colors found somewhere between life and death.

SEVENTY-THREE

I sipped the double espresso and checked the headlights in my rearview mirror more than I wanted to as I drove out of Miami, north up I-95. Each time a pair of lights came too close, I found myself touching the Glock between the seats. I didn't think Santana was following me, but then I wouldn't have thought he could snap the neck of a Special Forces paratrooper.

I saw a text message flashing on my phone, which was charging in the cradle. I picked up the phone and read the message. It was from Dan Grant. *call me when u get this . . . urgent . . . slater's going down.*

It was almost 1:00 A.M. I called Dan. He answered after two rings.

"O'Brien, you okay? I saw the news. They had video of you, FBI types, couple dozen Miami PD, all coming out of a ritzy South Beach condo. An officer killed?"

"Neck broken. A good cop is gone, and we have one hell of a problem walking the streets. Pandora's box is open and the baddest of the bad is out."

"So this perp is our bad guy?"

"He's the serial that's calling the shots. Slater is, no doubt, on Miguel Santana's payroll. How he got there I haven't figured out yet. We nailed Santana's connection when we got a DNA match from the hair on the duct tape near the vic I found. A fingernail matched to the missing dancer, Robin Eastman. Santana knew we'd made him. After we got that far, he turned the tables. He called me. The psycho in him figured he had nothing to lose. He'd make a game of it."

"What'd he say?"

"Something about my days on the planet expiring. He wants me to start writing my own epitaph. I think he's a little pissed we cut into his business and his perverted world. What do you have on Slater?"

"We searched his place while he was out. Canine found the jogging clothes. He'd put the stuff in a plastic garbage bag and set it out by the curb with the rest of the trash. It would have gone to the dump, but one of the county's trucks on that route was broken, so the trash was late in getting picked up. Dog found the scent in a matter of minutes. Grass and water stains matched, and there was a trace of Leslie's blood on the sweatshirt. Ballistics says the gun used to kill Leslie was the same that killed the club owner, Tony Martin. We haven't found it yet, but we have enough to bury Slater. I got a warrant earlier tonight. We have his place staked out. Pulled his DNA from the skin sample on the sidewalk."

"Let's hope he shows. Any results back from the gator-processing house?"

"Lab found traces of alligator blood that matched the blood found on the female vic's hair. Luminol indicated human blood all over the damn place. Like Frankenstein's lab. The liquid in the stainless steel canisters is a combination of human glucose and water."

SEVENTY-FOUR

Miguel Santana avoided a security camera at the gatepost by slipping under the fence. He blended with the long shadows as he approached the Brennen estate. He remembered the layout of the house. Little had changed. Except now, Josh Brennen had security cameras hidden discreetly inside the home.

Santana tried a side door. Unlocked. A very stupid thing to do, he thought. But the old man did stupid things. That was his way. Let the chips fall. Somebody else could sweep them away.

Santana closed the door softly and started toward the center of the house, more hidden cameras recording his movements. He could hear the television playing, the noise sounding like a war movie.

The old man was alone. He slouched in his leather recliner, feet up, a bottle of expensive scotch half gone. He watched a Bruce Willis movie, his eyes barely open.

Santana entered the room and stood there, observing. He could easily walk over and snap the bastard's neck, look him in the eye and watch him die. Or he could make it more spectacular. Maybe burn the house down. Let the ashes fall where they will.

Santana lifted the empty glass out of Brennen's hand and stood there as Brennen's eyes batted a few times before he was fully awake. He looked up. His mouth opened but there were no words, only a gurgling sound coming through vocal cords thick with mucus and sleep. He cleared his throat. "Who the hell are you? This some kind of robbery?"

Brennen started to stand, but Santana pushed him hard on the chest. Santana laughed. He lifted the bottle and poured some scotch into the glass and handed it to Brennen. He then stepped to the bar, got a second glass and poured scotch into it, and walked back in front of Brennen's chair.

Santana said, "Shall we toast?"

"Get the fuck outta my house!"

Santana smiled. He lifted his glass and said, "To you . . . and everything you are . . . Father."

SEVENTY-FIVE

Josh Brennen looked like he'd seen a ghost. "Where's Richard?"

Santana laughed. "Am I my brother's keeper?"

"What'd you do to him?"

"Father, what makes you think I'd hurt a hair on the favorite son's head?"

"What do you want?"

"Nothing from you. I wanted something a long time ago, but you refused to give it. I wanted a name. I wanted a home. I wanted you to take care of my mother. She was one of the many young Latino girls you fucked and spit on. You seemed to like her a lot. Made her your favorite. Fucked her over and over until she got pregnant. She was seventeen. I know that she came to you for help. Not for herself but for her baby, your son. Me, Papa, me! And where were you when I was raped at age ten, Papa?"

"How much do you want?"

Santana backhanded Brennen across the mouth. Blood spilled down the old man's face and into his two-day growth of white whiskers.

"You think I came here for money? You stupid old man! I learned how to make money. How to survive. I had no choice. You learn or you die. The streets of Guadalajara are where I got my education in people. Rich tourists. Corrupt police. My mother became a street whore. After you destroyed her spirit she didn't care about her body. She'd have sex with anyone for a dollar. Didn't care if I was in the house or not. She made me hate her! You made me hate her! She died from AIDS, but mostly she died from abuse. Abuse started by you, Papa. When she died, she still had scars on her legs from when your contractors beat her with a fishing rod. I was thirteen when she died in the streets. I rode with the coyote into California. Lived in the barrios of south Los Angeles. Fought gangs. Stole. Learned. Survived. When I got to Florida, I came to find the man my mother had talked about when the drugs were making her crazy. I only wanted to see you . . . to talk with you. And I saw your true colors through the blood spilled and running into my eyes. Your blood, Papa!"

"Shut up!" Brennen screamed.

"No! You listen to me, old man." Santana laughed. "I figured out how to get a scholarship and began medical school. Imagine, a doctor in the family! You could brag to your rich friends, 'my son the doctor.' You must remember when I came to you. It was fifteen years ago. You had one of your men teach me a lesson, as you called it. He beat me so hard I still have problems in my head. You let him beat me, your own son, almost to death, and you stood there and watched. The last thing I remembered, before he kicked my teeth, was looking up at you, Father. Lying there in the mud and horseshit in one of your pastures, looking up at you and hoping you'd stop the man from hitting me. From hurting me, your flesh and blood! But all you did was stare, those eyes burning through me. Guess what, Papa? We have the same eyes. I see yours are covered in cataracts, but I remember when they had color. They say the eyes are the windows to the soul, Father. But what if you have no soul? What do you see through those windows? You see hell. Evil can exist in many forms. When it's inherited in the spirit, it can be disguised. And that's the art to true evil. You've succeeded at it for years, Papa. Making people believe you're just a good ol' card-carrying rancher. In reality, you're a man who can slit the throat of a human as easily as a lamb."

"Shut up!" Brennen said, throwing the scotch in Santana's face.

"Oh, I know it's hard to listen to, Father, but it's time you admitted it. I'm just like you, a man without a soul. That's what you gave me. Like father . . . like son."

"Like fucking hell! Get out!"

"You don't give the orders, old man! Pick up that phone by your side and call your other son up to the big house. We can have a little family re-union."

"No!"

There was a slight noise in the foyer. Santana looked up to see Grace Brennen in her motorized wheelchair. He grinned, walked over to her, and pushed the wheelchair in front of Brennen's chair. Santana placed both hands on her neck. In a voice barely above a whisper, he said, "Call him or I'll snap her neck. It's a painful way to die—and you can sit there and watch it. Call him now."

SEVENTY-SIX

Richard Brennen wasn't sure what to think. The old bastard rarely called him to the house this late, and for no apparent reason. He sounded drunk, but then he always sounded drunk after 10:00 P.M. He entered through the side door that led through the kitchen. He picked a banana out of a fruit bowl.

He rounded the end of the hall and stepped into the great room, then stopped abruptly. "Mother?" he said, dropping the banana at his feet. "Daddy, what happened? Did you fall?" Brennen approached his father just as Santana stepped out from behind an alcove.

"Greetings, my brother."

Richard Brennen turned around to stare at a strange man with a pistol pointing at him. "Who are you?"

"I'm your brother."

"Like hell you are!"

"I am. Father is in denial, but he knows it's true. True as the color of my eyes."

Richard looked at the man's eyes, and then he looked at his father's eyes. "Who is this? What's this about? Some kind of half-ass blackmail? My opponent, Charlie Matthison, must have sent you."

Santana laughed. "Half-assed blackmail? Come on, little brother. I think larger than that. If I'd wanted to blackmail you, I could have sent these to your opponent."

Santana ripped open the packet he was carrying, took out the eight by ten photographs and tossed them in Josh Brennen's lap. The old man lifted one of the photos. It showed his younger son having sex with a man. He looked at another, the disgust building on his face after each picture. He threw the photos at Richard.

"You're a damn queer!" he said, standing to face Richard. "My son, the man who came out of my loins, is a fucking faggot."

Richard started for Santana but stopped. "I was set up! The condo!"

Santana said, "Usually it's reserved for heterosexual encounters, but I made an exception in your case, my brother. Cain and Abel. Guess who's Abel?"

Richard turned to face his father. "I tried to tell you. You didn't want to listen."

"Listen! How can you justify this? Damn you to hell and back, Richard!"

Grace Brennen sat in her wheelchair, stoic, her face someplace beyond sad. She pressed the small control with a finger on her right hand and the wheelchair began going backward. It crashed into a large porcelain vase, smashing it and knocking over a houseplant. Josh Brennen got up, his heavy cocktail glass breaking on the marble floor. He hobbled over to his wife.

"It's okay, Gracie. It's gonna be all right." Her breathing came in gasps, her head twisting as if she were in pain. "Your mama might be havin' another stroke!"

Santana was amused. It was better than he imagined. He put the small pistol in his pocket and said, "The wealthy American family at its

312

very dysfunctional best. But then again, Father knows best. I was going to kill you, Papa, but that would be too quick. Too easy and too final. This way you'll be in pain a long time. Just like my mother, from the first time you made her body bleed to the last time you bled her spirit." Santana smiled, turned, and left.

SEVENTY-SEVEN

The next day, late in the afternoon, I made Cuban sandwiches for Max and me. We walked down to my dock to eat. The river was tranquil, motionless as smoked glass. An anhinga swam less than fifty feet from me, bobbing in the water like a feathered torpedo. I thought about the investigation. The cloud wouldn't part, I knew, until Santana was caught and prosecuted along with Davis, Ortega, and Slater.

I scooted a paper plate over to Max. "Let's eat." She gulped down the meat and small piece of Cuban flatbread I'd cut for her.

I sipped a Sam Adams and watched the water bugs dart in circles. The river reflected a sky of cherry red clouds mixed with patches of blue. I heard the two-stroke engine before I saw the boat. In a few seconds, the small fishing boat came around the three-acre island in the center of the river. The boat's pilot throttled back for about twenty seconds, than accelerated and came in the direction of my dock. Max barked.

"Max, it's okay. Don't scare off the locals."

There was one person in the boat. As he came closer, I could tell he was middle-aged, deeply tanned. He wore black jeans and a black short-sleeved shirt that was completely unbuttoned and not tucked in his pants. In the sun, I saw the flash of a gold chain around his neck. There was something else on his chest, but at that distance I couldn't tell what it was.

Within thirty seconds, the boat was a dot around the bend, and the man dressed in black was gone.

THE LIGHT ON MY PHONE was blinking. I checked the messages. "Sean, this is Lauren. I finally came up with a photo of Santana. At least we think it's him. He's got movie-star good looks, with the eye of the tiger, so to speak. The Bureau found a picture in the *Herald*. Santana was with Congressman Lloyd Becker when Becker made the rounds during his campaign last October. Herald ID'd him in the cutline as 'Miguel Santana, local businessman and philanthropist.' I've e-mailed it to you. Please call me when you get this message. Oh, by the way, we've released the photo to the media."

As I started to open my e-mail, the phone rang. It was Dan Grant. He was almost breathless. "Where the hell have you been?" he asked.

"A walk down by the river and then dinner."

"A walk?"

"Yep. With Max. It's quality time. Found a large spearhead in the roots of a willow tree blown over in a storm."

"Look, O'Brien, here's what happened in the world while you took your dog on a field trip. Security cameras in the Brennen mansion caught it all. Too bad those cameras weren't monitored by a service. Everything digitally recorded to computer hard drives. Our team is streaming the video to the feds right now."

"What happened?"

"Santana, he slipped in the Brennen house and confronted Josh Brennen. No audio, but you could see the old man losing his shit when Santana and Richard Brennen had a little discussion apparently about Richard's sexual persuasion. Photos on the floor of the scene show Junior favored young men. The old man went ballistic. After Santana left the room, Brennen shot his son, and then he shot himself in the head. Did it in front of his invalid wife sitting in her wheelchair. He was so close to her when he shot himself, blood splatter hit the woman's face and she couldn't wipe it off. He fell dead at her feet."

"Why would Santana go there? Can she speak at all?"

"Her stroke makes speech difficult. She managed to garble out something that sounded like 'Papa.'"

I could feel my chest muscles tighten. I said, "That's it!"

"What's it?"

"Josh Brennen is Miguel Santana's father! The ostracized prodigal son returns. That helps explain Santana. I'm betting he's the son of one of Brennen's former workers, probably someone trafficked here, held as a sex slave. The mother could be a woman Josh Brennen used, impregnated, and tossed. In tossing her, he threw away any paternal responsibilities or links to Miguel Santana."

"Media will go nuts over this. They're already swarming in packs from all the major networks, and from England and South America, too. O'Brien, you were right about Slater being connected to Santana. He tried to cop a plea, but finding the stripper's body in the field with the others pretty much brought this around to Slater and Santana. Slater admitted he got sucked in because he was so overextended at the casinos and gambling boats, and he was about to have his balls removed by guys with no sense of humor. He says Santana bailed him out and wiped the debt clean as long as he, Slater, was occasionally 'on call' for Santana. Of course, one call led to another and another. Soon, Slater was Santana's enforcer in the rough-and-tumble world of strip club acquisitions and Internet porn. Slater's willing to take a life sentence for Leslie's murder if the DA drops charges in the strip club killing. Prosecutor is going full bore. Slater is looking at the death penalty. By the way, the sheriff is running unopposed."

I was silent.

"You still there?"

"Now we find Santana," I said.

"Got any ideas?"

"He's not where you think you'll find him."

"Between us, the FBI and state, we have major airports and bus terminals watched."

"What about private airports or boat transportation? In an hour, he can be in Bimini off the coast of Miami. If terrorists can get in, Santana can get out. This has to be the biggest dragnet in the state's history. Keep me posted."

As I opened Lauren's e-mail, I clicked on the attached photo. The picture was in color. I could see the yellowish eyes of Miguel Santana staring back at me. My mind flashed to the picture of Sandra Duperre's cat in Jacksonville. *I still hear his voice sometimes*, I remembered her saying.

I called Lauren. "Got your e-mail."

"The picture seems very anticlimactic after watching the video feed the Volusia sheriff's office sent. Santana was in total control playing Josh and Richard Brennen."

"Josh Brennen is Santana's father."

"Oh my God!"

"The night I was with you and received the call from Santana, you had a trace put on the call. Did you get a number? And was it different than the one I had?"

"Yes and yes. But in light of all hell breaking loose right after that, especially since Santana left us that note in the condo, chasing a cell phone number seemed moot."

"Can you find the number?"

"You know Santana's either tossed the phone or certainly won't answer your call, assuming he's still in the country."

"Do you have the number?"

"I've got it here on my desk."

She gave me the number. I wrote it on the back of a boating magazine. "Thanks. I'll call you later."

"Sean, what are you going to do?"

"Extend an invitation to Santana."

SEVENTY-EIGHT

I didn't expect Santana to answer. Maybe he was watching his caller ID in some international airport. Maybe I'd have a chance to bait him before he stepped on a plane. I had to get it right. Had to offer something he couldn't get or find for himself.

After one ring, the call cut immediately to a short beep and then into voice mail. I said, "Santana, this is Sean O'Brien. You said the next time we talked the words would be my last on earth. You wanted me to think about what I would say. I know what that is. My last words will be what your father told me about you. You want to hear what Josh Brennen really said about you, about your mother? To hear those words, you have to hear them from me. And, to do that, you have to come find me. If you don't, I'll go on Larry King and tell the world why Josh Brennen turned his bastard son away."

I hung up. Now what? *You've sent out the invitation, O'Brien, and you're all alone for the party.*

I slipped the Glock into my belt and stepped out on the porch, Max following at my heels. The frogs and cicadas were chanting their nightly sonatas. I placed the Glock on the table next to the large spearhead I'd found. Joe Billie would appreciate it. Maybe it was one of those rare paleo spearheads he mentioned. I sat in the wicker rocker, and Max jumped up on my lap. I scratched her head and watched a yellow moon rise above the river in the east. I could hear a coonhound chasing something at least a half mile upriver. The bellowing carried across the water on a night with no wind.

I knew it was a night I wouldn't sleep.

IT WAS AFTER MIDNIGHT when I took Max outside to let her do her business. We walked around the house. I had the floodlights turned off. The bellow of a bull alligator came up from the river. Although there was no wind, the mosquitoes weren't biting.

As we approached the porch, I could hear my cell phone ring from the table where I'd left it. I lifted it off the table next to the spearhead I'd found. It was Lauren.

"Don't tell me you're still at the office," I said.

"Sean, are you alone?" Lauren sounded out of breath.

"I'm here with my favorite lady, Max."

"Get out of the house!" she ordered.

"Why?"

"CNN ran a shot of Santana's photo. A man watching in Daytona Beach recognized the photo and called us. The man works for Hertz. They use GPS to help track cars—lost or stolen. They have a tracker on the car that Santana rented. Hold on, Sean. I'm on the other line with Hertz." Her breathing was quick. To the person on the other line she said, "What are the coordinates?" There was a pause, and Lauren asked me, "Where exactly do you live?"

"St. Johns River Road, off Highway 44."

"Sean, Santana's car, a Ford Fusion, is less than five miles from your house."

SEVENTY-NINE

I t's okay, Max," I said. "I'll be right back. No barking." I stepped out
the screen door into the dark and locked her in the house.

I tried to put myself exactly where Santana sat. I'd drive by, not
too fast or too slow, see if lights were on, maybe a car in the drive.
Then I'd return with the headlights off, park a good distance away,
move stealthily under the cover of darkness and enter the home. It
was all about surprise.

I wasn't Santana, though, and I couldn't be sure how he would
plan the assault. If surprise was part of it, I'd already removed that el-
ement. I jumped up to a low-hanging limb of a live oak tree and
pulled myself to a thick branch. I climbed another ten feet until I had
an open view of the road from both east and west.

The moon was higher, the soft light almost beaming through the
tree limbs. Shadows from the oaks connected like gnarly fingers in-
terlacing across my yard.

A horned owl called out, its series of hoots traveling up from the river. The call seemed to come from somewhere near my dock. Horned owls always sound like they are chanting, *who's awake . . . me too.* I wondered if it was the same owl that had captured the cardinal, the owl that had pointed me in the direction of Angela. If it was, maybe the bird would point me toward Santana.

The owl called out again, stopping after only two hoots. I've heard these owls often, and they always finished their statements. This one stopped in midsentence.

I saw the headlights in the distance, three-quarters of a mile away and coming toward my house slower than the speed limit. I touched the Glock and watched the car. The interior was too dark for me to make out whether Santana was behind the wheel.

It was a Ford. The driver kept the same speed as the car passed my house, but before the road began to curve I could see the brake lights tapped.

The driver slowed and turned around. The headlights went off. The car moved stealthlike, inching its way back toward my house. Within about fifty yards of my driveway, the driver pulled the car into a wooded area, state property.

There was no movement. I saw a tiny orange glow. The driver must have used the car lighter to light a cigarette. Why would Santana be smoking if he was about to kill me? Calm a nicotine itch? Something didn't feel right. I dropped from the tree and stayed in the shadows to move toward the car. I stopped every few feet to simply listen. Nothing. Not a sound from a horned owl. Not even a sound from a mosquito. In less than a minute, I'd slipped up on the car and approached the driver from the rear.

The window was open. He was a silhouette in the moonlight. He tossed out the cigarette, the red ash sparking in the night. Dumb move.

I came up from a crouch and touched the barrel to Santana's left ear.

"Put both hands on the wheel! Now!" I ordered.

Santana immediately lifted both hands to the steering wheel. I jerked open the door. "Get out! It's over, Santana."

"Don't shoot, man! Who the fuck's Santana?"

A young black man trembled with fright.

EIGHTY

I thought of Max alone in the house. I held the gun in the man's face and said, "Don't even think about lying to me. If you do, I'll shoot you between the eyes. How'd you get this car?"

"Dude gave it to me!"

"What dude?"

"Don't know his name. I work at Riverside Marina. Dude rented a boat today. He said he'd give me five hundred dollars to drive his car down this road at midnight and park right past that house back there. Said for me to keep the lights off and about one o'clock he'd come meet me. I'd get another five and he'd drop me back at the marina."

"At one o'clock, you would have been dead and your body dropped right here."

"What? The dude seemed real cool, man. Didn't seem like no crazy sex shit."

"His clothes, what color?"

"Lemme think . . . black . . . yeah, black shirt and pants."

I thought about the man in the boat I'd seen earlier. "Give me the keys."

"What?"

"Give them to me."

"No problem, man. What's this shit all about?"

"Start walking."

"It's after midnight. I'm a black man walkin' in dumb-fuck nowhere."

"It's the only way you will live though the night. Move! Walk the opposite direction from the house. There's a crossroad five miles west."

He looked at me, shook his head, and started walking west.

AS I APPROACHED MY HOME, I knew why the owl had stopped its night call. It had seen something. Something coming up *from* the river. I melted into the dark shadows next to the trees and crept down to my dock.

I almost didn't see it. Tied up behind the weeping willow tree was a boat. I could tell it was a small boat. In the moonlight, I knew it was the boat I'd seen earlier.

Santana was at my home.

EIGHTY-ONE

I stayed in the dark of the tree line next to my property as I moved closer to my house. I knew that locks would not keep Santana out. Where was he? On the porch? Hiding somewhere in a room? Or was he behind the next oak tree?

As I stepped out from cover and started for the porch, I was blinded by all of my floodlights. My backyard was like a Friday night high school football field.

"You move and you die." Santana's voice was calm. It was more a matter-of-fact statement than a death threat. "Throw the gun toward the river, and I won't snap your dog's neck. Remember that I have a gun pointed directly at your chest. Come on your porch, O'Brien. We're going to sit down to hear you speak your last words on earth."

I tossed the Glock and came up the steps onto the porch. Santana sat in a rocking chair, holding Max in his lap, her eyes wide. He pointed a pistol at me and kept the other hand clapped on the back of Max's neck. She was nervous, her tiny body trembling. She looked at me with pleading eyes.

"No reason to hurt the dog," I said.

"Dogs were my competition for food. As a child, I used to have to compete with them for scraps from garbage cans. Let's make this quick, O'Brien. I have other matters to attend to. Places to go. But I wanted to hear your last words, especially since you mentioned Josh Brennen. No one, at least no one alive, knows that Brennen is my father. How did you find out? Doesn't matter. You're about to die, so the secret remains with me. The bastard son, as you called me."

"That's what he called you."

"How did you know him?"

"We had drinks together. He always spoke his mind around me. Funny how too much single malt can open a man up. Open up his most hidden secrets." I slowly inched closer as I spoke. The spearhead I'd found was sitting on the table where I had left it. It was the best thing that I had for a weapon.

"That's far enough," he said, standing.

"Let Max go. Let her go outside."

He lowered Max to the porch. "Let's hear what the old man told you."

Max looked up at me. "I'll put the dog outside," I said.

"Don't touch the rat! What did he tell you?"

"He told me you'd never cut it in his world. He said he wouldn't be surprised if you had a dozen bastard brothers and sisters." I inched closer to the table. "He was proud of his conquests with dark-skinned women. He said no matter how you tried, Santana, you could never be better than Richard."

"He's the weak son! The gay son!"

"And you were the Hispanic bastard child! Richard fit in. You, Brennen said, never would. Never could."

I was less than five feet from the spearhead. "He told me that the only thing you two had in common was the color of your eyes. He said you may have had his eyes, but you'd never have his balls. Never be the man he was. He loathed you, Santana. No, he pitied you. Said you'd never be more than a tomato picker. Said you didn't have the intelligence to cut it in his world. He never even knew your mother's name. Called her a brown whore."

"You're a liar!" He kicked Max in the side like he was kicking a football. I sprang for his gun, but I was a second too late. The shot tore into my gut, like a baseball bat had hit me, knocking me to the floor. I rolled toward the table, grabbed the spearhead, and came up, hitting Santana hard in the center of his forehead. The sound was like an axe striking a piece of treated lumber. Blood squirted. I slashed out again with the spearhead, the thrust tearing his shirt, exposing his chest. Looking back at me were two large tattoos of cobras. Eyes glowing like coals.

He wears the mark of serpents on his body.

Santana laughed. "You can't kill me! Survival is what I do. A gut shot is a slow, painful way to die, O'Brien, but it's most fitting for a detective like you. When you see my old man in hell, tell him his tomato-picking bastard son said fuck off."

My eyes couldn't focus. Santana stood over me. "I might just sit here in this rocker and watch you die. All that nasty bacteria flooding your bloodstream. You're swimming in your own blood and shit. By the time they find you, your dog will have starved to death, or maybe the rat will eat your body."

My mind was spinning. The frogs and cicadas sounded like they were in my brain. They changed their singing into chanting, pulsating chants like an angry crowd at a boxing match. I felt a darkness closing in on my consciousness. Then I heard Max's frantic barks, almost like howls. I crawled on my hands through the stickiness of my own blood. My mind was racing and a dimness enveloping me as I crept toward the kitchen. I shook the encroaching dark shadows from my mind and tried to sit up. Max's barking was growing weaker or I was fading. I wasn't sure which. I stood, held my hands to my wound, and limped into the kitchen. My long bow was in the corner with the single arrow next to it. I picked them up and staggered out the back porch door. Max went ahead of me. Barking and limping down to my dock.

The full moon was at a forty-five-degree angle to my back. The moon and floodlights illuminated my entire yard in a soft light that carried beyond the river. On the dock, I could see Santana untying a boat. The look on his face was of disbelief and then amusement. He said, "Are you a walking dead man?"

I notched the arrow shaft in the bowstring. I kept inching closer. I was about seventy feet behind Max as she approached the dock barking.

"I like your fighting style, O'Brien. You rise from the grave, break out an antique killing tool, and you want to do battle again. But it is your last fight!"

I was now close enough to see the red eyes of the snake tattoos on his chest.

He pointed his pistol at Max. "Your dog will be dead before you could ever shoot that thing. And then you'd probably miss me by twenty feet. It's dark. You can barely stand. You're bleeding to death inside. Am I looking a little blurry to you right now, O'Brien? My, you don't seem well. You've resorted to a primitive bow. You're dying. Say good-bye to your noisy dog."

My mind played back Joe Billie's voice. *Keep both eyes open, block everything else out but the spot—then let go.*

As Santana pointed the pistol, I pulled the bowstring back to the side of my cheek, elevated the tip of the ancient arrowhead, focused on his chest, and let go. The arrow hit dead center between the snake eyes. Santana fell backward into the river. He tried to swim on his back against the current. His body jerked as if electric jolts were hitting it. Only the feathers on the shaft protruded out between the tattooed snakeheads. His arms flailed, slapping the water.

There was a loud splash from the water's edge. In the moonlight, I could see a large alligator swimming fast toward the dying man. The gator attacked Santana in the midsection, its jaws and teeth popping ribs, bone, and cartilage like twigs. The animal lifted Santana out of the water, tossed its massive head back, and rolled.

I wobbled back to the dock. I could feel vomit rising. My legs felt like they weren't part of my body. My eyes couldn't focus. I stumbled, dropped the bow, and fell next to Max. She was crouched in the grass, and I couldn't tell if she was hurt. I crawled to her and held her trembling body in my arms. "You're okay now . . . hold on, Max . . ."

I coughed blood. The murkiness swirled in my brain. The sound of crickets faded. Lying on my back, I clutched Max to my chest as a meteor shower burst across the dark purple sky, the afterglow locked in my retinas, the silence of heaven's fireworks falling on my ears. I watched a gray cloud slowly consume the moon, the light fading like a dying flame at the end of a match.

It was now very dark, and a cool wind blew across the river, sending a chill through every nerve in my spine. I felt my body shivering. The ink silhouettes from the river were rising all around me. I was soaring with no horizon. No control. Tumbling from an abyss and free-falling through a black hole where no one kept records. I was the product of my being, falling or soaring on the sum of who I was. There were no limbs to break my fall. There was only the sense of absolute nakedness. Nothing could be concealed or canceled. Nor did I care to try.

Sherri stood on the bowsprit of our sailboat, her hand reaching out toward me, the wind blowing through her hair. God, she was beautiful. I tried to call her name, to tell her I loved her, but I had lost my ability to speak. There was the sound of a woman's voice. Someone far away singing. Then a dark fog came off the sea from nowhere and I could no longer see Sherri.

There was a cool sensation deep inside my gut, like a drug was being released inside the skin. I opened my eyes and saw Joe Billie kneeling next to me. In a slow-motion voice, a strange voice, I heard myself say, "You're not real . . . you're a dream . . . none of this is real . . ."

He watched me without speaking, and he looked at the wound in my stomach. The sensation in my bowels went from cold to fire and back to coolness.

The darkness rose again. I was below the surface of the ocean at night trying to swim to the lights of my boat. I held my breath and kicked. I was rushing toward the light at the top. In a second I would breathe! I broke through the translucence and gulped in air.

THE LIGHTS FROM AN AMBULANCE and police vehicles raked across the limbs of the live oaks. I could hear a helicopter circling, and my thoughts dissolved to the dark valley of Afghanistan at sunset, the choppers like black locusts against a purple sky.

As they were lifting me onto the stretcher, a paramedic said, "You're gonna make it! Hang in there. Your dog will be okay, too."

EIGHTY-TWO

Nick's voice sounded like a dream. "He's waking up!" I heard him say. "Sean, about time you stopped sleeping."

I opened my eyes, blinked a few times, looked at the tubes running into my arms, the digital graphics monitoring my heart, and I glanced at the foot of the bed. Nick stood next to Dave, and both had big grins on their faces.

I said, "So, where's the Tin Man?" My voice sounded like it came from Oz.

"If that's Dan Grant, the detective," Dave said, "he'll be back."

"How you feelin', Sean?" Nick asked.

"Better than the last time I looked. How long have I been in here?"

Dave crossed his arms and said, "Three days. You were in IC for the first day. Lots of blood loss. When the EMTs got there, they said you looked like your body had gone into some kind of hibernation, sort of like those wood frogs we were talking about. Looks like your system had shut down somehow before it could bleed out. Santana did a number on your lower extremities."

"Don't tell me . . ."

"You're okay there, old friend, but he tried to rearrange your intestinal tract."

"How bad?"

"It's all stuffed back in there. Surgeons sewed you up in a lot of places internally. Flooded you with a few liters of bacteria-killing agents. You ought to have one hell of an aftertaste in your mouth until that bleach gets out of your system. The docs checked for polyps while they were in there. Clean as a whistle." He laughed.

"Where's Max? Is she okay?"

"Fine," Dave said. "Vet put some stitches in her. She's waiting for you."

Nick grinned and said, "I take her swimmin' when you get all well. I know she's a hot dog but she thinks like a Lab." He laughed, and then his face became creased with concern. "What happened, Sean? Where's the bad guy, Santana? Did he get away?"

Dan entered the room. I could tell he was worried. He said, "Sean, it's good to see you awake. How're you feeling?"

"Considering the circumstances, I'd say okay."

He smiled. "Must have been one hell of a fight. Lauren Miles called us when she heard Santana was heading for you. We found the rental car near your house. A patrol unit picked up a kid who said some crazy white dude pulled a gun on him and made him walk away from the car. That wouldn't have been you, would it, Sean?"

"My memory is a little hazy."

"Don't see how Santana got near your place if he didn't come by car."

"Came by boat."

"That how he got away? Using a damn boat?"

"He didn't get away."

"He didn't? There wasn't a body. But we did find drops of his blood on your dock. It was within six feet of the blood from you and your dog. So what the hell happened to Santana?"

"Best I can remember, he seemed to have lost his balance on the dock, fell in, and couldn't swim very well. Then he got in the mouth of a big gator."

"Sean." Dan sighed. "We found blood all over your porch, a big damn spearhead covered in blood. On the dock, we found a bow lying next to you and your dog. Looks like you had some kind of Custer's Last Stand going on, a one-man war against Santana. Did you shoot him with an arrow?"

"I was shot in the gut. How could I pull back a sixty-pound bow?"

"So, for the record, since we may never recover a body, Santana shot you, you hit him with your spearhead, he lost his balance, fell in the river, and was eaten by a gator."

"It's all kind of a blur after I was shot."

Dan closed his notepad. "I'll just get a statement on tape. You took out the most prolific serial killer since the Green River Killer."

We talked about all the multiple investigations into the murders. A half dozen agencies, including the FBI, ICE, Border Patrol, and the sheriff's departments from three separate counties in Florida, two in Texas, and one in Los Angeles were sharing notes, files, and extradition proceedings. In addition to the arrests of Silas Davis and Hector Ortega, others that worked for them were arrested and charged with dozens of counts, including trafficking in human beings, slavery, prostitution, and murder.

Nick was late for a date with a schoolteacher whom he'd been eyeing since she moved into the new condos across the street from the marina.

After he and Dan Grant were gone, Dave looked at the wires,

tubes, and bandages holding my body together. He lowered his voice and said, "You could have died, you know that?

"Yeah, I know."

"It's very noble to offer yourself as the bait, but not smart, especially with someone like Santana. You should have had backup right there at the house with you."

"I did. Max bit his ankle."

Dave grinned. His week's worth of stubble was a bluish gray from the lights of the monitors. His eyes were red-rimmed, heavy, with dark circles from worry and lack of sleep. "Sean, is he dead? Is all that about the gator true, or is it some metaphor you're using to explain something that's unexplainable?"

"What do you mean?"

"Santana resurfaced once before. Could he do it again?"

"Not this time. His evil will resurface, but his body won't rise up again."

Dave nodded as a nurse entered. She was in her fifties, hair beginning to gray, and she had lines on her face traceable to her compassionate heart. "Are you hungry?"

"I could use something to get the taste of a nuclear meltdown out of my mouth."

She laughed. "I'll see if I can find a good meal for you." As she took my pulse, she looked at my hands. "You still have a little of that dirt under a couple of fingernails. Thought I got it all out. Hands were filthy when they brought you in."

"I guess I had some blood on them."

"Yes, you did. You also had something else on them."

"What?"

"The same stuff that was in the wound on your stomach. Mud! Some kind of dark mud. Lucky that didn't kill you! Who in their right mind would risk infecting a wound with mud?"

EPILOGUE

They'd wrapped it in newspaper. I took it out of my Jeep, careful not to drop it on the parking lot. It had been a month since I got out of the hospital. Still, lifting the weight of the headstone, I could feel the beaded scar on my gut pull a little.

Max followed at my heels, sniffing the ground as we walked to the gravesite. The morning sun was edging above a tree line to the far right of the county cemetery. The grounds smelled of fresh-cut grass, crushed acorns, and wet dirt.

The grave marker, county issued, was a small white cross with a seven-digit number on it. I pulled it out of the ground. Then I unwrapped the newspaper and set the headstone on her grave. It read:

ANGELA RAMIREZ

1989–2008

I stood there a minute longer, said a silent prayer, and made the sign of the cross. Then I heard a bird start to sing. A cardinal, its feathers the color of a ripe strawberry, jumped between branches on the lone oak as it sang. Its voice sounded like a flute warbling in the wind, its head and shoulders moving side to side like a rock singer's.

I smiled and said, "Sing on, bird. Sing on."

I picked up the discarded grave marker and the newspapers and turned to Max. "Let's go, Max. We have some sailing to get to."

I RENTED THE FORTY-TWO-FOOT Beneteau from a bareboat charter company out of Key Largo. I'd brought enough groceries and ice to last for two weeks, if I wanted to stay out that long. I thought about sailing over to Bimini, find a quiet cove, listen to good music, catch a lot of fish, and simply do a lot of nothing. Then again, I might sail down beyond Key West to Fort Jefferson and spend some time where the waters of the Atlantic and Gulf became one sea. But there was a place I wanted to visit first.

Once clear of the marina, I wanted to turn off the Perkins diesel, open the spinnaker, and hoist the mainsail, but I kept her under motor for a few miles. I punched the coordinates into the GPS and followed the satellite toward the place where I had said good-bye to Sherri. Max hopped from one seat to another in the cockpit, barking at the soaring pelicans and enjoying the movement of the boat.

After a half hour, I went below and opened the refrigerator, taking out the long-stemmed red rose I'd brought aboard. Back in the cockpit, I checked the coordinates. I was within a hundred feet of where I'd released Sherri's ashes into the sea. I cut the diesel, stepped to the bowsprit, and stood there for a moment.

"I miss you," I said. "Max misses you." I tossed the rose into the ocean. It floated on the surface and began to drift away in the current. I watched it until the red bloom was a dot on the horizon.

Then I raised the sails. But there was a dead calm. No breeze. Not even the clouds seemed to move, and little Max was still. "Well, Max, what do you think? We were going to do some sailing down toward Fort Jefferson or over to Bimini. Thought I'd let the wind decide. Maybe it has. Maybe we ought to be back home, take *Jupiter* out and catch some fish if we can't catch some wind."

Suddenly, out of the west, a breeze started, picked up, and kicked with a strong gust. "Max, looks like we're heading to Bimini!"

I made my way back to the cockpit. As I stood behind the wheel, the wind was steady, the sails expanding, leading the boat toward the east. I reset the GPS for Buccaneer Point on Bimini. In less than thirty seconds we were doing ten knots.

I reached down into the ice in the cooler and retrieved a Corona. I turned to Max. "All right, first mate, we're heading across some blue water to an island I visited a few years ago. Enjoy!"

We had the sun to our backs and the islands somewhere over the horizon. Max quickly became used to the movements of the boat. She made it all the way up to the bowsprit, adjusting her balance by spreading her front and hind legs a little farther apart. She watched the spray off the bow and sniffed the salty air.

I listened to the boat cut through the water, felt the wind on my face, sipped the beer, put a Jack Johnson CD in the player, sat down, and steered the wheel with my toes. It felt good to be sailing again. I'd forgotten how much I'd missed it.

Max was walking back to the cockpit when something caught her eye. Two porpoises loped alongside the boat, easily keeping up with us. Max barked and scurried around the boat, keeping her eyes on the strange creatures. They swam less than twenty feet off the starboard side.

I remembered Sherri saying, "I love it when they join us. I believe it's the same pair we saw yesterday."

"How can you tell?"

"Their attitude. Maybe it's those smiles. I don't know. But they seem to want to travel with us."

These two did travel with Max and me for another two miles and then left us. They left us with their attitude, their smiles, and their sense of adventure.

"Keep an eye out for pirates!" I yelled to Max. "That's the mate's job, growl at 'em."

She turned and looked at me, her face animated in a swashbuckling dachshund kind of way. I grinned, watching Max as she stood near the bowsprit, her ears flapping in the breeze, her wet nose sniffing the trade winds.

Maybe I didn't need the GPS. I had my little watchdog to point the way.